ESCAPE FROM DANGER ISLAND

The Silencers Series

Whip Lipsey

Etherege and Wycherley

ESCAPE FROM DANGER ISLAND

In a jungle – evening

A narrow trail weaves through a jungle thick with vines and loud with the chatter of monkeys. On this trail: a Running Man. He pants heavily. He wears a business suit, now soiled and tattered. He looks scared.

No. He looks terrified.

He runs down the jungle path knocking vines and giant leaves out of his way. The odd monkey scatters, screeching complaints. The Running Man looks back often. Something chases him. Something really bad. He runs on in terror, glancing behind him as he goes; an act more desperate than athletic. But give him credit because it is no mean feat to run pell-mell through a jungle at night while looking both ahead and behind.

Then, behind him, over his shoulder, appears a Second Running Man. Running Man Two also wears a business suit, also now in dirty tatters. Running Man Two looks as panicked as Running Man One, but he does not look back. For a few moments they race through the jungle. Number Two catches up to Number One and they run side by side, shooting terrified glances at each other until Number Two starts to pull away. It's a dash for first place, and Number Two runs like a man inspired. Number One's pace fades. He watches Number Two take the lead.

As Running Man One slows to a jog he hears, above the ordinary din of the jungle, the sound of loud, deep barks, as if coming from a giant mastiff. As, indeed, they do. Running Man One looks back in terror at the jungle behind him. It looks just like the jungle ahead of him. But the barks grow louder from behind.

The barking inspires Running Man One. His feet fly beneath him. Ahead of him, he sees Running Man Two again. Running Man One catches up to Number Two. Running Man One shoots him a terrified glance, and gives us our first bit of clever dialog: "Aaaahhhhhhhhhhhhhhhhhhhhhhhhhhhhh!!!!"

Running Man One bolts past Running Man Two. Number

Two watches as Number One sprints off ahead of him on the jungle trail. Number Two hears the loud, low barking now. He gets it. He adds his own opinion on the approaching menace, "Aaaaahhhhhhh! Aaaaaahhhhhhh!" On he runs.

Ahead of him on the trail, out of Number Two's sight, rushing through the vines and bushes, under the jungle canopy, Running Man One reaches an opening in the verdant forest. Exhausted from his sprint, he staggers to a stop. Out of breath and nearly spent, he leans against a narrow tree. Then: BOOM! Out falls another man from the tree. He is Running Man Number Three. He wears a business suit, also soiled and also tattered.

Running Man One is taken aback, both by the suddenness of Number Three's appearance, and by the absurdity of businessmen falling like fruit from the trees. For a moment they stare at each other in frightened disbelief, then they hear: the barking of a giant mastiff! They look to each other.

Running Man One, "Aaaaaahhhhhhhhhhhhhhhhh!"

Running Man Three, "Ack! Ack! Ack!"

Number Three leaps up. His fresh legs carry him ahead, stumbling through the jungle. He can't help but look back at the unseen danger behind him. Number One follows, practically limping from fatigue. Running Man Three turns around, back-peddling as he scans for the danger threatening to emerge from behind Number One.

In this manner he steps into ... quicksand! His panicked look tells us all we need to know. Though it helps to see him sinking into the ground.

Running Man Three, "Ack! Ack! Help! Quicksand!"

Number One looks on in wide-eyed amazement as Number Three sinks past his waist, and then to his chest, struggling to get out. Number Three grasps for vines out of his reach. Running Man Three sees Number One and offers him a suggestion, "It's a little out of reach! Help here?"

Perhaps the thought of helping crossed Number One's mind, but the renewed sound of deep barking re-focuses him on the danger at hand. Number One looks back at the jungle behind him. The barking grows louder. The bushes rustle.

That's it. Running Man One takes off like a lightning-bolt hit his feet. He runs fast to Number Three.

An encouraged Running Man Three, "Oh good! Yes! The vine right there." Number Three points to a vine overhead as Number One bounds toward him. Number One leaps in the air, kicks off of Number Three's exposed head and over to the trail past him. He never looks back.

The step on the head has pushed Number Three further into the quicksand. Now his shoulders barely rise above the gunk. Number Three, immobilized by the sludge, looks at the jungle from which Number One just ran. The barking grows louder. The bushes rustle. The Second Running Man emerges exhausted onto the trail.

Running Man Three, "Oh! Wonderful! A little help?"

The Second Running Man races toward Number Three, leaps in the air before him, steps on Number Three's head, and leaps to the other side of the quicksand.

Running Man Three, "Ack!"

And now his trouble really begins. On the trail from which Number Two just appeared, a giant mastiff heaves into view. The most giant, bring-a-man-down-and-eat-his-liver hound from hell ever seen on earth. What kind of owner keeps this dog as a pet? This must be a working dog, and his work must be very nasty.

Running Man Three shows a keen appreciation for his prospects, "Ack! Ack! Ack! Ack! Ack!"

The dog races toward Number Three, leaps over the quicksand, kicks off Number Three's exposed head, and clears the rest of the quicksand without ever breaking his stride. Number Three has now been pushed down to his neck in the consuming muck.

Down the trail, Running Man One presses on through the narrow jungle path. Hard behind him, Running Man Two closes the distance between them. And right behind him, the hard working, mission focused mastiff charges relentlessly towards them both.

Number Two runs right up alongside of Number One. They run together, both looking behind at the pursuing mastiff. The mastiff seems to favor eating Number One. Number Two can't help but smile slightly. But Number One has a great idea. He points to Number Two and shouts: "Sick 'em!!" The mastiff shifts ever so slightly to chasing Number Two instead of Number One.

Number Two notices this, "No! Him! Sick him!" Number Two points vigorously at Number One, but the mastiff pays no heed. One order suffices. Now *Number One* smiles slightly. Second in the office pool; first in the jungle.

The two Running Men begin to separate; Number One down the left fork in the trail, Number Two down the ever-narrower right fork, the mastiff hot on his heals.

Number Two flags, but the mastiff does not. Now almost upon Number Two, the mastiff leaps.

Back behind, on the trail, Running Man Three—now turned into Stuck-In-Quicksand-Man—struggles to keep his chin above the mire. From his desperate eyes we see the jungle bushes rustling. From the foliage shapes appear. Two men and a chained mastiff emerge from the jungle. Running Man Three pleads his case, "Yes! Help here please!"

The lead man in the emerging group is the real and ultimate object of all this fear. He is Ivan Karloff. He stands medium height, lean, fair-skinned but with jet black hair, and a lightning strike scar on his face. He has an aristocratic bearing, like a man born to command and accustomed to obedience. He wears hunting clothes of a casual Cossack kind; long coat and high boots. Very sporting.

He carries a blow-gun.

Running Man Three recognizes him, "Oh."

Behind Karloff, holding the chain of a mastiff, stands Karloff's henchman, Boris. Boris looms like a dark, giant mountain hovering over Karloff. Boris is huge. Really. He is what huge becomes when it gets really big. Boris sports a thick black beard and a brow that would make a Neanderthal grimace as being

4

a bit too much. He wears a classic Cossack coat and looks the perfect image of one mean Russian giant from about a century ago.

Karloff inspects the pathetic sight of the slowly sinking Running Man Three. His lip curls in disdain. From the distance we hear a cry of pain and fear. It is Running Man Two meeting his new mastiff friend, "Aaaggghhhh!!!"

The mastiff held by Boris on the long chain howls. Running Man Three goes blank with terror. Karloff sniffs.

Running Man Three, "Perhaps you could..."

Perhaps he could, but he won't. Karloff skips over the quicksand onto Number Three's head and off again onto the trail, sending Number Three down into the muck to his chin. The mastiff skips off Number Three's head, pushing him down a bit further. Boris skips off Number Three's head, sinking him all the way beneath the muck. The pursuers carry on through the jungle toward the horrid sound.

Further up the jungle trail, an exhausted Running Man One pauses to catch his breath. Again. He needs a good deal more breath for what lies ahead, so it is good that he catches a bit now. The jungle darkens as night falls. Monkeys chatter just beyond sight. The wind rustles the branches. A bug crawls over his toe. A scream pierces the growing gloom. It is the death gasp of the Second Running Man. Then a baying of a dog. Number One jumps at the howl of the mastiff from the trail behind him. He takes off again at a meager jog.

Suddenly, from a tree above him, a man swings down from a vine!

Running Man Four shouts as he swings, "Ahh Haa!" Running Man Four wears a soiled business suit ripped to shreds by the jungle. He holds a vine in one hand and a sharpened stick in the other. Swinging down upon Number One he—misses! Instead of hitting Running Man One, Number Four swings past him and hits the base of a tree. He lets out a cry, "Owww!"

They look at each other for a moment. Number Four's shoulders slump as he realizes he has wasted his ambush on the wrong target. Number One just shakes his head in disbelief. A mastiff emits a low howl behind them. Number One takes off. Number Four considers his options for a moment. He sets an aggressive pose toward the trail behind, spear shaft ready for battle. The mastiff howls again. Running Man Four lets off the war cry of the Running Men, "Aaaaaaaaaaaaaaaaaaaaaaaaaahhhh!" Then he drops his spear and charges after Number One.

Up the trail, in a tree in the jungle, above an opening in the canopy, hides Running Man Five, the last of his kind, wearing the uniform of these desperate men: formal business attire, rendered to shreds, covered in filth. Number Five distinguishes himself with a pair of impossibly thick glasses. How did such a blind man even climb this tree?

Number Five looks—at least so far as he is able—down at the ground below him. Through his squint he sees, disguised in the leaves, a looped rope. Following its length with his eyes (such as they are) he checks to see the rope tied off onto a cunningly bent tree. A classic rope-trap! Number Five jumps up in his tree branch at the sound of men running toward the clearing.

Sprinting by first, Running Man One. He dashes through the clearing, barely missing the rope trap. Number Five grimaces at the miss. He then hears the approach of Number Four. Running Man Four enters the clearing, steps in the loop, and trips the trap. It hauls him up abruptly, ass-over-tea-kettle, to hang in the middle of the clearing by one foot.

Running Man Five whoops in victory, "Whoooop!"

Number Five leaps from the tree and does the Dance of Ecstatic Victory around the hanging form of Number Four. He shouts, "Caught in your own trap! Not so smart now! Whooooop!"

Running Man Four responds, "Hey! What? What! Hey?"

Realizing that this doesn't quite sound right, Number Five decides to take a closer look at his victim. Number Five holds the upside-down head of Number Four steady and looks at him eye-to-eye through his bottle-nose glasses. Number Five has the terrible realization that he does not now stare at the face of an aristocratic master hunter.

Number Four sees the recognition and nods angrily, "Right! Now get me down!"

The sound of a mastiff barking emanates behind them in the jungle from which Number Four had emerged. They both look. Or Number Four does; Number Five just jerks his head around in that general direction wishing he could see that far.

Running Man Four, "Get me down!"

Running Man Five, "Aaaaahhhhhh!"

Number Five flees down the trail away from the sound of the barking, bumping Number Four into a spin as he goes. The spinning Number Four sees only a jungle whirl, but he hears the approach of someone, "Uh? Hello? Could you help me?"

A hand reaches out and stops Number Four's spinning. Number Four smiles. His world stable again, he sees the inverted face of Ivan Karloff. One could describe Number Four's own face as, well, disappointed. "Oh."

Karloff motions to Boris the Giant. Boris pulls out the world's largest scimitar. Number Four smiles hopefully, perhaps they mean to cut me down. Then he realizes the absurdity of this idea. "Aaaaaaahhhhhhhhhhhhhhhrrrrrrggghhh!"

Up the jungle trail we see, once more, the form of Running Man One, running ... slowly. He hears a scream in the distance behind him: "Aaaaaaahhhhhhhhhhhhhrrrrrrrrrggghhh!" He picks up his pace. He runs until, abruptly, he disappears down a pit dug into the dank jungle earth. A classic tiger-trap! He hangs onto the side by his fingertips. He struggles to climb out. He almost makes it. But then the legally blind Number Five falls into the trap on top of him, sending him down.

Number Five manages to hold onto the edge of the pit. He conducts the same struggle as his now displaced brethren did before. He looks almost to clear of the pit. But something seems to have a hold of him from below.

Number Five looks confused. He starts to sink back into the pit. On Five's back, the ever-determined Number One climbs out of the pit over Number Five. Number One clears the pit kicking off the head of Number Five, sending Number Five back down out of sight. Number One dusts himself off. From the pit he hears a faint voice:

Running Man Five, "I could use a hand."

Perhaps Running Man One considers this for a moment, but then the howl of the mastiff sends him headed off into the jungle.

Number Five struggles to climb out of the pit on the vines that have fallen into it. Although not the athletic sort, he makes progress. He smiles. He is going to make it all by himself! He grasps the edge of the pit. He sees a figure above him. He squints. He squints harder. He sees Ivan Karloff. Karloff raises a blowgun to his lips. Number Five frowns.

Up the jungle trail Running Man One runs. He runs like a man possessed. But he has reached the end of his reserves. Ahead of him lies no trail now, just thick jungle and inky darkness. The howl of a mastiff drives him on, but he has no breath to carry him. Then, ahead of him, he sees something. The moon? Yes, the moon. Running Man One leaves the jungle.

Out of the jungle and onto a rocky precipice he goes. The moon and stars shine above; the waves crash at the cliff bottom. He staggers to the edge of the sea cliff. He looks down to the ocean far below. The waves pound the rocks in the moonlight. And still the mastiff howls behind him. He turns to the sound. A great mastiff, now off his chain, charges toward him. Number One backs up to the very edge of the cliff. What now? He has a thought. His last great thought. He yells at the mastiff: "Sit!"

The mastiff sits!

For a moment. But just as Number One sighs in relief, the mastiff barks his deep bark. This is enough, just enough, to back Number One up another half inch. He waves is arms in an impotent effort to arrest his tipping over. He tilts over the cliff. He shouts, "Aaaaaaaaaahhhhhhhhhhhhhh!!!"

We don't have to hear the "splat" at the bottom to know what happens. But let's listen anyway: SPLAT.

On the cliff, Karloff and Boris arrive. Karloff pets the head of the mastiff. Karloff looks down at the sea. Karloff shrugs and walks away.

Common sense tells us that a book cannot have a theme song. But I urge you now to listen to *Rock Fort Rock* by the Skatalites. There we have it; our theme song.

At Interpol USA HQ – Washington D.C. – day

A man sits at a desk, studying a paper. The desk is made of solid oak carved from the mast of the fleet flagship sailed (only in port) by Henry the Navigator. It has the sheen of a thousand polishings. It rests atop an inch of carpet with a thick Persian weave. It stands beside a globe of the world last updated in 1835. Behind the desk hangs a tapestry depicting unicorns at dangerous play with wary nymphs who dodge mischievous horns. Before the desk sit two leather chairs crafted with such delicate care as to nearly ensure the comfortable lethargy of any who sit on them. The office is paneled in wood of the deepest grain, and the window looks out on the manicured lawn of Interpol's North American headquarters. In other words, the office declares unambiguously the authority, competence, humanity and intelligence of the man who sits behind its desk.

So you know he must be an idiot.

Lester Halftrain, the man behind the desk, stares intently at a paper. He is middle aged and possessed of a solid chin, an air of casual authority, a sonorous voice and an avuncular smile. He is masculine, sincere, decisive, hapless, easily diverted and a dangerous accident always ready to happen. At this moment he looks baffled and perplexed by the paper in front of him. "I can't understand it." He stares at it harder, trying to coax meaning from the paper. "Is it in English? All our papers should be in English."

Across the desk, sitting on the edge of a leather chair so as not to be sucked into its soporific comfort, Marcy Gainer sighs deeply; not a contented sigh, but the sort of sigh a prizefighter lets out as the bell rings. She is a woman in her late twenties, business pretty and dressed in executive secretary business wear. She is patient, competent, quietly determined and right this moment stoically managing to suppress her impulse to explode. Halftrain is just the sort of man nations select for their leaders; Marcy Gainer is just the sort of woman you want holding the nuclear codes and thus ensuring that the nation's leader does not nuke China while trying to order chow mein. Marcy watches Halftrain staring at the paper just a moment longer than she thinks she should, then reaches across the desk, takes the paper from his hands, turns it right side up and gives it back to Halftrain.

Halftrain, "Oh yes, English." Now transformed from hieroglyphics to English by simple inversion, Halftrain can comprehend the document. "So this is about the special infiltration team you've been advocating. Not sure I see the need."

Marcy, "Arms smugglers, international counterfeiters, mad hunters—"

Halftrain, "Yes, but Interpol is more an information and advisory organization. We leave commando raids to sponsoring nations."

Marcy, "This would be a secret team. Specialists. Just for information gathering. No guns. No explosions."

Halftrain, "But don't we have a team like this now? Didn't I just send them on a mission last week?"

Marcy smiles prettily at him. This is how she stops her anger from exploding like a flamethrower into the boss's face. "No sir. That was not the special infiltration team you sent in. In fact, we really need to fast-track the formation of the special infiltration team in order to investigate that—" she pauses here to find the right words—which is to say the correct wrong words —"improperly vetted action order you sent to the Hidden Assets Investigation Group."

Halftrain studies the document again. A Halftrain document-study is not really a *reading*, not even a quick scanning. It is more a facial pose of serious concern followed by a look a stern determination. "Very well, proceed. But—"

Marcy has already cleared her seat when the "but" stops her.

Halftrain, "This prospect here," he points to the paper, "he's some sort of artist? Is that what we need?"

Marcy, "He has many talents. And a lot of spirit."

Within an art gallery – evening

Opening night for a new art exhibit at the Saville Gallery. People in formal wear mill about with cocktails in hand while others nibble at food from a buffet table. They must mill about carefully because the canvases are not on the walls but laid out randomly on the floor. The canvasses are blank, pure white and untouched by paint. Also placed about the room, around the blank canvasses, lie buckets of paint in primary colors: red, blue, and green.

This, naturally, confuses the patrons a bit. But it also adds to the excitement. They have come to see the premier of the young, and to date unknown, new artist, Kip Carson. Having heard nothing about him, they assume him to be a genius, which is not a bad assumption in its way. Though he is not perhaps the kind of genius they or he imagine.

Kip enters the scene. Young, energetic, filled with nervous excitement. Handsome in a fresh-faced innocent manner. Any mother would be happy to see her daughter bring him home as a prospect; until discovering his occupation: conceptual artist. Don't worry Mom, he takes side gigs as well. But tonight he has arrived as an artist. Kip wears an artist smock and black sneakers, a selection that requires only modest foreknowledge rather than genius. A gallery assistant follows on his heels.

Kip, "This is fine! This is great! This is exactly what I envisioned!"

Gallery assistant, "There's a call for you Mr. Carson."

Kip waves away the offered phone. Nothing must come before art. He calls his new admirers together, "Gather round everyone, gather round. This is art, so I'll need to explain it to you."

The assistant puts away the phone and tries to rush an introduction to the now gathering patrons, "Everyone, everyone

—mind the paint buckets. Everyone, I wish to introduce you to the gallery's latest new find. Formerly a fabricator for some of the biggest names in abstract structural art, our latest discovery has now stepped up to the big leagues. Ladies and gentlemen, I present to you Mr. Kip Carson."

Mild applause as patrons try to avoid stepping on blank canvases.

Kip shines, "Thank you. Thank you." He launches into his explanation, waving his arms excitedly as he speaks, "What is art?" He pauses dramatically, "Never mind that, let's ask a different question," more drama pausing—Kip's art takes a lot of set up, "*when* is art? Is art a thing done and accomplished? Or is it the very moment of its own creation?"

The patrons look intrigued. It'll be idea-art tonight, not the stuff you have to look at.

Kip, "You see here the ingredients of the moment of art's creation: the gallery, the canvasses, the paint, the patrons. But the moment is not-yet. And it's not-yet-ness is simultaneously its own almost-upon-us-ness. Will it be brilliant? What are the odds?"

Kip pauses to let the questions sink in. And the patrons pause along with him.

Kip, "You have heard that if a hundred monkeys typed on a hundred typewriters for an infinite time they would eventually write the works of Shakespeare. Well I ask: what if they were given even less time? Would they write something more original than that?"

The patrons find all this pleasingly baffling. The gallery assistant seems no more enlightened but equally excited about the deep conceptual territory already staked out. Kip reaches for his dramatic conclusion, "Tonight we will find out. Tonight, we will experience art in its very moment of self-becoming. Tonight, we shall truly BE THERE FOR IT!"

Kip raises his hands dramatically and shouts: "Release the monkeys!" Mild nervous laughter throughout. Until the monkeys come screeching in. Yes, monkeys. At least a hundred angry, frightened, shrieking monkeys. They leap everywhere. They upturn paint cans and scamper across canvases.

Kip, "Watch! Watch as they create!"

They climb up dresses and evening coats, spreading paint everywhere. Patrons scream and curse. Vervet monkeys swing from silk ties. Squirrel monkeys gnaw frantically at diamond broaches. Capuchin monkeys become entangled in extravagant hair-styles; making them even more extravagant. Howler monkeys—well, howl—like the damned of the Ninth Circle. A proboscis monkey tries to mate with a pygmy marmoset on what now looks remarkably like a Jackson Pollock.

Kip seems just a bit concerned, "Yes, there may be a few casualties for art."

The assistant stands looking on, mouth agape. Her resume flashes before her eyes. Most definitely delete this.

Monkeys assault the buffet table, throwing food, and what is surely not food but something of the monkey's own production, at all and sundry. Patrons dash about in panic, upturning paint cans and battling off baboons. Sustaining Members of the Saville slip and crash into pools of paint as art critics dive for the door.

Kip, "Yes. Sorry. A bit more than I expected too."

Women cry in the corners; men barricade the bathrooms. Who do you call for a monkey invasion?

Kip, "I think if you just think about it for a moment ... really..."

Monkey-art chaos reigns. The trauma-therapy bills alone will bankrupt the gallery. And that's just for the monkeys.

Kip losses heart. His shoulders slump. He turns to the assistant, "Okay, I'll take that call now."

Within the executive washroom at Interpol HQ

We see the face of Mr. Lester Halftrain, head of Interpol's North American Operations Division. He smiles and talks in an up-beat manner to someone, "I have the highest possible regard for you. More than that, I admire you. You're a patriot, a leader, and frankly, not a bad looking fellow into the bargain. I wish— and this is not easy to admit—I wish I could be more like you."

Halftrain talks to his reflection in the mirror of the restroom. "You're a natty dresser too. And you have a way of talking to people that puts them at ease, makes them speak frankly." Over his shoulder Marcy Gainer steps in. Clearly she feels uncomfortable being here. Halftrain notices her in the reflection, "Mrs. Gainer! Should you be in here?"

Marcy, "It *is* the women's washroom."

Halftrain, "Is it?"

It is. Halftrain looks about confused.

Halftrain, "But it has urinals." Halftrain motions toward the sinks. "Well, as long as you're here, you can brief me on how the team building goes."

Marcy winces at the word *brief* in the current context but presses on, "I reeled in our tech specialist, and I have high hopes for our master cat-burglar."

Halftrain looks alarmed, "Kidnapping kittens?!? Do we really need a specialist in just that? Are we even authorized for—"

Marcy raises a reassuring hand, "I didn't mean—I meant —we are about to recruit our master Exterior to Interior Repositioning Specialist with Special Skills in Secured Deposit Extraction Technique man."

Halftrain looks happy now.

Within a parking garage – night

A limo passes through a guard-post at the entrance to the garage. It glides to a halt before an elevator. Two men in tuxedos, kings in their world, get out and head to the elevator. They share some salty joke as they enter it. The elevator doors close. The parking garage descends into silence. From the car: a slight sound. Then the trunk pops open. A third man in a tuxedo gets out and looks about. He is Trevor Sinjun-Tunsby, English gentleman-thief extraordinaire. He looks like, well, look up the actor Terry-Thomas, famous player of upper-class toffs. Our man Trevor looks and sounds just like this man. He would be pleased to note the resemblance himself. For now though he is all business, and his business is cat-burglaring.

To the sounds of the James Bond theme, he makes his way to the elevator. (No one can charge royalties for imagining a song —yet—so go on and imagine the James Bond theme.) From the cummerbund around his waist, he pulls out a wire and attaches it to an air-gun pulled from his pocket. From his sleeve he slides out a flat metal rod.

He draws the metal rod up the gap in the elevator doors until he trips the mechanism for the doors. They open to reveal the elevator shaft, the elevator car now rising up.

PING. The sound of the wire from Trevor's cummerbund shooting up and attaching to the bottom of the rising elevator car. Trevor deftly swings out beneath the elevator car's floor as it rises. He looks every bit the dashing double-O agent. Trevor counts off the floors until he arrives at the outer door to the floor he wants. Drawing another wire from the tuxedo sash about his waist, he loads the air-gun again and fires the second wire at the shaft wall above the outer elevator shaft door. Disconnecting the first wire, Trevor swings out on the second to the outer door of the elevator shaft. He uses the metal rod to trip the mechanism on this door, and it opens onto the hallway of an elegant apartment building.

With cat-like grace our tuxedo wearing burglar swings into the hallway. Trevor disconnects from the second wire as the elevator door closes. He adjusts his suit, an air of confidence never failing him. He walks around a corner, past Romanesque planters, and into another hallway. He takes a glove from his pocket. He admires the gold letter L emblazoned on it. He puts on the glove and with the gloved hand reaches up and unscrews a hallway light-bulb. He moves to the other side of the door next to this light fixture and unscrews another light-bulb. He thinks a moment. Then tip-toes to a further light fixture and does the same. Returning to the door, now cast in darkness, he bends down to the doorknob and the keyhole below it. He pulls out a head lamp and puts it on. How the hell does he carry all this in a tuxedo? Secrets of the trade.

He pulls open a lock-pick kit, selects several metal picks and deftly places them in the lock on the door, one above the other. He moves the picks carefully in the lock. Then: CLICK CLICK. He looks about one last time to see that he kneels alone in the hallway.

He turns the knob and pushes the door open, revealing: A party! Jammed with shouting, happy people. Confetti and steamers everywhere. What fun!

Trevor's face falls in disbelief. A reveler in a party-hat takes him by the elbow, "Welcome friend! Come on in! Everybody's welcome!"

The party-goer walks him into the gorgeous two storied apartment decked out in the most stylish, stealable, objects d'art imaginable. Trevor still can't believe his eyes. He nervously tries to suggest he belongs here, "Hello, old chap. Trevor Sinjun-Tunsby, here. Invited you know." The claim would be more convincing if he weren't still hearing a head-lamp. No one seems to care though; everyone's too drunk and happy. What a story anyway. That guy that showed up in the embroidered glove and headlamp; costumed like *The Lurker* cat-burglar everyone talks about.

Trevor pushes through the throng until he arrives in front of a large and valuable painting; a Gainsborough depicting a ruby faced woman with a deliciously bemused expression.

He stares at it longingly. It stares right back at him, defiant.

He pulls off his glove and puts it away. A reveler pats him on the back, "Beautiful isn't it? And they say it's worth a fortune."

Trevor sighs. His phone rings. He answers it. He listens a moment, then, "Finding myself at odd angles I do believe I'll accept your offer."

Within an office hallway at Interpol HQ

Halftrain and Marcy walk through the hall. This might seem too mundane an action to mention, but with Halftrain anything can become an adventure.

Halftrain, "I thought we already sent in an extraction team?"

Marcy, "Yes, the wrong team. The accountants. It was a

miscommunication."

Halftrain, "Well what idiot did that?" Halftrain attempts to enter his office but runs into a window to it instead. Jumping back, he reaches out a hand to feel the glass. What is this strange force-field between him and his office? Marcy takes his arm and eases him around through the door.

As Halftrain passes through the door he turns and reaches out to feel the glass of the window from this side. Yes, the invisible wall is still there.

Marcy, "Sir, perhaps we should sit?"

Halftrain enters and sits in a chair in front of his desk. He waits. Marcy indicates the chair behind his desk. Ah yes, that one. Halftrain takes his proper chair, "So we're bringing in the proper team now?"

Marcy, "Yes." Marcy hands a file to Halftrain, opened to the first page. Halftrain can see the picture of a stunningly attractive woman with jet black hair. Marcy explains, "Our next prospect, Natasha Raskalitkanof,"

Halftrain grins sheepishly at the picture, "My but you are a looker, aren't you Ms. Raskalitkanof?"

Marcy, "It's a picture sir, she can't hear you." And give thanks for that; one less memo from Human Resources.

Halftrain, "I suppose she is the glamor model of the team. The seductress. The honey trapper." He licks his lips in just the manner Human Resources warned him against.

Marcy, "Well, I suppose she could double as that. But that's not why I'm trying to recruit her from the Russian Clandestine Services."

Halftrain, "Russian Intelligence? Do you think she would come work for us?"

Marcy, "I think she may have some ethical issues at her current job."

Within a dark hallway – Moscow – night

Natasha leads a man to her apartment door. He is Yuri Preshcov, and he makes a point of being easily led. Natasha wears an all-black form-fitting body suit with a shawl-like sweater gracefully draped over it. Yuri wears a stupid grin. Natasha turns to him and cocks her head just so before asking, "You are sure you have told no one of our rendezvous?" Yuri is sure. He has never been so certain of anything in his life. God himself does not know about their rendezvous. Frankly, it came as something of a surprise to Yuri. Natasha opens the door. They enter.

Nice apartment. New build. One bedroom with den off the entry, and a kitchen with a bar looking over the den. Bedroom in the back. One could describe the décor as Casual Nihilism: modern chairs for correct posture rather than comfort; paintings of black squares framed in black on the walls. They might have brought to Yuri's mind images of a black widow's lair, if Yuri had his mind currently doing any of his thinking.

Yuri tries to take Natasha into his arms, but she stops him, "I have a special request." She slowly walks to a cabinet and removes a pair of handcuffs.

Yuri, "You want me to handcuff you?"

Natasha returns to him. She takes his hands. "Silly boy." In a flash she has cuffed his hands together.

Yuri, "What?"

Natasha pushes him back into a posture-perfecting modernist chair. She walks to the door and opens it. Three large men brush past her to Yuri. They are Vadim, Serge, and Gleb. Vadim leads the group.

Yuri, "What have you done? What is this?"

Vadim, to Yuri, "Now you just listen journalist, we ask the questions, you take the beatings." Vadim loves this distribution of responsibility.

Natasha, to Vadim, "What do you mean *journalist*? You said he was a terrorist."

Serge, "All journalists are terrorists."

Natasha, "Where is your authority?"

Vadim, "Shut up bitch. Your job is over."

Take a moment to consider, as Vadim did not, that for most of us the world does not flip from black to white in an instant. We live in a world of careful hesitation. Most of us.

Vadim roles up his sleeves, the better to reduce staining. Serge cracks his knuckles, because health experts advise warming up before exercise. Gleb leans back on a wall, because rest matters before your shift starts. Yuri whimpers, because now he knows why he has been brought here. Natasha walks to the bathroom. None of the men bother to notice her leaving.

Natasha enters the bathroom. It is sparse and clean. She opens the medicine cabinet. Within she sees toothpaste, cold medicine, eye drops, antiperspirant, baby powder and decongestant. Seventeen different ways to kill a man. One should outlaw these things. She takes the eye drops, removes her sweater, zips the form-fitting outfit down a bit to reveal her cleavage ever so slightly, takes the lid off the eye drops and turns to leave.

Down the hall, on her way back to the living room now filled with the sounds of a good old fashion Russian beating, Natasha snatches a bottle of vodka from the hall cubby and removes the cap. She stands at the hall door looking seductive until Gleb spies her (elapsed time: 2.2 seconds). She shows him the bottle and nods back toward the bedroom. Gleb is no fool. Well, he is, but he doesn't know it yet; point being: he checks that Vadim and Serge are not looking before he heads back to Natasha.

She leads Gleb back to the bedroom. Walking in, with him behind, she motions for him to shut the door. He does. She takes a great swig on the vodka bottle and gives Gleb a look of good times ahead. She approaches Gleb. She runs a finger across his temple. Gleb likes. She also empties the eye drops into the vodka bottle with just the one hand she holds it with, but this Gleb does not see. She steps back and offers the bottle to Gleb. Gleb shows what a man he is. His vodka down-take doubles Natasha's. Natasha nods; impressive. Gleb takes another pull and hands her back the bottle. She puts it on the dresser. She approaches Gleb. He reaches out to touch her. But he doesn't.

Instead, he grabs his throat. His eyes go wide, and his body starts to twitch. He looks at Natasha much as an insect looks at a praying mantis when it's already too late. His body begins to seize up, and she turns him toward the bed and pushes him silently onto it with one finger. "You rest," she says.

Natasha picks up the bottle and leaves the room. She goes to the kitchen and looks across the counter into the living room where Vadim and Serge take turns beating Yuri. She asks, "Would anyone like a drink?"

Vadim, "No."

Serge, "Bring a towel to get the blood off."

Natasha shrugs. She turns the vodka bottle upside down into the sink and tosses the eye drops away. She opens the cabinet underneath the sink. There she sees an extension cord, dishwashing detergent, a brush, a dishtowel, a pair of rubber gloves, a box of steel wool, a role of duct tape, and a sponge. Practically an armory. These things should be banned.

Natasha dumps the steel wool balls onto the counter along with the rubber gloves. She spreads the extension cord onto a cutting board. She uses a serrated knife to cut off the attachment end and to strip the plastic insulator from the wires. She wets the steel wool and ties the exposed copper wires to the steel wool balls. She pours a glass of water. She puts on the rubber gloves. She takes the contraption, the duct tape, and the glass of water and walks into the living room. No one notices her, because who wants to miss a good beating? (Well, Yuri does, but he finds himself in no position to notice things.)

Natasha plugs in the extension cord. She holds the steel wool in the palm of her rubber gloved hand, covered by the dishtowel. On her way to Serge she draws out the extension cord behind her. She places the duct tape on a table. She says, "Serge."

Serge turns to her. She drops the water at his feet. She says, "Sorry," and offers him the towel. Instinctively he takes it, grasping the steel wool instead. As the electricity courses through his body, two thoughts come, almost simultaneously, to Serge. One is "She ambushed me!" and the other, "Holy crap, electricity is coursing through my body!" He does not say any of this. He does not make a sound. Electricity will do that to you. Natasha pushes him into the chair. She removes the rubber gloves and picks up the duct tape. She finds her best position as Vadim pulls himself away from the fine beating he delivers. He notices that things have changed a bit.

He sees Serge, jittering on a chair. He sees Natasha holding a role of duct tape. What exactly does that look in her eyes mean? Natasha pulls out a long strip of duct tape.

Vadim, "You bitch!" Sticks and stones, Vadim, sticks and stones.

Vadim charges Natasha, throwing a crushing punch at her. Natasha deftly entangles his arm in duct tape, and judo throws him to the floor. He lands on his hindquarters, and she has tied his entangled hand to his head before he knows which side of up he sits on. Foolishly, Vadim uses his free arm to pull at his restrained arm and Natasha tapes this one to his head as well. She ties his legs together and flips him face up. She kicks him once in the ribs because that is how they teach it in duct tape jujitsu school.

Natasha pulls the extension cord from the wall freeing Serge from its icy grip. He looks at her and says, "Thank you." She knocks him cold with a right cross to the jaw. "You are welcome."

Natasha frees Yuri. She says, "Do not go home, they will wait for you. Go abroad. By train. Now." Yuri nods and leaves; bruised, bloodied, but oddly grateful.

Natasha collects a few things and starts to leave herself. Vadim, flopping on the floor, shouts as she heads to the door, "You bitch! I'll find you! Wherever you run to, I'll find you!"

Natasha stops. She leans over the trussed-up Vadim. She says, "I am not running, I am leaving. Now hear my threat: I have defeated you with duct tape. If ever you cross my path again, I may choose to use a pair of scissors or a sharp stick. You may include this in your report to headquarters, along with my resignation, and, I'm guessing, your own."

Vadim meet Natasha. She woke at dawn when you slept till ten; she saw you coming before you left your house; she broke your will before she struck your body; she beat you senseless before you knew to fight. When you play checkers, she plays chess, with a machine gun.

Natasha leaves the apartment. On the street she makes a call. To the voice on the other end of the line she says, "Da. Your job I will take."

Within an Interpol HQ hallway

We see Halftrain pondering a file as Marcy leans over his shoulder correcting him.

Halftrain, "So we're now gathering the *A* Team?"

Marcy, "Technically, they will be the *C* Team."

Halftrain, "Who was the *B* Team?"

Marcy, "That would be whomever you sent to Danger Island last night without forwarding the memo to me."

Halftrain, "And the *A* Team?"

Marcy, "That would be the bookkeepers sent in after your first memo went out. Which raises the issue of *countersigning orders* we talked about."

Halftrain stares meaningfully into the middle the distance, "*Team C.* I like it. But let's just use initials: *TS.*" He collects himself for an official announcement. "Marcy, gather *TS!*"

Marcy, "We have just one more to recruit," she points to the paper.

Halftrain reads, "Rafe Riley, confidence man." Halftrain nods in approval, "I like that. A man with confidence. I have confidence. I reassure myself of it every morning. A man can go far on just confidence. This fellow might have the makings of an executive. Upper management."

Marcy, "I'm hopeful we can get him before he goes to prison."

Halftrain, "Very much executive material."

On a country road – Texas – day

A dreary country road. Very country. Dilapidated shacks consumed by kudzu, framed by broken tractors in varying states of disassembly. You can hear the birds chirp, the branches shift with the wind, the sound of one man running, the gunshots going off, and the bullets plinking about.

The running man is Rafe Riley; tall, well-built, handsome, late thirties, and clearly in a hurry. Running for his life, frankly. Hardly admiring the bucolic scenery at all. Rafe's phone rings to the tune of *I Got the Power*. He answers, still running, "Hello. Rafe Riley here." More gun shots. Rafe flinches, "I'm a bit occupied right now."

Angry voices shout from behind him. Four men chase Rafe, all wearing red-neck tactical fashion apparel, firing pistols and swearing. One of them has scorch marks all over his face and wears tattered, smoldering clothes.

Rafe, "Running from gunmen." More bullets whiz past. "Well, that is a tale."

So let us see that tale.

On that same country road – earlier

Rafe Riley, now calm, in mid sales pitch, "Every item here has a ten-year warranty with a no-lemons policy for the first two weeks. Plus we have a help line, twenty-four/seven, to get you through any start-up issues." Rafe speaks to four rather scruffy looking men in red-neck tactical wear. Which is to say that Bubba Joe Bob, LeRoy, Rooter and Duke Boy wear flannel shirts cut off at the shoulder under Vietnam era tactical vests. Bubba and LeRoy sport mullets stolen from the early eighties, while Rooter has a facial tattoo of a peace sign—crossed out— in what must count as one of his top ten most embarrassing semiological errors. Duke Boy wears a bib. All in all, not the best of Texas. They listen attentively to Rafe, rather than chasing him with guns blazing. No one is scorched yet.

And what is it that has this ten-year warranty with a no-lemons policy? Rafe stands before cases of weapons. Handguns, assault rifles, grenades, and, what? A bazooka? Do they even make those anymore? Rafe carries on with his pitch, "I'm talking a good old American help line here; not some bitter out of work engineer in Bombay sniggering to his friends at your accent while giving you the run-around."

Bubba, "Yeah, I hate that."

LeRoy, "Damn foreigners. They ought to go back home!"

Rafe puzzles at this for a moment, "Of course, if he's in Bombay then he's already home and not really a—" Rafe recalls his purpose, "Point is, you won't be left wondering which is the pointy end. Some fellow with an accent you can understand, who feels about guns the way you do—" Rafe checks himself here, "We do. Who feels about them the way we do—will walk you through shooting at whatever God in his good grace tells you to shoot at." One of the men click-clicks a rifle like he knows what he's doing. Raising the question, "What are you fellows looking to do with all this anyway?"

They look at him like he just laid a turd in front of them.

Rafe, "Just asking to see if I can guide your purchase. I'm all about customer service."

They accept this. Bubba lays down the master plan, "We're gonna assassinate the government."

LeRoy, "We're the Texas Liberation Force."

Rafe, "Never heard of you."

Rooter, "Well if you had we'd have to kill ya!" They all laugh at this. What fun. Rafe laughs too, what else can you do?

LeRoy, "Course, we are good Americans. We're gonna bring Texas back to America." Rafe tries not to puzzle over this additional geographical conundrum.

Bubba, "We gonna save Texas."

Rafe, "From what?"

The men speak virtually as one, "From the government!"

This chorus of agreement brings little enlightenment to Rafe, but he has his own agenda to press, "Well you couldn't do better than this stuff boys. This is some of the best anti U.S. Government weapons technology available. And every bit of it U.S. Army surplus. Made and guaranteed by the good old USA Army. The best anti-government government equipment money can buy."

They nod, very impressed.

Rafe pulls up a bullet proof vest, "And let's not forget that the government might shoot back."

They look on, interested.

Rafe, "This sucker will stop a round from a Glock 41, and you'll have to ask if anyone even tried to shoot you. I can put you in full suit body-armor. Government bullets can't touch you. You can just stand there taking rounds and sipping tea."

They look at him funny.

Rafe, "I mean drinking beer. Hell, I can sell you a full armor beer-cozy, so the government can't even break your bottle. And *you*," Rafe points specifically at Duke Boy, as the most unlikely of the group to tie his own shoes, "*you* can shoot back if, and when, you feel like it. Take pictures of it on your fully armored cell phone. I got everything. The best body-armor anywhere, and all of it U.S. Government certified safe and effective."

They nod, impressed.

Bubba, "Still, the price. $100,000?"

Rafe, "For the lot. All of it."

Bubba, "Might be too much."

Rafe, "Don't forget the rebate." They hadn't heard about the rebate. Rafe hauls up a duffle bag and unzips it. Full of cash. "Just for you boys, today only, I'm giving a $20,000 rebate. You pay me the hundred grand and you get the guns plus this twenty-thousand-dollar cash bag as a rebate straight back to you."

They nod. Rooter looks through the cash, somewhat to Rafe's dismay.

Bubba has a thought (perhaps his first ever), "Why don't you just keep the cash, and we give you $80,000?"

Rafe shakes his head at their innocence, "Boys, boys, I hear you. I wish I could do it that way. But it's the god damn government regulations. All the red-tape. The paperwork. It's got to be this way. Damn government."

Three of them nod knowingly. But Rooter has noticed something. He holds up a bill, "Who's on the fifty-dollar bill?"

Rafe, "Grover Cleveland. Very underrated president. Now, remember, I'm throwing in the antitank weapons as pure bonus.

Plus, the flame retardant ammunition."

Rooter, "I thought Ulysses Grant was on the fifty."

Rafe, "That's right. Damn Yankee."

Rooter holds up a bill to Rafe's face, "Well who's this?"

Rafe inspects the bill, "Well that's Grover Cleveland. And I can see why you're confused, but these are the new bills. Grant was on the *old* fifty."

The entire Texas Liberation Force rummages through the bag. Rafe starts to back away.

One of them holds up a twenty-dollar bill.

LeRoy, "Who's this on the twenty-dollar bill?"

Rafe, "That's Warren Harding. Jackson was very bad to the Indians; he's out now."

The hardy men of the TLF appear to have recalibrated their Rafe-confidence level rather severely.

Rafe, "Boys, come on! Would I be crooked enough to deal in counterfeit bills with the wrong presidents on them?"

This doesn't take long to answer. They pull guns.

Rafe backs further away, "Okay, okay. Just don't do anything ironic like shoot me with my own weapons. That wouldn't be sporting."

Now that inspires them. Shoving their own weapons into their belts, they each pull guns from Rafe's selection.

Rafe continues backing up, "Boys. You shoot those at me it's going to void the warranty."

Duke Boy picks up an anti-tank weapon with a big grin on his face. The others take aim with assault rifles. Rafe takes to his heels. The three with assault rifles take aim and fire.

BOOM!

Not *bang* like a bullet comes out, but *boom* like a defective weapon blows up. Scares the hell out of the would-be shooters. Ear-bleeds all around.

Duke Boy looks on at the damage done to his comrades-in-arms. Now he is mad. No brighter than before, but madder. He levels the antitank gun.

Bubba, "Uh, Duke Boy, maybe—"

Duke Boy doesn't listen. He never developed the habit of listening, so he hasn't the knack for it now. Duke Boy fires the antitank gun.

BOOM!

I mean really big *Boom*. Smoke everywhere. Duke Boy's face is scorched. His clothes smolder. They all draw their own guns.

On the same road – now

And so now Rafe runs, holding his phone. The liberators of Texas give chase, shooting.

Rafe, "So what I could really use is an airlift."

Ahead of him, Rafe sees a pick-up truck parked on the roadside. A young woman stands next to the truck speaking into a cell phone while a man sits on the roof of the truck with a remote control.

Rafe looks perplexed, not knowing who he sees. But that pales beside the puzzlement to follow.

A drone whizzes past him. Down the road the drone hovers before the advancing phalanx of the Texas Liberation Force. They stop, not knowing what to do. The drone carries a loudspeaker and from this emerges a robotic voice: "Drop your weapons! Surrender! Lie prone on the ground!" The mean men of the TLF look at each other a moment, then, as one, they raise their guns and blow the drone out of the sky.

From the drone ruble on the ground the loudspeaker speaks: "This will make my big brother very mad." A rumble and buzz comes from behind the truck on the road. Into view flies another drone. Bigger. Much bigger and painted in ice blue lightning bolts against a black background. Very ferocious looking for a drone, but quite an unnecessary embellishment given that the large missile the drone carries conveys more than sufficient menace. This drone flies to the armed redneck army. This drone does not talk. But it speaks eloquently: FOOSH!

Foosh, as in a missile launches. And the subsequent explosion scatters the bad guys unconscious across the road.

Rafe puts away his phone and walks to the woman next to the

truck. She puts her own phone away and offers her hand to Rafe, "I'm Marcy Gainer, behind me, Kip Carson. Welcome to Interpol Mr. Riley."

Rafe shakes her hand. He looks back at the smoke behind him, "I really, really want one of those."

Interpol conference room – Washington D.C.

A mid-sized room whose chairs form a semi-circle around a lectern; coffee available in the back. Today it holds only four people: Trevor, Rafe, Natasha, and Kip. They all sit or stand alone and in silence. Rafe retrieves a cup of coffee and brings it to Natasha. "Hi. Coffee? No? Right." Rafe puts down the coffee. "I'm Rafe Riley. I'm the truth management specialist here. I oversee the presentation and distribution of truth. Or truth's near cousin, plausibility." Rafe can see that this does not sound very plausible. He's an expert like that. "I also run the poker games."

Natasha looks away from him with only a vague aspect of annoyance on her face.

Rafe, "You really rock the black. Your specialty is what? Not being seen during a power outage?" Nothing. "Is that a uniform or something? I only ask because I designed the uniform here at Interpol. I don't know if you've seen it ... blue and yellow ... with a great big silver helmet. Hasn't been released to the public yet."

Natasha looks unmoved. Unmoved is her typical look, but she looks especially that way now.

Rafe, "Does any of this seem at all charming to you?"

Natasha, "I infer that you are a child who has wondered among the adults. Go away child."

Rafe, "Ouch. Okay. I sense some initial skepticism. I get that a lot. Ever heard of the Belmont Hustle? A classic."

Natasha, "No."

Rafe, "I invented it. It's a four man grift with the mark taken by the shill after a three-part swap. It's like ballet. And wholly original. Most grifters use hustles dating back to the stone age—but I'm an innovator."

Natasha could not seem less interested.

Rafe, "Ever heard of the Mishnu Ponzi Scheme? A big deal back in the day, brought down a whole government. That was mine too. It was textbook. Literally, you can find it in a textbook."

Natasha, "Some might say that a criminal of deception whose work can be found in textbooks failed as a criminal."

Rafe leans back into his seat, "Valid point. Are you sure I can't get you any coffee?"

Natasha, "I am sure."

Trevor approaches bearing cups, "Coffee anyone?"

Natasha takes a cup. She doesn't drink it, just holds it in plain view.

Trevor, "Just talking to that Kip fellow over there. It's been yonks since I've had such a beastly time wringing lucidity from a chap. I'm sure he's an absolute brick, being all present and accounted for, but jolly hard to fathom. Plumbed for the depths, mind you, came up all mud-cakes. Might as well blister a raisin as push the tiddle with him."

Rafe, "Your English is harder than her Russian."

Trevor, "Well, Queens own." Trevor walks away to another seat. Kip approaches with two cups, "Coffee?"

Natasha takes another cup and so now holds two in plain sight.

Kip thinks of something witty to say to her, "I bet you take it black." Natasha walks her cups to another seat.

Rafe slaps his head, "Why didn't I think to say that."

Kip finds a seat far from the others.

In the hallway just beyond these deepening rifts, Marcy walks behind Halftrain to the conference room.

Halftrain, "And how's our team coming together? Just fine, I'm sure."

Marcy, "I left them alone for a while, I figured they could start getting to know each other best in a relaxed, informal atmosphere." She opens the door to find each member of the team facing away from all the others in a silence of the damned.

Halftrain, "Well, at least they're not shouting at each other." Halftrain makes his way to the lectern. He introduces himself,

"I'm Lester Halftrain, your supervisor. This is my assistant, Marcy." He points behind him in the wrong direction, then looks at his notes, "Though unqualified and poorly trained and led, you've been selected for this team because you are expendable—barely be missed really. Your names aren't even in the computer. Why if you were all to die, we could even stop payment on your first checks."

Marcy clears her throat and leans in, pointing at Halftrain's notes, "Red colored notes for your eyes only; blue colored notes for your pep talk."

Halftrain looks over his notes again, reading off the blue ones to himself, "Highly qualified ... credit to the force ... well prepared ... thanks of a grateful nation ... yes, this looks much better. We'll go with the blue notes." He looks around to the silence of the room. Halftrain carries on, "I want to congratulate you on the successful completion of your training." Marcy steps up and points to the right part of his notes, "Ahh, I want to encourage you to successfully complete your training." Halftrain leans toward Marcy, "They've filled out all their forms? The liability releases? Good. That should about do it." To the team he offers parting wisdom, "Carry on." Halftrain leaves. Marcy looks at her creation.

Rafe, "Training?"

Kip, "What do we need training for?"

Within a trophy room – night

Heads of animals stare blankly—or is it accusingly?—into a room of elegant, tufted armchairs that could double as small thrones. In one sits Karloff the hunter, inspecting his glory walls. He sees deer, antelope, bison, a cape buffalo, an elephant (it is a very high-ceilinged room), two lions—he and she—a whole family of marmosets, and a kangaroo, stuffed baby in pouch. Karloff's feet rest upon the head of a tiger now turned ignobly into a rug. A great fireplace casts flickering shadows across the room. Karloff pokes a feathered pen at the wooden table beside him. Boris the giant sits across from him on the edge of a sofa made from a leopard's hide. Karloff sighs. He drifts into the open arms of memory. Back to the old country.

On a cold day, outside in the snow, a bearded old man calls out, "Ivan, come look." A young Ivan Karloff runs over; he must be just ten years old. "Look here Ivan. These are the tracks of the male wolf. You can tell by the spacing and the occasional brush of the tail. He has hunted, you can see by the blood flecks." Ivan looks on with awe. "And here, further he goes, leaving his mark." The two walk on in the snow. "Mind your own steps Ivan, do not disrupt the trail." Ivan minds. "Ivan, look here now. New tracks. What are they?"

Ivan, "Also a wolf, Grandpa."

His grandfather offers a tone of rebuke, "A she-wolf! Note the lesser gap in these steps, a shift in the displacement of the hind legs typical of the female. Notice everything, Ivan! Everything! Four paws become eight paws, and now we have wolves he and she."

Ivan looks hard and notices, "Grandpa, what does it mean when eight paws become just six paws? And why aren't they walking anymore?"

His grandfather stumbles a bit, "Uh, well, when one set of paws loves another set of paws very much, uh ... Look! Bear tracks! Follow me!"

Sweet memories. In his study Karloff nods. "A great man. A great teacher." Karloff stares into the fireplace and pokes at the table.

Outside a rustic farm, a thirteen-year-old Karloff carries his rifle past two attractive girls his own age. One girl asks, "Did you kill anything today Little Ivan?"

Little Ivan stands stock still like a deer asked a question by an attractive other deer, "I have hunted in vain on this day, though I shall prevail in my great work and many a woodland creature shall fall to my rod!"

The girls laugh. "Your rod did not fell any?"

Ivan nervously strokes his rifle's barrel.

The prettier of the girls approaches, "Oh great Ivan, may I

touch the rod that will smite the woodland creatures?"

Ivan's voice cracks, "Yes."

They laugh and run off.

Karloff stares at the mantle above his great trophy room fireplace. Stuffed birds and rodents. A Marmot, a prairie dog, a muskrat and a flying squirrel that no longer flies. It serves instead to introduce the mantle's dead birds: falcons, eagles and gyre-hawks. Birds of prey, preying no more.

Karloff takes a drink of vodka from a shot glass, "My destiny, the hunt." His mind turns back again to the past.

A thick flock of birds flies in a clear bright sky. Karloff hefts up a shotgun with an extension clip. He shoots birds down, letting off twenty shells in quick succession, two to three birds downed with each shot. The sky rains birds down onto Karloff.

Karloff stalks a giant bull elephant. It roars and shakes dust from its head, tusks swinging. Karloff brings down a bull elephant with a single shot. He poses with the body standing between the tusks.

Karloff chases a rhino; he carries only a spear! Karloff runs from a barely speared Rhino. Learning curve. Karloff tracks the prints of a mountain lion, armed only with a bowie knife. He tracks the lion to a rock. He looks up, the mountain lion leaps! An epic struggle. Karloff prevails and raises his bloody knife high.

Karloff, charged by a silverback mountain gorilla, stands his ground and brings the mighty beast down with his tricked up sling-shot. He beats his chest over his prize.

Karloff kneels on the extended prow of a ship shooting arrows one after another at the sea below him. The dolphins gliding ahead of his ship go down, one after another. Behind Karloff the fishing crew looks on, aghast.

Karloff tiptoes on the pack ice wielding a club. A white coated baby seal looks sweetly at his approach. Karloff lets out a war cry and clubs the baby seal to a pulp. A baffled Inuit guide takes a picture of Karloff holding the dead seal over his head.

Karloff swims in scuba gear armed with a speargun. A penguin swims past, halting its pursuit of fish to welcome a land creature to his crystal-clear world. Karloff spearguns it down. No fish for the baby penguin now!

Karloff soars on a hang-glider next to eagles on all sides. Hunters flying together. An eagle tips it's wing at the flying man. Karloff pulls a pistol. Down go the eagles.

Karloff sits on a mustang, holding a rifle, surveying the scene before him. Buffalo, twenty adults and seven young, stand in the field in front of the mounted hunter, eating grass, as buffalo will. Karloff checks the wind with his finger. He spurs his horse to run parallel to the buffalo herd. The buffalo take notice. They become antsy. Karloff turns and spurs his horse the opposite way, still parallel to the herd. The buffalo become highly agitated. Karloff fires his weapon in the air. Mercy to buffalo? No. His shot sets them running in a panic. Karloff gives chase, firing in the air to channel the buffalo just where he wants them. And does he channel them to a safe buffalo preserve lush with green grass? No. They run off a cliff. One after another, adult and young alike, crashing at the bottom to become a pile of dead bones and meat. Karloff dismounts and stands on the cliff above the carnage. He lets out a war whoop. He scrambles down the cliff face to the bottom. He pulls his knife and cuts, from a single dead buffalo, a single tail. He does a war dance which he regards as a tribute to the traditional hunters of the plains, but which they, were they to see it, would regard as a particularly egregious case of cultural mis-appropriation.

In his trophy room, Karloff smiles as he holds up the buffalo tail. "Who says there are no more worlds to conquer?" Boris doesn't say that. Boris says nothing at all. He just sits, watching Karloff absent mindedly poke at something on the side table. Boris watches Karloff poking with a feathered pen; cutting off the legs of a wingless fly, one at a time.

Within a room – night

Marcy looks serious, "Mr. Halftrain, you must be the most incompetent, self-serving, glad-handing, nit-wit executive I have ever worked for. You took over my concept for this team, and I resent that. You also wear stupid looking ties."

Chris Gainer, Marcy's husband, looks on a bit panicked as he listens.

Chris, "You told him this?"

Marcy shakes herself out of the spell, "Of course not. I wiped his nose as usual. But the day will come. Do you have to look so relieved?"

Chris, "No, I hope you do it. Take the camcorder to work that day because I want to see him faint. It's just, if you're going to do it tomorrow, let me know so that I can go out and find a job pumping gas or something. I don't think our creditors would understand an act of conscience at this stage in our financial history."

Marcy heads for the kitchen sink and leaps into a violent dish washing spree, "He'll blow this for me! He'll say the wrong word, drool on his shoes—something. Months to get approval, and then finding the right people, making contact—" She throws a dish into the sink, breaking it, "Christ! Couldn't you have done these while I was at work?"

Chris walks to her, carefully, as one would a caged tiger that just discovered how to lift the latch. He puts his hands on her arms, "I'm sorry. I was ... uh ... I was watching my soaps all afternoon. You know how I love my soaps."

Marcy stares into his eyes. Her anger breaks and she laughs a bit, "Soaps my ass, you were working on that damn dissertation."

Chris smiles, "Yes. But I feared that if I told you that you might start making more dish shards. You have busted my kitchen budget for the week already."

Marcy puts her head against his chest. Then she pulls herself away, just tired now. She sits down again at the kitchen table, "How is the Magnum Opus coming?"

Chris starts doing the dishes, "Good. Good. I got three more pages done. But I think I'm going to have to throw out chapter five."

Marcy, "Oh no! You worked two years on that."

34

Chris, "I know, I know. But the field has passed that chapter by."

Marcy, "The field? Semiotics in Cultural Anthropology? I didn't think there were more than half a dozen people in your field."

Chris, "Evidently some of the others get more work done than I do." A child cries in the background. "Ahh, they're playing my theme song."

Marcy jumps up from her seat, "Oh, let me!"

Chris, "Consider yourself the front of the line."

In the nursery, Marcy opens the door to find an eighteen-month-old toddler named Katrina, the pride of the family Gainer. A moment ago she pitched a fit at being left two minutes too long at nap time, but on seeing her mother she starts bouncing up and down in joy. Marcy picks her up, "How's my little peanut? How's my little Katrina?"

Katrina responds with, "Peanut!" This annoys Marcy slightly, but she will not let bad news break her good mood. Katrina handles mommy's face with sharp nails, which also proves a challenge to Marcy's mood, but Chris enters behind them to help out.

Marcy, "Wonder child needs her nails clipped."

Chris, "Sorry, I have calluses on my nose from her clawing."

Marcy, "Hmm, there's an attractive image for Daddy. Why don't you clip them?"

Chris, "She squirms. I needed Mom to hold her fingers so she doesn't lose any."

They set Katrina down on a changing table as Chris retrieves a small pair of scissors.

Marcy, "Ahh you such a sweety, you are ... you are such a sweety. A boo boo. A boo boo."

Chris, "I love it when you come home, and I can finally have an adult conversation."

Marcy, "Don't you talk to Daddy? Say Dada. Say Mama. Say Mama." Marcy seems just a tad insistent on this last point.

Katrina beams at her mother and follows her lead, "Dada."

Marcy, "Okay." Marcy watches Daddy trim Katrina's nails as if she means to fill out a work evaluation form when he's done.

Marcy, "So what did I miss today?"

Chris, "Toy throwing."

Marcy, "Skip the little stuff. I want to hear about firsts that I've missed. Developmental milestones I only get to hear about.

Chris, "We do our best to keep you in the loop."

Marcy, "I missed rolling over, sitting up, first crawl, first pull to a stand. First steps! I've missed all the firsts. I've missed just about the whole baby Olympics."

Chris, "I knocked her down so many times trying to keep her from taking her first step without you. I practically tied her feet together."

Marcy, "Did she say the word?"

Chris shifts uncomfortably. He finishes clipping Katrina's nails, "There. All done. She's safe to snuggle with now."

Marcy picks Katrina up and rubs noses. They walk down the apartment hall to the living room, a space filled with books and stacks of papers. The debris of Chris's dissertation efforts. Marcy plays with Katrina while Chris picks up the TV remote, "So now that you have your team together."

Marcy, "Halftrain's team."

Chris, "So now that you have Halftrain's team together ... will we be seeing more of you at Castle Gainer? Home by dinner occasionally?"

Marcy, "We have four talented individuals who have hardly even met yet. Turning them into a team is the hard work ahead. And I don't give better than even money for our chances."

Chris, "I thought that welding random individuals into a cohesive unit was the special talent of paramilitary organizations."

Marcy shoots him a nasty look, "Interpol is not a paramilitary organization. We don't even carry guns. Normally. And these are not random individuals. I selected them specifically for their ability to improvise and work without supervision. I chose them to be agents who could move at the zig zag rather than the straight line."

Chris, "So now all you have to do is straighten them out."

Marcy, "That's what Halftrain thinks. But we need to do something harder than that. We need to keep them bent, but all bent in the same direction. And the right direction at that. While keeping our eye on the silverware."

Chris, "And you selected their initial mission to do just that."

Marcy, "So I thought. Perfect first job: important enough to justify a special team, but outside the authority of local police in San Monique. Just a quick two punch infiltration to find unlicensed exotic animals. An easy, quick justification of my concept."

Chris, "But."

Marcy, "Everything that crosses my desk goes to Halftrain's. Now he's lost a fraud detection team, has ordered in our Best of the Best Agent of Chaos, and put us in the spotlight before I had the team properly collected, much less trained. Ick! She spit up on me! Help."

Chris brings a burp cloth and towels Katrina and Marcy off. Katrina has a big smile on her face.

Chris, "So you have a hard job ahead of you."

Marcy, "Yes. She looks awful proud of herself."

Chris, "Yep. A hard job. But not as hard as keeping little Mrs. Spitupilus from wolfing all over every stitch of fabric in the house."

Chris cleans off Marcy's pants. Marcy looks at her husband. She puts a hand on his face, "No. Not as hard a job as that."

Out at the training grounds – day

Trevor and Kip stand at the top of a tall platform strung with repelling ropes next to the repelling instructor.

The repelling instructor asks Trevor, "Ever done rope work?"

Trevor smiles, "Confine your concerns to the young man there." Trevor gracefully takes the rope and smoothly glides to the ground like something out of Cirque de Soleil.

The instructor looks impressed. Kip looks ticked off, "Give me the rope." Kip takes the rope awkwardly. He slides down a few feet. "Arrghh! My hands have caught fire!"

Repelling instructor, "Use your feet!"

Kip loses a shoe trying to snag the rope. He slips further, "Arrghh! My feet are on fire! You bastard!" Kip slips the rest of the way down in palm-burning jerks, falling the last five feet to land on his back.

Trevor waits at the bottom, "Most bold descent."

Within the Interpol gym

A judo instructor faces off against Rafe. Others watch, including the rest of the team. Everyone wears the classic judo uniform. Off white for the judo instructor, thanks to many washes. Pristine white for the trainees.

Judo instructor, "It could be life or death. You or the scum-punk. Take your stance."

Rafe tries to imitate the judo instructor's stance but looks obviously out of his element.

Judo instructor, "Now, I pull a knife on you. What do you do?"

Rafe, "If you kill me, you'll never find the gold!"

This throws the judo instructor a bit. He straightens up, "What gold?"

Rafe, "See, it's working already."

The judo instructor just shakes his head, "Sit down." The instructor looks around and happens upon Natasha. He orders her forward, "You, come here and take a stance." Natasha comes and stands. The instructor throws a punch that stops just short of her nose. He asks, "I do that. What do you do?"

Natasha, "Laugh."

Judo instructor, "This is no laughing matter, little girl. I'm going to grab you from behind."

Natasha, "I do not like to be touched."

The instructor moves behind her, "You'll be touched and like it. Now class, supposing an assailant grips you like so..." He grabs Natasha.

Deftly she pivots and throws him on the mat. She then puts

him in an arm lock and strikes his neck.

Judo instructor, "Aggghhh! Okay, class is dis—"

Natasha pulls him up with a pain control hold then flings him again to the mat. She puts him in an arm bar and strikes hard at his kidneys.

Judo instructor, "Aggghhhh!!!" The others form a neat circle around the two as Natasha twists his arm and grips his eyes with her other hand. The instructor screams in agony and pleads for his life.

Rafe, "I think that ends today's lesson."

Natasha, "Not for him."

Within the Interpol psychological evaluation office – day

Marcy watches nervously as each prospective member of her team undergoes a rigorous evaluation from Interpol's Department of Psychological Profiling. A psychologist in a white lab-coat prepares a Rorschach test. She holds up inkblot pages to Kip.

Psychologist, "Just tell me what you see. Give your impression."

Kip looks at the inkblot excitedly, "I see a profound commentary on the fallen nature of man. The struggle of self-overcoming in a bleak and unforgiving world crushed by small minds and brought low by the suffering of the tender heart. Yet, also, a faint hope rising, suggesting that all can be transformed by the power of love."

The psychologist offers another ink-blot, virtually indistinguishable from the last, of course, "And this one?"

Kip, angry, "Mawkish derivative twaddle peddling the same sentimental bourgeoisie nonsense about the redemption of the soul that we have all seen *so* many times before."

Marcy feels relief, noting that the psychologist passes Kip. Apparently, a frenzy for novelty does not indicate psycho-pathology.

The psychologist holds up an inkblot to Rafe, "What do you see?"

Rafe, "I see a psychologist holding up an inkblot."

Psychologist, "No, I mean *in* the inkblot."

Rafe, "Right, *in* the inkblot I see that."

The psychologist holds up another, "And what do you see in this one?"

Rafe, "I see a psychologist wondering how seven years of graduate school and ten years of clinical work led to finger painting."

That is, of course, what the psychologist always sees in the inkblots, so Rafe gets a big check mark.

The psychologist holds up an inkblot to Trevor, "What do you see here?"

Trevor, impatient, "A smudge."

Psychologist, "Yes, but what does it suggest to you?"

Trevor, "It suggests that the designer of this particular work, if we might call the person such, could readily be replaced with any random four-year-old. It further suggests that said designer —if such a person even exists—might well be color blind, given that if one *must* spill ink on paper with so little regard for representational content, one ought at least to make it colorful to the eye."

The psychologist holds up another, "And what do you see in this one?"

Trevor, "A blotch."

Psychologist, "Yes, but what does it indicate to you?"

Trevor, "It indicates a general decline in standards, both in the world of art and in the science of human understanding. It indicates in fact—as long as you've asked—a fundamental decline in Western Civilization altogether. One that I'm in no way certain we can ever overcome. If you must know my opinion."

Marcy breathes easy. She knows with certainty that no one gets screened out of Interpol for either literal-mindedness or Old-World values.

The psychologist holds up an inkblot to Natasha, "Now what does this look like? Take your time."

Natasha, "Death."

Marcy looks worried.

The psychologist tries another, "And this one?"

Natasha, "Disease."

Marcy looks really worried.

Psychologist, "And what does this one look like to you?"

Natasha, "Two men have killed each other with knives and are dying."

The doctor notices Marcy's concern, "Oh no, don't worry, she's absolutely right. Highest scorer I've ever seen."

Well, there it is then, in case you've ever wanted to know.

Within an Interpol lecture hall – day

Interpol agents attend a lecture. The blackboard reads: "Ethics for Agents—The Morality of Intelligence Gathering." An ethics instructor speaks, "So in the past, we have had issues relating to conduct in the field and the ethics of intelligence gathering for law enforcement. In its wisdom, Interpol has called for the completion of this mandated course." He holds a thick spiral bound book aloft. "In here you will find the rules and regs relating to ethical conduct in the field. Read it carefully." An audience member laughs. "What's that about?"

Rafe, "Page 47, on the don'ts' of video surveillance."

Ethics instructor, "You find those funny?"

Rafe, "Check out page 63, on the misuse of sex in sting operations." Trainees start thumbing their copies with new interest.

Ethics instructor, "This wasn't put together for your amusement."

Rafe, "Well it works anyway."

The instructor looks to change the subject. He notices Natasha, "Mrs. Raskalitkanof; I understand you once worked for Russian Intelligence. You must have seen one of these before."

Natasha, "Da. But not so thick." Her fingers indicates a two-page pamphlet at best.

At the Gainer house – night

Katrina tries out vocabulary, "Boom!"

A small party. Attending are the team and the three Gainers. Natasha holds little Katrina at arm's length. Rafe looks on over her shoulder.

Natasha, "Such a sweet child."

Rafe, "That's not how you hold one of those."

Natasha, "What would you know of it?"

Rafe slowly coaxes Natasha's arms into bringing Katrina close to her, "Three brothers, four sisters. In my house you had to negotiate your way into the bathroom."

Natasha now holds Katrina awkwardly, but close. Katrina locks her legs around Natasha.

Rafe, "Now isn't that better? Baby likes it." Katrina frowns at *baby*. Independent minded toddler if you don't mind.

Marcy flits by, "Oh, you look so cute together."

Natasha, "She has erupted upon me."

Marcy has a towel ready, "Sorry, she does that. Apparently, it's her idea of a thank you gift."

Marcy goes for more snacks, passing Trevor and Kip.

Trevor, "Yes, I think I understand. You're something called a conceptual artist, and you use explosives as your palette. Is that it?"

Kip, "Yes. Well, no, not exactly. The explosives are more like my brushes. Ideas are my palette."

Trevor, "I thought ideas were your canvass?"

Kip, "No, the world is my canvass."

Trevor, "The world? So what portions of the world have you painted with explosives?"

Kip, "Not painted. If you have to call it something, call it ... *ideaed*."

Trevor, "Ideaed."

Kip grows really excited now, "Right. Take my Munich project. From a hot-air balloon I exploded a giant vat of blue paint over the heart of Munich during the lunch hour. I covered four city blocks in blue."

Trevor, "That's just my point. You dyed Munich in blue paint."

Kip, "No, you're not getting it. The paint was just a vehicle for the idea of blue. A metaphor. The blue is the omnipresence of depression that can fall on one and all. The city is a symbol of modern urban alienation which lies under our—call it what it is: our *Blueness*."

Trevor, "And the lunch hour?"

Kip, "The lunch hour was just lunch hour—the winds were right then—but get this: After I covered the city in blue—I released a pair of white doves."

Kip seems well satisfied; Trevor looks bewildered.

Kip, "Hope ascending. Get it?"

Trevor, "What about the people you sprayed with blue paint?"

Kip becomes a bit uncomfortable, "There were some complaints."

Marcy takes shrimp to Trevor and Kip, passing Rafe on the way. Rafe holds Katrina now and stands next to Chris and Natasha.

Chris, "At first I focused on ethnography. For my field work I went to study the Hagerati of West Central Africa. Turns out they smoke this local herb most of the day and won't talk to anyone who doesn't. After a few days of smoking their herb I was in no shape to talk to anybody. Can I get you a drink or anything?"

Natasha, "No."

Chris, "Right. Well, then I shifted my focus to Polynesia. I heard of this stone age tribe, the Tatacom, living on a small island in the middle of French Polynesia. But by the time I got there they had just won a lawsuit against an internet startup using their name. They had given up stone tools for computers. Had their own web site. So I gave up on living cultures altogether. Now I work in theoretical archeology. In between toddler training and sweeping out the cave."

Natasha, "You work in house like woman?"

Rafe, "What a way for *you* to talk."

Chris, "I get that all the time. Not usually so direct." Natasha blushes at having failed to navigate a cultural difference. But Chris understands such failures almost as much as he understands toddler developmental psychology, and he is about as immune to gender shaming as a man can be. "It's okay, really. Also, Marcy is looking to get me some consulting work as a researcher with your group. Not quite a secret agent. No kung fu. But maybe I get a decoder ring."

Natasha, "What is this decoder ring?"

Chris considers how to navigate the gap between American cereal-box toy culture and covert operations nomenclature.

Marcy pulls Chris away, "Excuse us, Natasha."

She retrieves Baby Kate from Rafe, "Thank you, Uncle Rafe."

Rafe, "Like being at home again."

Marcy pulls Chris away to the kitchen with her. In the kitchen Chris offers his impressions of Natasha, "She's really quite something. Doesn't talk much, but she says something to you with her eyes."

Marcy, "She knows twenty different ways to kill a man." Marcy hands off Katrina to Chris.

Chris, "We stayed off that topic. No shop talk, just like you ordered."

Marcy, "I think my plan will pay off. They seem to be getting along."

In the living room, Natasha grows impatient with Rafe, "Covert agents gather data, they do not give it out."

Rafe, "I'm not gathering intel on you, I just asked about your family."

Natasha looks at him impassively.

Rafe, "Don't give me your interrogation resistance look. We call this a party. At these you drink too much, share too much, and stay until the host comes out carrying a toothbrush."

Natasha, "I have no information to offer."

Rafe, "I don't want your social security number, just how many siblings?"

Natasha says nothing.

Rafe, "It's zero now, right? Because you murdered them all."

Across the room Kip speaks to Trevor in a state of shock, "Turner! Gainsborough! Are you kidding? You'd compare some English landscape to what I'm talking about?"

Trevor, "Well, not to exploding cans of paint obviously, but to those ghastly tomato soup cans."

Kip cannot believe his ears. He charges over to Rafe, seeking vindication, "Where do you stand on Warhol?"

Rafe, "I need a Warhol policy?"

Trevor approaches, chewing shrimp, "Don't mind him, he's just inhaled too many paint fumes."

Kip, "Ideas! That's what I inhale." Kip turns to Rafe, "What do you think of Turner?"

Rafe, "What exactly is your super-power here kid? Post-modern kung fu?"

Kip, "Painting with missiles, what's yours? Running slower than bullets?"

Trevor, "If we did need to engage a resident artist, we might at least have picked one with refined taste."

Natasha, "Decadent Americans."

Marcy and Chris make their way from the kitchen into the lion's den.

Chris, "So is it working? Whatever you're trying to do with them?"

Marcy, "I'm trying to make a team out of them. I'm trying to pull them together."

They enter a scene of bedlam; everyone shouting at everyone.

Chris, "Yes, well, we'll need to pull them apart first."

Outside above the jungle – night

Agent 117 falls fast from the dark sky toward the jungle canopy. Ten seconds before the nick of time, his chute opens jerking him in the air. He continues, slowed but still fast, toward the thick of the trees. Ordinary paratroops would fear to break their necks dropping into trees, but Agent 117 stuffed ordinary into a body-bag and threw it out years ago. In the nick of time (ten seconds having passed) he pulls a second ripcord. His chute detaches as a six foot round globe of hydrogen inflates above him, slowing him to a gentle landing in the tree tops. He pulls the cord on this and drops to the ground beneath the jungle canopy. Banish fear; Agent 117 has arrived.

See the living embodiment of advanced tactical gear merchandizing: The soles of his boots can automatically deploy three different kinds of treads depending on the terrain or the need to alter his tracks. They lace up for a classic look (and to provide steel laces as garrotes should the need arise) and end in Velcro, for that modern touch. And not ordinary Velcro, but special silenced Velcro, in case anyone should be listening when you need to take your boots off in the jungle, or in a lady's boudoir—Agent 117 can handle any environment. His midnight black pants resist puncture, retain or dispense heat at the push of a button, and show off his thighs to good effect. Black kneepads protect his knees (the knees always go first for a secret agent), and above the knees Agent 117 wears equipment pouches hooked to a utility belt that Batman would gasp at in wonder. On his hips, Agent 117 has strapped two automatic pistols. They each sport extended ammunition clips and telescopic sights and small bayonets protruding from under the barrels just in case. (Take care sitting down in the boudoir.) His Kevlar tactical vest screams manhood so loud it requires an extra level of silencing. His black gloves have different fabrics for each finger, designed for different tactile tasks: trigger pulling (no slip grip), gun-grabbing (extra sticky), map handling (stubby, for turning pages), and brail reading (very thin fabric). Agent 117 wears a full head-covering black mask (he's balding, and a little sensitive about it), and night vision goggles cover his eyes, extending a full three inches from his face in two lenses. Agent 117 looks like one exotic animal.

And in his hands, well gripped, he carries the PR .46 caliber Mag-master Machine Assault Rifle/Survival Kit. Radar aiming sights, regular-to-hair-trigger conversion button, full noise suppressor, single, rapid and random firing modes, a locator system synced to your cell phone (in case you leave it somewhere), and companion mode with internet connection, so you can verbally order it to shoot—or ask about restaurants in your area. It also has a compass and full surgery kit in the stock. No weapon not contained on a jet fighter looks scarier or costs more than the PR .46 caliber Mag-master Machine Assault Rifle/Survival Kit. Best of all, you can order it online.

Agent 117 scans the jungle through his night vision goggles. The jungle in day looks green. The jungle at night looks dark. The jungle at night through night vision goggles looks green again, but a fuzzy "what exactly am I seeing here?" green. What, exactly, Agent 117 sees in a green haze is: leaves and tree limbs, then a puzzled bamboo rat, then a man with a bow and arrow pointed at him, then an armadillo rolled into a ball, then—wait. Back up. Agent 117 goes back to the man with the bow. Then: PRANG! Which is the exact sound a high tensile hunting-bow arrow makes when it shoots straight through a single night vision gog. For a moment Agent 117 jerks his head around trying to make sense of the hazy green static electricity he sees. Then: PRING! The sound of a reinforced blowgun bolt taking out a second night vision gog.

Agent 117 rips off the goggles. This leaves him in complete darkness. Now his training kicks in. He lets rip with the assault rifle, chewing up bark and leaves. SNAP! The sound of a bullwhip ripping a PR .46 caliber Mag-master Machine Assault Rifle/Survival Kit from a secret agent's hands (thus voiding the warranty). Agent 117 looks about frantically, which does not help since frenzy produces no light. So he runs. Not a run of glory but a bid for survival.

Running blind through a jungle is functionally equivalent to crawling, blind, through mud while harassed by mosquitos. After a few minutes floundering in the jungle mud, he collects himself. He remembers who he is, and more to the point, what he has brought. From one of his many pockets he produces a pair of infra-red goggles. Putting them on, he sees the jungle as a spectrum of haloed light and darkness—the brighter parts betokening the heat of an animal. Agent 117 pulls his pistol and clicks its mechanisms a few times as a confidence building measure. He walks through the mud, or slogs through, as his boots do not have a mud-repellent feature. He looks for roughly man shaped red images.

He passes a log covered in mud. No sign there. Agent 117 passes on. But from the mire arises a man whose cool carapace of mud conceals his heat signature. This man watches Agent 117 tactically point his gun at every chirping cricket as the secret agent makes his way through a jungle clearing. The mud-covered man stalks Agent 117. He takes out a bent object and begins to carefully wipe the mud from it. The moonlight in the clearing reveals the object: a boomerang.

From a tree above, a howler monkey lets out a loud hoot. Agent 117 nearly jumps out of his tactical gear. He lets loose with his pistol. Thirteen shots go off at the tree before a boomerang crashes into Agent 117's hand, knocking the gun out of it. The boomerang made a sound, but no one could hear it over all the gun shots. Agent 117 quick-draws his other pistol. Now we hear it: WHOOSH WHOOSH WHOOSH. A boomerang takes out the second gun.

Sticks! Flying sticks! Agent 117 cannot believe he has been beat by flying sticks. Why has he no defense for this? It just confirms what he has always said: you cannot take enough equipment into the bush with you. He runs, stumbling in the jungle. He tries to climb the nearest tree—no mean feat when looking for hand-holds on the basis of differential heat signatures. Fortunately, he finds a vine to pull himself up to a fork in the tree. Unfortunately, the vine is a tripwire, and just as Agent 117 gets comfortable on the branches he sees an object swinging toward him; a log on ropes which looks to him like a log shaped blueish halo with a bright red frog-shaped figure in its center. The log hits Agent 117, knocking him from the tree, with a beautiful midair somersault, onto the trail behind the tree, and smearing dead frog all over his face.

Agent 117 props himself up. He shakes his head to clear it.

He wipes off some frog. Ick. He sees before him the growing red of a man approaching. Agent 117 stands up, shakily, and pulls a knife (the Bushmaster S11 with laser sights and self-sharpening case). WHUMP ... WHUMP ... WHUMP. Argentine bolas give a man plenty of time to worry about what's coming. When they arrive, they entangle Agent 117, pinning his arms to his side and delivering three ugly blows, knocking him to the ground. From this disadvantaged tactical position, Agent 117 watches his foe approach. First a red man in halo, then a red face looking down on him. A demonic vision painted in heat with an expression one might describe as:

Disappointed.

Halftrain's office – day

Halftrain looks gravely across his desk at Marcy. He has worked for the last half hour on his *grave-across-the-desk* look, and he is rather proud how well it seems to come off. Marcy looks very buried in his grave look. Halftrain intones his bad news—proud at the tone his intoning sets—and he periodically points to a piece of paper to back up his argument. The paper contains no writing. "Cost benefit issue. Budgets. Expenses. I'm sure you understand. Interpol does not print its own money. Why, I only just finished the redecoration of this office, and that went well over-budget. We're just not sure this new infiltration team will meet budget. Given costs and expenses. Things maybe you do not appreciate."

Marcy, "I have a Master's in Public Policy Budgeting from Princeton."

Halftrain nods in agreement, "That's just what I mean. You ladies major in home economics and that just doesn't apply to the real outside world."

Unable to think of smaller words to use, Marcy tries a different tack, "This team could save us money. For instance, by not disappearing like the last one did. Think of the accountants lives it might save."

Halftrain, "I have taken care of that problem."

Marcy braces for impact.

"I've sent in Agent 117." He says this gravely, then leans back, task completed.

Marcy, "I was developing this team to avoid use of 117. Agent 117 tends to go in with hand grenades and a camera, blow everything up, and then take pictures of the rubble. Interpol needs to take pictures for evidence and then *not* blow things up. That way the things match the pictures. The 117s of the world are blunt weapons. I designed the new team as a precision instrument, as befits an organization not legally entitled to start small wars."

Halftrain, "I am certain that Agent 117 will succeed. You should have seen how confident he looked when he left my office. And just dripping with high-tech. On the other hand, I have grave doubts about your team's ability to work together. They do not fit my idea of team players." Halftrain furrows his brow in just the manner Interpol executive training videos recommend.

Marcy knows that she has all of two seconds to save her project, "Put them to a test. Let me show you what they can do."

Halftrain, "Not a bad idea. Their failing a test would really help justify termination costs. What did you have in mind?"

Marcy had not a thing in mind when she made the suggestion, but now, "Infiltration and extraction. We agree on an item," she snatches up a metal globe from his desk, "you secure it. We find and extract it by a deadline."

Halftrain loves this idea that he just came up with, "Brilliant idea. We'll use that globe as the item. I'll hide it at my estate, and your team must extract it from the estate by Sunday morning."

Marcy, "Sunday morning?"

Halftrain, "Perfect. I'm having a big party there Saturday night, all the top people in attendance. Airtight security. It would be a wonderful addition for everyone to have a good laugh at your team floundering around the grounds. I could fire them on the spot for cause." Halftrain leans back, beaming at how much a man can achieve with clean living and grave looks.

"Marcy, I do not know what you would do without me."

At the Interpol briefing room – later that day

The team pours over papers, photos, blueprints and schematics. None of it seems to cheer anyone up.

Kip, "And no later than Sunday morning? I don't see a way."

Trevor, "A globe? A little medal globe?"

Marcy holds up a picture of the globe.

Kip, "Couldn't you have picked a statue or a chair? Something big? We'll never find that thing."

Marcy hauls out three small black metal boxes with antennas attached to each. "The globe has a transponder in it. I gave it to Halftrain months ago as an example of what our tech division was working on. For his approval. He took it for a paperweight, and no matter how many memos I forwarded from the tech division he never took it for anything but a way to control paper in a draft. So now we use his lazy reading habits against him."

Kip picks up one of the black locators, stretching out its antenna, "You call this tech?"

Marcy, "If we're close enough they will blip. Maybe only very close enough. The transponder signal might be quite weak by now."

The team pours over the photos. Kip says, "Look at the cameras. What I wouldn't give for his equipment."

Marcy, "He has top of the line security at his villa. And considering his guest list, the best in Interpol security personnel."

Natasha, "With a team of commandos, you could take it—maybe."

Marcy, "No, it has to be quiet. And nothing in the press. The whole point of this team is that we operate in silence. Under the radar. No attention." She looks at Kip, "What about you Kip—any technical solutions?"

Kip, "Do we have any Whisper-Jet helicopters available to us?"

Marcy, "We have us. Maybe some rope or something."

Trevor, "I have a pretty good nose for safes and such. But I prefer to be invited past the armed guards."

Marcy, "I looked into finding some invitations."

Everyone perks up.

Marcy, "But no luck."

Everyone perks down.

Rafe laughs, "He's having a party and you guys worry about how to get in. Special Squad for Interpol Infiltration and you worry about how to crash a party."

Marcy, "He'll have a lot of security there."

Rafe hops up and takes the lead, "Good, that will make them feel very secure. The more security at a party the easier it is to get in." Rafe looks at Kip, "Kid, can you make up a big camera, very professional looking, with flash bulbs that will blind a man at ten feet?"

Kip, "It's *Kip*. Only my dad calls me a kid. And I can blind a man at twenty feet. What color lights do you want?"

Rafe, "Ten feet is fine, and no colors, just flashes. Don't give me any of that art crap—just painful flashes to the eyes." Rafe turns to Trevor, "Wall-crawler, can you carry your gear inside a tuxedo?"

Trevor, "I prefer to be known as ... *The Lurker*. And I *always* carry my gear in a tuxedo."

Rafe, "Great. Natasha, you just need a nice dress and a push-up bra. You can even wear black."

Natasha, "And tell me, just who made you the leader?"

Marcy's smile fades. Their moment of teamdom now on the cusp of derailment.

Rafe, "I'm not the leader, I'm not the leader type. I'm the idea man."

Kip, "Hey, I want to be the idea man."

Rafe, "Okay. You're the idea man—I'm the problem solver. Okay."

Natasha, "So who is the leader?"

Rafe looks around. Then points to Marcy, "She is."

Natasha considers Marcy for a long, hard moment. Then nods her agreement.

Marcy asks Rafe, "What will *I* need?"

Rafe, "To go in? Just papers. Lots of papers."

At the Halftrain estate – night

The sounds of a posh party at full tilt drift out to the large circular driveway. Valet parkers open doors for arriving guests. Beautiful people in fantastic clothes spill out of elegant autos; each party-goer glad to be one of the in-crowd. Interpol doesn't throw banquets often, but when it does, it recruits the best of the Euro-trash party-set to fill out the guest list. Your average Liechtensteinian duchess may not know Interpol from the EU Commission on Cheese Inspection, but if its Washington office throws a party with free drinks while she's in town, she goes. Likewise, German beer heirs, Romanian diplomats, French fashion brand developers, and a whole slew of dodgy characters just rich enough to dress well and find a place on a rolodex at Interpol. Halftrain has probably invited as many subjects of investigation as friends and allies, but then he used only one criterion for denying an invitation: *named Marcy.*

And security? Super-villain level. Interpol's budget for special infiltration teams may not amount to much, but the service spares no expense on Site Safety Officers. Less training, one supposes. As the valets open doors and the guests head up the drive to the house, big men in suits wearing earpieces check for invitations. They have the serious look of men whose job consists mostly of looking serious. Probably, though, they practice judo on the weekdays and carry guns that keep spewing out bullets for as long as you hold the trigger.

Into this scene a limo drives up. From that limo comes the latest (prospective) Interpol elite forces team: *The Silencers.* But right now they practice a loud sort of silence. They all burst from the limo. Natasha, dressed to kill (figuratively this time), carries on like a movie star. She leans on Trevor, who in his tuxedo and British manner comes off credibly like a louche member of a dying aristocracy. Kip plays the photographer, snapping their picture for the tabloids. Marcy acts as a personal assistant, juggling papers, a briefcase, two cell phones, and other electronic instruments of mis-scheduling. Rafe herds them toward the guards at the front door.

Rafe, to Kip, "Are you getting her? Her left side. Her left side is her best side. More on the left side." To Natasha, "Sasha! Baby! Make love to the camera! This is for *Movie Times*. Your public baby, this is for your public. Make love to the camera!"

Natasha hams it up well. The guards start to take an interest.

Rafe, to a guard, "You. Big and good looking; you want to be in a picture with Sasha Liminsky? *The* Sasha Liminsky! Right over here. Bring your friend. Put your arms around them Sasha, they love you, they're your fans! They're your public!" Natasha poses with the guards. Kip points the camera at them. He gives a signal to Natasha, and she closes her eyes. This time the flash is blinding; the guards are dazed but too self-conscious to say anything.

Another guard addresses Rafe, "Your invitation sir?"

Rafe, to Marcy, "Mrs. Peabody, the invitations, over here please. Sasha! A picture with this fellow here." Rafe asks the guard, "You don't mind, do you?"

Happy man to pose with *the* Sasha Liminsky, "No. My pleasure." Like a ballet troop the team moves together. Natasha puts her arm around the guard while Marcy offers him the phony invitations, dropping them just as Kip blinds him with another flash.

Rafe, "Come along. We've got set-ups inside."

Natasha smiles at a final guard; Kip flashes him. They enter the house.

And what a house. Decorated in a style suitable for European royalty, Interpol clearly only loans this place to Halftrain as its Washington D.C. director. Even bureaucrats at his level can only afford this as a perk. It must have been repossessed from a jailed oil sheik. Persian rugs on the floors and French baroque chairs by the fireplace, all now festooned with party-goers in mid-revel.

Marcy marvels at their success, "It worked."

Rafe, "No one stops an entourage."

Marcy gets down to business, "As planned, Kip to the basement, Natasha covers the lower floor, Trevor and Rafe search the upper level. I'm going to take over the security cameras." Marcy waves some papers like a commando showing her weapon. "Now comms on and go to." Earpieces enter ears as each team member heads out.

Marcy herself walks through the busy kitchen and up the stairs to the security room. The room sits above the six-car garage and has been stuffed with a hundred closed circuit television monitors plus one man whose special Interpol skill-set consists entirely of watching boring TV. Marcy enters against the security man's objections, "You can't be in here!"

Marcy pounds papers down on the small table between the man and his monitors, "David Devney? I'm with HR. We've had complaints!" David Devney sees his life flash before his eyes. He scratches his memories, new and old, for which on-the-job misdemeanor might have put him into the gunsights of Interpol Human Resources. Marcy shows no mercy, "Multiple complaints! Your future is at stake! your pension is at risk!" She locks him in her eyes, "I am your friend, but I am not a patient friend."

All Mr. David Dead-As-A-Doornail Devney can think to say is: "Thank you?"

Marcy, "Don't thank me yet, you have forms to fill out." She slams more forms on the table. "Take these downstairs to a quiet place and fill them out, carefully." She adds another thick stack of forms. "All of them; spelling counts."

Devney, "I have to stay by the monitors."

Marcy, "I'll watch the monitors."

Devney, "But I'm not supposed to leave them."

Marcy touches his shoulder with a compassionate hand. She leans in reassuringly. Tears of pity well up in her eyes, "I can still save you. But we don't have much time." Devney snatches up the forms as Marcy hands him a pen on his way out. Alone now, Marcy takes the seat before the monitors. She searches for her team on the cameras. Natasha has passed beyond the party on the ground floor and taken out her locater. Rafe and Trevor walk up opposite stairs into the dark to the second floor. Marcy sees Kip pass a camera on his way to the basement. She presses her earpiece and speaks into her collar, "All team, security monitors taken."

Within the Halftrain estate – second floor

Rafe touches his ear, "On the second floor. Searching." Rafe creeps, no other word for it, into a bedroom. All the lights are off, and Rafe is under strict orders not to turn any on since security agents on the grounds outside can see the windows. So the lights stay off and Rafe stumbles in the darkness. Rafe slams his shin into an ottoman and his crotch into a dresser corner. He becomes familiar with the room's edges while seeing only the red blips on his transponder locator. The red blips come infrequently enough to tell Rafe he has a lot more tripping to do before he runs down his quarry. So Rafe creeps on.

Trevor, also upstairs, navigates eighteenth-century furniture in the dark like a pro, which he is. On the other hand, he does so by walking on his tip toes, an old cat burglar technique, or so he maintains, so that he looks like an alley cat stepping over an octopus. In and out of the upstairs rooms they move, visible in the dark to Marcy's monitors only in the faintly lit hallway.

Within the Halftrain estate – basement

Below, in the basement, Kip has found the control box for the alarm system. Into his communications mic he tells Marcy, "I'm on the security system." He works to rewire it. From the shadows a drunk approaches. Some poor inebriate lost in the basement while returning from, one hopes, the bathroom for which he had searched (rather than returning from, say, the pantry). The drunk lurches toward Kip, his tux coat in his arms. Kip offers to help him out, "Here, let me get you turned right."

The drunk nods, "Thanks pal."

Kip helps the drunk on with his coat but puts it on backwards, with the buttons running up his back. Then he maneuvers the drunk toward the basement stairs and gives him his instructions, "You are the Dark Clown, symbolizing the omnipresence of Death in the Revels of the Blind. You, in your stupor, see what they miss, and in seeing it, you miss it." The drunk begins to speak but Kip puts a finger on his mouth, "Speak not. *You* are the symbol."

The drunk man acknowledges his new responsibilities, or maybe just belches.

Kip pushes the drunk on his way, "Back to your friends, Dark Clown. You stagger now, for Art."

Within the Halftrain estate – second floor

Rafe steps out into the dark hallway, creeping forward. A figure on tip-toes slowly closes the distance behind him. Marcy sees this, dimly, in the monitor, "Trevor? Someone's behind you."

The figure on tip-toes stops and looks to his rear, whispering, "I don't see anyone."

Marcy corrects herself, sort of, "It's Rafe."

Trevor, "Rafe is not behind me. No one is behind me."

Marcy hits a button on her communicator, "Rafe, someone is behind you." On the monitor Rafe stops as a man tip-toes up behind him. Rafe turns to face his attacker. Rafe lunges with an "Ah ha!" (which, according to training should have been a *Kia ahh!*—but he is new to this). Rafe judo flips the man behind him. His instructor would be so proud.

From beneath him Rafe hears the voice of his victim:

"What the bloody hell did you do that for?"

Rafe, "Trevor? What are you doing down there?"

Trevor, "I've just been judoed if you must ask!"

Marcy clicks onto both earpieces, "You two quit fooling around!" Good cover Marcy.

Within the Halftrain estate – billiard room

While the boys execute Pink Panther level follies upstairs, Natasha enters the billiard room below. She sees a mahogany pool table covered in green velvet, surrounded by bookcases filled with books too sophisticated for dustcovers. The billiard table lies under a small chandelier and a large man with a small earpiece watches over it. The security man's mother named him Richard, but his buddies on the Interpol Safety Force call him *Beasty*, so Beasty he will be. Beasty puts a hand on his side arm and a finger to his earpiece, "Four nine, pool room alert." Beasty asks Natasha, "Lost?"

Natasha instantly becomes the seductress, "Oooo." She puts the locator in her purse and her purse on the pool table. She slides toward Beasty hips first, "No. I have found what I look for." She walks toward him with a hip swing that discourages shooting. Beasty has waited his entire life for something like this, so he will not ruin it now by any sudden movements.

Beasty says, "Hey baby." Which represents a misunderstanding of the situation on so many levels.

Natasha embraces him. He pulls his hand off his side arm to embrace her. She kisses him deep into his mouth. They seem to be sharing the same piece of gum. Then Beasty's face turns to a mask of pain. Natasha has his tongue in her teeth, and she bites it hard. He pulls away, spits blood. He screams, "You Bitth!" He pulls his gun, but she kicks it away.

Natasha, "Oh, are we not in love anymore?"

Beasty grabs a pool cue and motions it in rapid circles like a fighting stick, graceful and threatening. PLUNK! An eight-ball strikes his forehead, right between the eyes.

Natasha, "Your baseball bores me. Let us now wrestle." Beasty attacks with the stick. Natasha side steps his first strike and breaks the stick in two with a karate chop. Beasty attacks with a blur of punches as Natasha blocks and counter-strikes. It's fast and furious. Until Beasty hits the floor with a thud. Natasha walks over to him to retrieve her purse. He trips her, taking her down. She dodges a blow, then flips back to her feet. Beasty launches a punch, but she catches his fist.

Beasty, "You're good. You're very—" She hits him square in the mouth.

Beasty, "Damn! That wath my tongue again!"

Natasha, "Let me kiss your boo-boo." In Russian covert operations they call this taking the psychological advantage. Beasty looks panicked. Not a good look for him.

Within the Halftrain estate – security room

Marcy sees none of this, partly for want of a camera in the billiard room, but with all the screens before her how would she notice in any event? Marcy *does* see Rafe and Trevor proceeding down a dark hallway; Rafe creeping and Trevor tip-toeing behind him. Behind Trevor another figure appears, stalking them. Marcy speaks into her microphone, "Rafe, someone is behind you."

Rafe, "Trevor is behind me."

Marcy, "Then someone is behind Trevor."

Rafe spins around. Marcy sees a figure appear now where Rafe had been heading, "Rafe, someone is behind you!"

Rafe, "Trevor is behind me, I'm looking at him right now."

Marcy, "No, behind you. Behind you! Behind you from before!"

Rafe notices something, "Trevor, is someone behind you?"

Trevor, "Behind me?"

Marcy, "No. Rafe! No both!"

Rafe and Trevor spin around, away from each other and toward their stalkers. Interpol safety officers fall upon them before either can deploy what little judo they know.

Marcy radios Natasha, who at this moment is stepping on Beasty's throat, holding him down. "Natasha, come in. Rafe and Trevor have been captured."

Natasha touches her earpiece, "One moment." She takes her foot off Beasty's throat. She looks on him with pity. She helps him to sit up. She says to him, "I am sorry." She knocks him cold with a left elbow. She speaks to Marcy, "Where have they taken the boys?"

Marcy checks the cameras and her map of the house, "I think they were taken to an office in the southwest corner."

Natasha takes out her locater and watches as the blips

increase. She moves to the corner of the room. The blips get stronger. She hears furniture moving above her. She presses her earpiece, "They are just above me. Also the target. Tell Kip to set off the perimeter alarms."

Within the Halftrain estate – second floor office

Above Natasha, handcuffed to their chairs, Rafe and Trevor look at their interrogators.

Safety Officer Bob, "Now you're going to talk."

Rafe feels better, "Name a topic, first one to run out of something to say losses. No repetitions."

Safety Officer Bob looks at the locator he took from Rafe. Its red lights blip furiously, "What is this?"

Rafe, "Geiger counter. This place is red hot with radiation. I suggest we all move quickly out of here before family planning becomes a moot point."

Trevor looks around and sees the metal globe on the desk. Safety Officer Bob moves the locator around the room till it blips crazily at the globe.

Rafe, "That's it! You've found it. Good work man. Now uncuff us so we can call decontamination. And for God's sake don't touch it!"

Safety Officer Bob almost picks the globe up when alarms go off outside. "Boundary alarms! We have intruders outside!" Security departs. Rafe and Trevor remain cuffed to the chairs.

Rafe, "I think I did some genius level work there."

Trevor, "Kip tripped the perimeter alarms."

Rafe, "That helped. I don't suppose you know anything about getting out of handcuffs?"

Trevor holds up his handcuffs, "I know everything about it, old boy."

Trevor frees Rafe, who picks up the globe. The door to the office opens. Rafe takes a karate pose, ready for action. Natasha enters. Rafe sees her laugh for the first time ever.

Rafe, "You should have seen the size of the two guys I just ran out of here."

Trevor looks out the window, "Unbelievable number of security men guarding the perimeter. How do you propose we escape this gilded cage?"

Rafe presses the earpiece, "Marcy, we have the McGuffin but have no way out of the building to the car."

In the security room, Marcy checks her screens. "Stand by." She sees Halftrain at the party, drink in hand, boring an elderly woman to the point of suicide. Marcy takes out her cell phone and hits speed dial. She watches Halftrain answer and hears him say "Hello." Mary lowers her voice in a parody of a man's, "Mr. Halftrain, head of security here. We have intruders. I need you to meet our security team at the stairs and exit the building with them." Halftrain pushes the elderly woman away as he looks around in concern. He puts his phone in his pocket and heads for the stairs. Marcy hits her earpiece, "Halftrain will meet you at the stairs. Have him escort you through security to the car. I'll alert Kip and meet you there."

Rafe hits his earpiece, "He's seen us. He'll recognize us."

Marcy, "Lester Halftrain does not recognize common employees. He calls security on the janitors. *I* have to reintroduce myself almost once a week. Just don't give Halftrain time to think, which, frankly, should be carved in stone above the main gate of Interpol HQ. Buffalo him."

That Rafe can handle.

They take off down the stairs, meeting Halftrain at the bottom. Rafe says, "Mr. Halftrain, stay with us, we need to get you and, uh, this radioactive globe, to safety."

Halftrain stays close to Rafe and as far from the mysteriously radioactive globe as he can. He shouts orders to clear the way before him. "Make way, open up a way. I must get to safety. Be careful of the radiation." The sea of security men parts before them. Marcy and Kip fall in with the group. They hustle Halftrain into the car and drive the car off the grounds; Kip driving, Marcy riding shotgun, Halftrain stuffed in the back. Rafe gives the globe to Halftrain.

Halftrain, "Is it safe?"

Rafe, "From everyone but us."

Marcy looks back from the front. Halftrain nods, still just a little perplexed. Marcy sits back and takes her first deep breath since this whole thing started. "I feel like we are ready for anything.

Atop a jungle wall – night

Karloff stands at the height of the barricade, moonlit from above; torchlit from below. He holds a whip. Next to him, Boris holds two giant hounds on heavy chain leashes. Below the barricade, in the view of Karloff, lies a village. It's crude huts formed of muddy straw, plastic tarps, and tightly stacked Gucci handbags. Around the huts stand painted soccer balls on sticks and great heaping stacks of stiletto-heeled shoes. Empty cans of peaches lie everywhere, along with piles of plastic forks and empty Dr. Pepper cans. The twenty foot high barricade upon which Karloff stands, made of mud, straw, wood and sharpened poles, rises high over the village.

Within the little village, gazing up in reverence at Karloff: The Lost Tribe. Men and women wearing grass skirts and feathered headdresses. The women have bras sporting coconut shells while the men are shirtless but for ties; three or four ties each. All the tribe wear costume jewelry around their necks. Some hold torches; others scented candles in jars. Of near to fifty people, half dance and half bang on drums. Every sort of drum. Bongos, snare drums, base drums, bodhrans, Djembes, tabla drums, goblet drums, a cajon, and a single, annoying, tambourine. The drums keep a beat, barely, but the dancing could best be described as ecstatic gyration.

Perhaps the most surprising thing about the members of the tribe, given that they are a tribe, in a jungle, dancing ecstatically, is their ethnic diversity. The large black man looking on as the others dance, presumably their chief judging by the abundance of feathers on his headdress and the numerous ragged ties sharing space with costume jewelry around his neck, could pass for a Nuba wrestler. But he heads a tribe which includes

Asians, Hispanics, Indians (New World and Sub-continental) and sunburnt whites. They are a Lost Tribe in virtue of being a tribe of the lost.

They all visibly share at least this though: a fear of the man on the barricade. A barricade whose sharped wooden poles face inward toward the people of the tribe, containing them, rather than outward, protecting them. They dance, not attending to each other, but stealing terrified looks at Karloff, watching his every move, adjusting their dancing, drumming and chanting to his glances. Karloff watches with a judging eye even in the poor light of the moon. The villagers see that he inspects them with the suspicious gaze of one looking for any transgression; not just of action, but of thought as well.

Karloff cracks his whip. The drumming stops. The dancers still their bodies. All attend Karloff above them.

Karloff, "What is the Law?"

The chief answers, "Not to swim from shore! That is the Law. Are we not prey?"

The crowd around him repeats, "Are we not prey?"

Karloff cracks his whip, "What is the Law?"

The chief answers, "Not to leave the stockade! That is the Law. Are we not prey?"

The crowd repeats, "Are we not prey?"

Karloff cracks his whip, "What is the Law?"

The chief answers, "Not to step on the orchids! That is the Law. Are we not prey?"

The crowd repeats, "Are we not prey?"

The chief finishes the ritual invocation, "His are the hands that feed! His are the ties that bind! His are the hounds that hunt!"

The crowd responds, "The hounds that hunt!"

Karloff nods, "You have done well. The time grows close. In two nights, as the moon grows full, I shall select my navigators. Be most worthy and faithful servants, and you shall serve my hunt. Fail in your devotion, and you shall feed my hounds."

Karloff cracks the whip, and the drums begin again. The

dancers race to retrieve stiletto-heeled shoes. They loft them in the sky and resume their dance as the chief shakes a rattle and dances with them. They dance in a frenzy. Karloff watches from the top of the barricade. The dogs howl.

Within a room – night

Marcy looks earnest—almost desperate—yet firm, "Mr. Halftrain, I've been working for you for over a year. And in that time, I have done a great deal for Interpol and for you personally. I have put out a lot of fires for you. And not just metaphorical fires. Remember when you set your desk on fire? *I* put that out. And the memos you send out—you should look at addresses before you send them. Don't just send me a copy with a note asking if you sent it to the right person."

She sighs at the thought, and then presses on, "And this latest action. You need to let me check the covert operations orders before you send them out. *Everyone* needs for you to do that. You have me re-typing all of your reports. Which are mostly just dinner orders until I fix them. But you issue orders with no—how to put it—oversight. Babysitting. Putting it honestly. And then getting you around in the halls and into the right restroom..."

She girds herself for the finale, "My point is, Mr. Halftrain, I need a raise. No, I deserve a raise. Actually, I deserve your job, if we are going to raise the issue of merit, but I will settle for a raise. I think double what I currently make would be generous. Meaning that I would be generous to accept just that. So, what do you say? Double what I make now?"

She speaks, in fact, to her husband, in their tiny nursery, almost a closet, in their small apartment.

Chris, "I already give you everything you make. I don't think I can afford more."

Marcy, "Do you think my boss would go for that?"

Chris, "I'd edit a bit."

Chris holds Katrina, who practices her new favorite game, point and name.

Katrina, pointing, "Table!"

Chris, "Good, Katrina, table. Yes."

Katrina, pointing, "Door!"

Chris, "Door. Right little girl."

Katrina, pointing at Dad's nose, "Nose!"

Marcy, "She's good."

Katrina, "Booger!"

Marcy, "You two must have the most interesting conversations while I'm at work."

Chris, "It's like the Algonquian Round Table."

Katrina, pointing at Dad's, "Chin!"

Chris, "Ooo! That's a new one."

Marcy girds herself yet again. She looks hard at little Katrina. She points at Chris. "Who's this?"

Katrina knows this one cold, "Daddy! Daddy! Daddy!"

Marcy and Chris smile nervously. Marcy points at herself, "And who is this?"

Katrina looks blankly on. They wait. No, she's lost.

Chris, "Come on baby, we practiced with her picture. Who's this?" He points at Marcy.

Katrina stares hard. Then the light bulb goes off. She grasps the collar of Marcy's blouse, "Collar!"

The parents are crushed.

Marcy, "Collar! She knows *collar* but not *mommy*?"

Chris, apologetic, "We were doing laundry today."

Marcy gives up, "I'm never home. I'm always at work wiping Halftrain's nose instead of hers. How *would* she know who I am?"

Chris, "It's not like that. She gets so excited to see you come home."

Marcy, "Yes, she's very good with strangers."

Chris, "It's just the *m* sound she struggles with."

Katrina, "Mammoth!"

Chris, to Katrina, "That's not helping." Katrina looks contrite.

Marcy shakes her head, "She's got to see me more, that's all there is to it. Halftrain is introducing a new *take your kids to work* policy.

Chris, "He is?"

Marcy, "He doesn't know it yet, but the memo goes out tomorrow."

Within an Interpol briefing room – day

A high-tech briefing room; plush chairs, a podium, a screen for showing slides (Slides? High-tech, yes, but on an Interpol budget).

Attending are the Silencers: Rafe in casual wear, Trevor in some sort of English riding outfit no one in England has worn in four decades, Kip in an Andy Warhol T-shirt, and Natasha in Ninja black skin-tights, holding a toddler. A toddler? Yes: little Katrina. Chris sits at the back wearing an empty Baby Bjorn child front-loader with a pink bag decked out in yellow and blue elephants, his complete Katrina care kit.

Marcy enters looking nervously at Natasha holding her child. If the kid is going to say *mommy* it had better be to the right woman. Marcy reaches the podium, standing just off its center, and steadies herself. Then she notices that she entered alone. She sighs off her frustration, and starts back toward the door. Halftrain enters with a big smile on his face. Marcy waits. Halftrain's smile fades. Why did he come in this room? Marcy waves him on in, like calling a lost puppy. Halftrain sees her. He smiles and marches confidently to the podium,

"Team, team." He nods at the team as he enters. Smiles at each in turn. Gives a little wave. Notices the toddler in Natasha's arms. Frowns as he arrives next to Marcy. He points to the toddler, "Who's that?"

She does not miss a beat, "That's our midget agent. Very hush hush."

Halftrain, "Ohh." Now he gets it. Halftrain puts on his glasses. Now he can't see anything. He squints around the room. He takes off the glasses. He seems very satisfied with himself. Marcy clears her throat. Halftrain begins. "A Team, you're all dead. At least we assume you are. Of course, we will try to recover your bodies; and we will bring your killer to justice. Or notify the proper authorities."

Marcy steps forward and speaks to him softly, "This is the C Team sir."

Halftrain, "What? Are we down to them?"

Marcy points down to his notes. Halftrain squints at them without recognition. Marcy puts his reading glasses back on him. Now he gets it, "Ah yes. An extraction. A rescue mission. I have slides."

Marcy looks panicked, "You didn't tell me about slides."

Halftrain, "Did them myself." He smiles knowingly at Marcy, "I'm not as dependent on you as you think." Halftrain picks up the remote for the slide machine as the lights go low. We see a picture of an island. Halftrain begins his presentation, "This is Danger Island." And, indeed, it does look dangerous. "It lies off the coast of the island nation of San Monique."

Halftrain clicks the remote. The image of a cooked lobster on a plate replaces that of the island. Halftrain frowns, "That doesn't seem right." He clicks again and we see an image of Halftrain eating a lobster. "That's better. The island is owned by a man named Ivan Karloff. Master hunter, very deadly." The image switches to show a very friendly Hispanic waiter holding a lobster plate. "Makes your blood run cold to see him."

Marcy leans forward and presses the remote. The image switches to an aristocratic and dangerous looking man; Ivan Karloff.

Halftrain, "He built a castle on the island and stocked the island with animals." The image of a swank Caribbean resort hotel flashes on the screen, complete the smiling valets. Halftrain grows enthusiastic, "Oh this was lovely, right on the beach." He clicks and brings up a frumpy woman holding a Mai Tai and waving at the camera. "That's Fanny, my wife." Next slide: Halftrain in Bermuda shorts. "Oh, that's me, got quite the tan."

Marcy desperately shuffles through his slide list, "Press in twenty-three sir."

He does, with effort. A slide shows a dark castle rising

incongruously from a jungle. Halftrain says, "Don't remember this." He presses the remote. A slide shows Karloff's mountainous henchman, Boris. "This must be my brother-in-law."

Marcy tries to save the briefing. She speaks to Halftrain but loud enough for the others to hear, "This picture shows Boris Bronsky, last of the true Cossacks and henchman to Karloff. A deadly wrestling champion; utterly without mercy."

Halftrain, shakes his head, "No, no, he wouldn't be involved in anything like that. Mind you, he's a bore at Thanksgiving, but not deadly."

Marcy sighs. She has an inspired idea. She takes out her cell phone and hits a button.

The phone in Halftrain's pocket goes off to the tune of *I'm Walking on Sunshine*. Halftrain answers, "Halftrain here."

Everyone in the room can hear Marcy talking into her phone, but Halftrain remains oblivious to this and concentrates on the voice on his phone. It says, "Sir, the building is on fire. We need a complete evacuation immediately."

Halftrain looks alarmed, "Right." He puts the phone away and addresses the group, "We must all evacuate the building. I'll lead." And with that he exits the room.

In the silence that follows Rafe claps slowly, "I didn't know we'd have dinner theatre."

Natasha offers Katrina to Rafe, "You will take the wiggly thing?"

Rafe takes Katrina, then Chris steps in and takes her, Chris says, "I've got her, I think you folks still need to be briefed."

Trevor, "Yes, I say, what is all this about? Are we going on vacation?"

Kip, "Did that guy receive a blow on the head? Because I know this doctor—"

Marcy tries to restore order, "Please, please."

Rafe, "Are you sure we work for him? He seems more like the problem we've been recruited to solve. We eliminate him. Save Interpol. Collect a bonus."

Kip, "I'm a little bit hungry, anyone for seafood tonight?"

Trevor, "I'm surprised he ate the lobster; I would have guessed that in a battle to the death with a lobster, even a boiled one, the lobster would have prevailed."

Marcy has to use her Voice of Command; her Mommy Voice: "All right, that's enough playing around." She even has Katrina's attention. A little harsh maybe. "Sorry."

Natasha, "Carry on. I will enforce order." The team sit now in silence.

Marcy, "Thank you." Marcy has looked over the slide list and figures she can cover this. "San Guanaco Island, code named Danger Island, lies off the coast of San Monique just out of sight from the capital San Monique City." A slide appears: an island with a rocky coast photographed from sea. "The island is owned and occupied by the big-game hunter Ivan Karloff." His image again. "And his henchman and fellow Russian ex-pat, Boris Bronsky." His image again. "We think they live alone on the island." We see the castle in the jungle. "Karloff bought the island around ten years ago, during the last stages of the post-Kananga administration. Since about that time, up till maybe three years ago, records show a steady flow of exotic, unlicensed animals imported into San Monique City. These would constitute invasive species on this small island. Further, the purchase of so many such animals, from five continents, suggests support for a large-scale poaching operation.

"But none of the animals ever left the port of San Monique City." A slide shows the modest harbor of San Monique City. "They appear to have all been turned around and sent to Danger Island." Marcy takes a somewhat more tentative tone. "I thought this would be a simple opening operation for this team. Go in, look around, and see if Karloff has a collection of exotic animals. Find out if he is re-exporting them, running a private game reserve, or one open to select clients. And finding any of this, we would turn it over to our local contact, Chief of Police in San Monique City, Pierre Baptiste." A slide shows a middle age black man in short sleeve khaki shirt with shoulder flashes. "He wants to move against Danger Island, but Karloff has paid off local politicians and they won't let Chief Baptiste move without slam dunk evidence."

Rafe, "So that's all? Show up and check for animal droppings?"

Marcy, "Simple, I know, but things have gotten complicated. My approval request passed over Director Halftrain's desk and he decided to send in an extraction team. What I meant to be your first assignment he gave to the Special Operations Accounting Fraud Unit instead." An image appears of five men in suits, mugging for the camera at an office party. A close look reveals them to be the Running Men in happier times. "They are crack accountants; our top money-finders. But maybe not the best team to parachute onto a place called *Danger Island* at a moment's notice. After they went missing, and before you were ready, Interpol sent in Special Agent 117." An image of Special Agent 117. He looks straight out of a James Bond movie. "His last and only message from the field was somewhat ambiguous. He said," Marcy gathers herself, "love, peace, and flower power." Marcy sighs, "That's it mostly. You're our Snafu-recovery plan. We want to send you to the island to find Agent 117, or the lost CPAs, or evidence of their deaths, or illegally trafficked endangered species."

Rafe, "You think they died?"

Marcy, "Seems unlikely. Not over an unlicensed game reserve. More likely they were offered a better pay package. Interpol can be remiss in pay upgrades."

Chris concurs from the back, "Hear hear."

Marcy shoots him a nasty look; wives should be seen and not heard.

Natasha, "If we do find them? Or find anything?"

Rafe, to Marcy, "Did you say something about jumping out of a plane?"

Trevor, "Yes, I was going to ask about that. I'm more of a rope man myself."

Rafe, "I like to stay on the ground pretty much. Firm footing."

Natasha, "You call yourselves men?"

Rafe, to Natasha, "Well you've had all that Russian covert ops training."

Natasha, "I jumped out of my first plane at twelve."

Rafe, "You learned to parachute when you were twelve?"

Natasha, "No. I did not start using parachutes till I was fifteen."

Marcy clears her throat, "We will set up a task force HQ in San Monique City. I'll liaise with the local authorities, and I've hired Chris to act as team researcher on San Monique. He will find further supporting materials for any case brought against Karloff. I plan to send in staggered teams, starting with the boys and progressing to Natasha if needed. Each entry team will have a satellite phone. Find anything funky, call for help, the cavalry will arrive. We keep it simple still. As for entry methods. Airdrops didn't work so well last time. We have other methods in mind for you."

Rafe does not feel reassured.

In San Monique City – docks – day

The island of San Monique rests as a lonely jewel in southwestern Caribbean Sea. French Afro-Caribbean to its core, its people have endured and overcome slavery, French colonialism, Spanish missionaries, Cuban communist brotherhood, US development aid, local dictators, and petty bureaucrats. Voodoo permeates every aspect of the island's culture; the one enduring strength of a poor people. The island, thick with jungle in the time of Columbus, sugarcane in the time of the French, and heroin in the time of Kananga, now mostly feeds itself with small farms, fishing, and a calculatedly modest tourist trade. It has only one small city, named after the island itself.

While the Port of San Monique loads and offloads shipping, and the San Monique Marina shelters yachts of the richer tourists, the docks serve just the local fishermen. These small boat operators provide food for local tables. Women and men on the wharf work at nets. Others refresh the paint on small boats dragged onto the shore. At the docks a small ship of the sort one might take out on a day's deep-sea fishing trip rests tied to a pier. It is an old diesel-powered boat far past its latest safety inspection. A thick set black woman in a white dress and red colored cloth splashes chicken blood onto the boat, stopping occasionally to chant. Rafe, Kip and Trevor watch as she carries on her ritual.

Trevor, "Quite the bit of local color."

Rafe, "Is she blessing it or cursing it?"

The woman turns to the men, "I am Mama Tambo de Tutu. I given license to this boat. You the white fools gonna take this boat out?"

Rafe, "I would describe us as merely folly adjacent."

Mama Tambo, "I would describe you as shark food if you gonna take this boat out the harbor. This boat doomed to die at the sea."

Trevor, "Can you see that through your ceremony?"

Kip, "Her gods tell her."

Mama Tambo, "Fools. I own three boats. This here one got cracks along the keel, rudder is loose in the rudder braces, and that there motor chugging inside ain't never gonna make it back to no harbor. The gods tell Mama Tambo to know her boats fore she take any out. Like the gods might tell you to know how to swim if you goin out on this here boat."

Well, that tells them. But Mama Tambo takes some pity on these doomed men. She takes out a great mass of feathers from her bag and sprinkles herbs on them. "These here feathers from a rooster, plucked when he in his fury." She holds the horde of feathers up to Rafe, "Blow." He does. Again, to Trevor, "Blow." He does. And last to Kip, "Blow." All having breathed on the feathers Mama Tambo completes her ritual with an incantation and stuffs feathers in the pockets of each man. "This here will protect you from all that may. You remember this spell in your dark hour and a blessing will come upon you." With this she returns to casting her spells upon the boat. Rafe, Kip and Trevor head off the dock toward their party on the shore.

On the shore, Marcy stands next to Chris. Chris holds Katrina in his front-load Baby Bjorn carrier, though Katrina seems to be getting a bit big for the rig. Chris holds his back under her weight. Natasha stands next to a man that those in the description business would term an *Old Salt*.

Marcy tickles Katrina's chin, making her giggle, and presses on with the language lessons. Marcy points at herself, "Mommy. I'm Mommy."

Katrina looks confused. But she would like to get this right.

Marcy, "Mommy. Say *Mommy*. I'm Mommy."

Katrina's confused look turns to joy. She points just where Marcy points and says, "Button!"

Marcy's face falls.

Trevor walks by, "A reasonable guess."

Kip passes, "Points for creativity."

Rafe passes, "At least it wasn't *buttocks*."

Aren't co-workers lovely?

Marcy turns to start the meeting, "To recap the plan: you three will turn up on Danger Island as distressed sport-fishers. The idea is to charm your way into the castle. Karloff must want for company. If we don't hear from you then we send in Natasha by submarine to back you up."

Kip, "Hey, why can't *we* go in by submarine?"

Rafe, "Explain *distressed*."

Marcy, "You'll be shipwrecked. That's the ship. We will wreck it on the island." She points to the hulk now filled with the blessings of the voodoo priestess. Being a wreck looks like what it would do best.

Rafe looks at it warily, "Like Kip said, why can't *we* go in by sub?"

Marcy, "The idea is to have two ways in; charm and stealth."

Rafe, "So send Natasha to lead this end. She can be charming." The others look skeptical. Rafe continues, "Anyway, at least she speaks Russian."

Marcy, "Karloff speaks English fluently, Boris is mute."

Rafe, "But why Natasha for the submarine?"

Kip, "Yeah!"

Marcy, "We needed someone who doesn't mind being shot out of a torpedo tube."

Silence all round.

Rafe, "Okay. Fine. Natasha for the sub. But how do you propose to wreck the ship on the island?"

Marcy smiles, "We have an expert."

She gestures past them to The Skipper. He is a salty old man in dungarees, classic sailor's blue-and-white striped T-shirt, and a captain's hat. He smokes a corncob pipe. He would inspire confidence on a box of cereal; not so much at the helm of a ship. Marcy says, "Gentleman, I give you: The Skipper." The Skipper nods. He winks. Given a little encouragement he would dance a jig.

Rafe, "He's an expert at wrecking ships?"

The Skipper, "Aye matey, trained and certified."

Kip, "Matey? Did he really just say matey?"

Rafe, "You wreck ships on purpose?"

The Skipper, "Not at first lad. At first I just wrecked them. But after a while, you do it enough, you get good at it."

Marcy, "The Skipper is very good at his special skill."

Rafe, "Good at wrecking ships!?!"

The Skipper leans in close to Rafe and makes his points with his corncob pipe, "Lad, I was wrecking ships before you were weaned. While you were just a little scuttle fresh off your momma's teat, I had run ships ashore across the seven seas. Why just in the time we talk here I could have sunk this one!"

Marcy, "Please The Skipper, we only have one ship. I'm sure everyone one here has complete confidence in you."

Rafe, "Wait! His name is *The Skipper*?"

The Skipper, "It's a title lad, you have to *earn* it. Like you might earn being called *The Wart on The Pygmy's Arse-Hole*."

Rafe, to Marcy, "I want to be shot out of a torpedo tube."

Marcy, "Gentlemen, the weather is turning on us. You need to shove off."

The guys look concerned, but Natasha clearly enjoys all of

this.

The Skipper, now wearing a pea coat, mans the wheel as Rafe looks out the ship's wheelhouse window at the growing storm. Rafe wears two life-preservers and looks like he wants a third.

The Skipper, "This ain't nothing matey. Just a brief squall. I once wrecked a ship off Barbados in a full-on hurricane."

Rafe, "Did you ever steer a ship you didn't wreck?"

The Skipper snaps back, "Ain't wrecked this one yet."

Kip enters with wind at his back. He drags a heavy black box marked: *Vital Gear.*

Kip, "It's getting rough out there."

Rafe, "Where's Trevor?"

Kip, "He said something about keeping a stiff upper lip and threw-up over the side."

The Skipper, "Chuck 'um on the leeward not the windward side lads."

Rafe, to Kip, "Are you getting this? Are you taking notes? The Skipper has tips for us."

The Skipper, "I'll have you eatin brine for biscuits by mornin, lads."

Rafe rolls his eyes, "Do we have a medical kit at least?"

The Skipper, "Lubbers! You see this eye?" The Skipper points to his left eye. "Lost it off the Barbary Coast. Took two men down with me in the fight. Never have missed the eye from that day to this."

Rafe, "The very fact that I can see the eye means you didn't lose it."

Kip, "It *is* there."

The Skipper, "Glass eye."

Rafe looks more carefully, "It follows me. Glass does not do that."

The Skipper, "Must be the other eye. Lost the leg off of the coast of Maine. Swallowed by a cod."

Rafe, "You have both your legs!"

Kip, "Look here," Kip rolls up his pants leg to reveal a long scar, "Monterey Jazz Festival, fell on a broken bottle."

Rafe, "Cods do not bite off legs!"

The Skipper holds up his hand, which he curves, fingers together, "Got this hook chasing the great red whale Motely Dink."

Kip lifts his shirt revealing at best a faint scar on his stomach, "Appendicitis. It's faded some."

The Skipper, "You're fit for the sea lad."

They both look at Rafe. Rafe shrugs in disbelief. He points to his chest. "My mom wouldn't pay for more acting lessons. The scars are emotional, but they run deep."

The Skipper, "Lubber!"

Trevor wanders in, looking pale. He stares for a moment at a lamp swinging from the ceiling. It sways back and forth, back and forth. Trevor staggers out. The swells toss the boat about. The wind casts waves onto the window of the steering house. The Skipper whistles the theme from *Oklahoma*.

Kip, "At least in this weather no one will see our approach."

Within a tower room – stormy night

Through the circle of a telescope a leisure fishing boat tosses about on a disturbed sea. At the other end of the telescope, Karloff watches. Karloff lowers the scope. Boris stands behind him.

Karloff, "We shall have guests soon. Prepare a welcome."

Boris grunts.

Within the boat wheelhouse – stormy night

The Skipper looks hard out the window into the storm. Before him, through the wind and rain of the squall, an island appears. "There she lies, won't be long now."

Rafe, nervous but game, "So what's the technique? An oblique approach? Do you back in and turn around or what?"

The Skipper, "No technique lubber. Just gun the motor and dash it on the rocks."

Rafe, disbelieving, "That's it? Ram the rocks? Years of experience just to learn that?"

The Skipper, "The years of learnin is to survive after the wreck!"

Rafe is pretty sure he missed that briefing.

The Skipper, "Grab your goolies, we're dead for the rocks!

Rafe, "I hate sailor talk."

Upon the brine – night

Rocks split the small ship apart, practically unzipping it, and disgorge its contents into the sea, including Rafe, Kip and Trevor. Waves toss them about like corks. Except that corks would have had the sense to stay off any boat Mama Tambo recommended against. They struggle mightily to make the shore. They make it, brine covered, drenched and exhausted, but alive. The storm passes over them leaving a calmer night.

Kip, "That was so much fun!"

Rafe, "I'm still alive." Rafe pinches himself in disbelief. It hurts. A good sort of hurt. A hurt you can count on. Rafe collapses in exhaustion.

Kip, "I want to do that again! Let's do that every time!"

Trevor looks at the stars. Never have they looked so beautiful. The Milky Way, what glory to behold. Astronomy, that would be a fine career. Sitting under a dome, drinking tea, looking through a telescopic lens now and again just to break the monotony. The lovely, dry monotony.

Rafe pinches himself again. He turns to Trevor, "Here, you pinch me, I'm still not sure."

Trevor, "I think I've missed my calling."

Rafe, "Not if you've been called to be shore buoy."

Kip walks about marveling at the sea, "Did anyone get that on camera? I forgot to take any pictures."

Rafe, "Where's The Skipper?"

They look around. Finally, Trevor points out to sea, "There. Paddling away."

They see that The Skipper has lashed together life preservers into a raft and paddles out to sea. You can just faintly hear him singing *Yo ho ho and a bottle of rum* in the distance.

Rafe, "Well good by *The*, and may the insurance detectives never catch you."

The three of them look in toward the jungle just beyond the beach. Tangled vines and broad draping leaves. Monkey chatter breaking the night air.

Trevor, "We should call in to headquarters. Let them know we've arrived safely."

Rafe, "Yes, do that."

Trevor turns to Kip, "Yes do."

Kip looks at Trevor, "Okay with me. Go ahead."

Trevor and Kip stare at each other for a moment.

Rafe turns around to face them, "We have a satellite phone."

Kip, "Yes, we do."

Trevor, "Quite right. We do."

Another moment passes.

Rafe, "Which one of us is *we*?"

They look about.

Kip, to Rafe, "*You* have the satellite phone."

Rafe, to Kip, "Me? You're the tech guy. You have it."

Kip, "You're holding the vital equipment trunk. It's in there!"

Rafe, angry, "Sure. I'm holding the vital equipment trunk. That's why I'm at the bottom of the sea right now!"

They both look at Trevor, "Don't look at me, gentlemen. If I can't carry it in my tuxedo, I can't carry it at all." In fact, Trevor wears a tuxedo under his life vest. And he has no satellite phone.

On a jungle path – early evening

The three walk together through the jungle on a wide path. The agitated jungle resounds about them. Macaws call, monkeys chatter, howlers howl, and, *what the hell*? Was that a roar? What roars on a Caribbean Island?

The three have ditched their life vests. Kip wears jeans, a T-shirt and a jacket; Rafe, slacks and a wind-breaker; Trevor, incongruously, a full tuxedo. Trevor picks a flower from a jungle plant and puts it in his lapel, Bond style.

Rafe, "Probably everything in this jungle will poison you."

Trevor tosses away the flower.

Kip, "I kind of like the jungle. So green and full of life."

Rafe, "Every living thing in a jungle wants to kill you. There isn't an ant out there that doesn't think it can eat a human. The bushes ooze toxins. Nothing survives long in a place so full of things needing food unless it can kill on contact seven ways to Sunday."

Trevor notices a monkey on a tree, "Oh I think the monkeys are a bit adorable."

Kip, "Let's not bring up monkeys."

They walk on in silence down the surprisingly broad jungle path. It must be the way to the castle given its convenience to castaways. As the men stride on, behind them, unseen and unheard, Boris falls into line. He walks after them silent as a tomb.

Rafe, "The worst part of a jungle is that you always feel something is watching you."

Kip shudders.

Trevor senses something following him. He looks back and sees Boris keeping pace six feet behind them. Trevor looks forward again, still walking with the others. He shakes his head to clear it and looks behind him once more. He sees Boris, still looming over him, still silently keeping pace.

Trevor looks forward again. "Has anyone seen anything unusual?"

Kip, "It's all new to me."

Trevor glances behind himself again. "No, I mean has anyone seen ... anyone else?"

Rafe, to Kip, "Not even a compass? You didn't save anything from that trunk?"

Kip, peeved, "*You* were supposed to take the trunk. The whole trunk."

Trevor, "I mean to ask, it was just the three of us that landed on the island?"

Rafe, also peeved, "Take the whole trunk? Tied to my back as I swam ashore? Look…" Rafe turns to face Kip, sees Boris, and nearly jumps out of his skin, "Holy back-scratching Jesus!"

Kip sees Boris now.

Rafe turns away from Boris and they all start walking forward again. Boris walks behind them in silence. He is the proverbial elephant in the room. Larger than most, really.

Rafe, "Okay. Now what?"

Trevor, "Then you *do* see him? All of us see him?"

Rafe, "See him? He blots out the sky."

They all steal a glance over their shoulders.

Kip, "Does he see us?" Boris makes no indication and the guys walk on for lack of another plan.

Rafe, "Someone should say something. We look ridiculous."

They glance again over their shoulders.

Kip, to Rafe, "You do it."

Rafe, "Me?"

Kip, "You're the talker."

Rafe, "To humans. Not to piles of ambulatory stone."

Trevor, "Dash it all, I'll have a go at it." None of them stop walking. Trevor doesn't try to face Boris. He just talks louder. "Well, I say, chappy, do you often perambulate the grounds?"

Rafe, still walking, wears an expression of utter disbelief.

Trevor, "That is, it's a fine evening for a walk, lovely in the moonlight. Terribly good for one's health. Do you ever, perhaps, escort a lady-friend?"

Rafe, "Jesus Trevor, maybe you should just take a knee and propose."

Trevor, "Well I'm bloody doing more than you are!"

Rafe, "All right, everyone just stop."

They do. They turn as one and face Boris. Boris lifts his arm, approximate in size to a tree trunk, and points forward.

They look about at each other. They turn and walk on up the trail as indicated.

Kip, "Well that worked brilliantly."

Trevor, "I think we might defeat him if we tried. There *are* three of us."

Rafe, "But how many of *him* are there?"

Ahead of them they see a clearing in the canopy revealing a castle against the darkening sky.

Rafe, "Oh good, Castle Frankenstein."

Karloff's stone fortress looks simple but imposing. The castaways stand before the double doors of the castle entrance. To the left a tall tower rises five distinct stories, to judge from its narrow windows. Attached to this, a rectangular building rises just three stories, it's windows more generously proportioned. The side windows each let out onto small balconies, one at the topmost floor with similar balconies beneath. A stone walkway of considerable breadth rounds the castle. The stone walkway leads round to steps on the far right. These lead down to what must be a large space beneath the balconies. A split-level castle with, one must assume, a finished basement. A retaining wall stands equal to the height of the first floor (that is, the floor of the double door Rafe, Kip, and Trevor now face) and thus encloses the lower level down the outside stone steps. From this lower level, which as yet cannot be seen, Rafe, Kip and Trevor can hear the baying of hounds. Hounds with rich baritone voices, and by the sound, large teeth and insatiable appetites.

On the great doors they see two door knockers. One depicts a mounted hunter stretching back a bow, the other a deer in flight. Choose your fate. The knockers look larger than any man could easily lift, each three feet across and a foot high, all iron. Boris walks past Trevor (nearly giving him a heart attack) and raises a knocker (the deer). He lets it go and it emits a great CLANG. This noise alerts anyone within the fort of the new arrivals, sets the jungle alive with new chatter, and sends the hounds in the kennels outside the lowest level into a frenzy of howls. Dinner has arrived.

Does one wait here for a gang of coolies to open the massive portal? No. Boris leans into the doors, and they swing, or rather they gradually sway, open. Boris gestures for them to enter. Not so much an invitation as an order. With trepidation, they walk in, followed by Boris.

Once inside they see the grand entry and receiving area. The room impresses powerfully in its old-school Boy's Own Adventure sort of way. The light in the room, though artificial, comes from decorative torches, and fills the space with a warm glow. Several full suits of armor stand in corners. Swords crossed before sashed shields adorn the walls. A knight from ye olde times could walk in and think he had fallen into a Mark Twain story. Animal skins cover most of the stone floor, providing soft purchase for the soles of one's feet at the expense of ease for one's soul. Someone killed a lot of zebras to decorate this floor.

Across the grand door a grand staircase leads to the second level. Halfway up the stairs, in formal wear, stands Ivan Karloff. Although he isn't such a fearful sight after being stalked down a jungle trail by Boris, the castaways have no doubt that he runs the place. Perhaps the scariest thing about Karloff is the fact that Boris so clearly defers to him, bowing his head low in Karloff's presence. Having made his obeisance, and with a great heave, Boris shuts the massive doors, giving Trevor another start, and Karloff a smile.

When Karloff speaks, he does so in a thick Russian accent much like Natasha's, but in no way sexy, "Gentlemen. Enter. You are my guests."

This sounds too much like Count Dracula for Rafe's comfort.

Karloff, "I am your host," Karloff straightens up, as if presenting himself to the Czar, "Count Ivan Petroski Ivanovic Belenko Gaspov Karloff, at your service."

Rafe, "That's quite a name to get through on one breath."

Karloff smiles. Not a comforting sight. He stands on the staircase awaiting introductions.

Rafe, "I'm Lance Hedrend," Rafe pauses for further inspiration, "the third. These are my companions," he gestures at Kip "Brightcot Dunderhill O'Malley," he gestures at Trevor, "and Lord Benington Billingsly Puetrise Harway Halfenhoff, Esquire."

Kip and Trevor work at trying to remember everyone's new

names. Mouthing them to themselves in a futile effort to even know what to answer to now.

Rafe, "I'm afraid we ran aground on your island."

Trevor, "Frightful bit of bad luck."

Karloff nods gravely in what could not quite be called mock concern—but more like a mockery of mocked concern, "Did you lose anyone?"

Rafe, "No, all safe." He, points to Kip, "Lance here steered the ship."

Kip desperately shakes his head at the name.

Rafe, "And fortunately for us Captain Halfling." Rafe gestures to Trevor, "Got a radio call off."

Trevor worries visibly as to who everyone is now.

Karloff feigns curiosity, "And Mr. O'Malley was not injured?"

Rafe, "I'm fine." And simultaneously, Kip says, "I'm fine, thank you."

Now even Rafe looks confused.

Karloff, "And what of Lord Benington Billingsly Puetrise Harway Halfenhoff?"

Trevor thinks he recognizes some of that.

Rafe, "Alas, our one casualty." Rafe lowers his head in respect for the newly departed.

Trevor frantically gestures that Rafe's creative impulses have run ahead of his story.

Karloff, "Gentlemen, we can clarify the introductions later. You are wet and tired. Hungry no doubt. My valet, Boris, has laid out some evening wear for you. Dry off. Dress. We shall speak again in my trophy room."

They are not entirely certain if Karloff means to feed them there, or mount them.

Karloff, "And I must ask you not to leave the castle. I have released the hounds to guard my island. They are most deadly to strangers."

He smiles. And one has to wonder if anyone could be stranger than Karloff.

Within the trophy room – evening

The castaways enter the trophy room. They wear silk pajamas and velvet lounging robes. Trevor takes naturally to this, but Rafe and Kip feel a bit uncomfortable as guests in sleepwear. All such discomfort vanishes upon entering the trophy room though—displaced by a new unease.

Before them they survey a room paying grand tribute to games of life and death. At one level it seems comfortable enough. A blazing fire in a large fireplace lights the space before comfortable chairs with side tables of glasses filled with the finest port. Karloff even provided a buffet table of fresh fruit on a fine dining set.

Yet, in spite of these minor comforts, the room stirs disquiet, for nothing in it fails to exalt the owner's deadly sport. Karloff has upholstered the chairs in hunting scenes, reminiscent of seventeenth century tapestries, but depicting the sheer goriness of a hunt: Animals vivisected by spears; bloodlust in the eyes of men and dogs. The armrests of the chairs end in bronze animal heads each in the form of a beast howling in pain. Relaxing a hand upon them, you grip the fear of the prey. The inlaid wood of the side table displays a tiger in its death throws. The port glasses are etched in scenes of stags butchered in the field. Pick up a glass, sip from it, set it down again, and you have imbibed the master's obsession.

No room accessory fails to incorporate its theme. Two elephant tusks frame the fireplace. In the corner a coat rack made out of deer skulls holds a bear-skin jacket. Beside this, lamps of ivory covered by shades of hide cast dim light on the floor. A chandelier of antlers hangs above. Below it sits a coffee table of gorilla skulls with a glass top (the better to see gorilla skulls through). Atop this lies a coffee table book: *The Mountain Gorilla; Man's Great Cousin*. The drink caddy beside it is made of arrows, fletches still on, tips piercing a row of monkey heads at the bottom.

And the trophies? Animal heads, of every imaginable kind,

cover the whole of three walls; Lions, tigers, leopards, rhinos, water buffalo, all stuffed and mounted. A stuffed penguin serves as a door stop. Stuffed eagles act as bookends. A stuffed condor looks from the ceiling for the stuffed cougar cubs hiding in a corner. A stuffed porcupine serves as a much-neglected footrest. If an animal can be killed, and any can, and its remains benefit from the art of a taxidermist, then it finds some place in this room, or some other in Castle Karloff. And the three large walls of the trophy room could not fit another preserved dead animal. They are stuffed with stuffed stuff. And although each specimen has been expertly rendered as alive-in-death, Karloff has maintained in all of them the hole right between the eyes that rendered each ready for taxidermy.

On the fourth wall: every kind of hunting weapon known to man. Rifles of course, but also boomerangs, blowguns, bolas, bows, blunderbusses; just to cover the letter *B*. And not just hunting weapons, but fencing swords as well; the man is an aristocrat after all.

Rafe, Kip and Trevor dutifully inspect the room for clues and prospects of escape, should the need arise. The trophy room offers abundant indications of Karloff's erotic devotion to the hunt, which clues one to something, but it does not offer a line item in a report to Interpol. As for escape routes, the only way out of the room, apart from the large entryway, is a balcony. Looking down from this, each man can see that below the balcony lies another balcony, and below that: the dogs.

Karloff enters, outfitted in greet-the-guest formal wear, making even Trevor feel awkwardly underdressed now. Karloff is either inept at making his guests feel welcome, or he plays an astute game of psychological warfare. So hard to say which.

"Gentlemen, be seated," he tells his guests, "enjoy some port to warm you." They stand next to a roaring fire, on a tropical island, in a room of death, so *cold* does not place high on their list of discomforts. Maybe *sober* does. They sit, hands uncomfortably cradling screaming heads. Boris brings round the tray with port and glasses. Boris offering cocktails feels more a threat than a courtesy, but Karloff looks like a man about to make an oration, so best to sit and have a drink.

Karloff, "I live devoted to the hunt. From every corner of the world, I have hunted every kind of game. I am unmatched in my hunting prowess. I, personally, shot the last of the Grey Rhinos." He pauses in memory of the last Rhino, then adds the coup de grace, "With a short bow."

Rafe nods in feigned approval.

Karloff, "I hunted the snow leopard in winter. Few men have ever seen one; I have killed five." Karloff gestures to a stuffed snow leopard rearing back like a scared cat. Behind it, cringes its stuffed snow leopard cubs.

Kip barely listens. Trevor would like to hire his decorator for some old English country house ideas he has.

Karloff, "You have perhaps heard of the Yeti of the Himalayas?"

Kip nods. He has heard of the Yeti. Saw a whole movie on the late show about it when he was twelve.

Karloff, "Yes, there were such creatures. Until Karloff came!"

Rafe pours some more port, "How *Count*? I thought the Russians had hunted down all their aristocracy."

The point wounds Karloff, "My great grandfather escaped during the revolution with the Czar's jewels. We Karloff's have never recognized the Revolution or its meager off-spring. We were of the old world. I am the last in a line of greatness."

Rafe, "Going extinct, are you?"

Karloff does not like this fellow. "I wonder if you can understand the hunt? The study of the wind and land. The oneness of man and nature. The subtlety of tracking the desperate creature. The joy of closing off all hope of escape. The ecstasy of the kill." Karloff is almost transported by the thought. "It is the most exquisite game."

Rafe, "Does the animal know it's a game?"

Karloff bristles, "Animals show wisdom in neither giving nor expecting mercy."

A slightly toasted Kip has a thought to add, "I like Grand Theft

Auto: Street Level."

Trevor, "Now hunting the fox, there's the thing. Sport of kings. Such lovely regalia. All the leather equipment. The trousers. Bright crimson jacket. Sounding the horn. Drinks after."

Rafe, "I picture myself as more the fox."

Karloff, to Rafe, "You see yourself as clever like the fox?"

Rafe, "More I see myself scared when hunted like the fox."

Kip, "But does the poor creature even have a chance?"

Karloff, "Exactly! Not against guns! Not against me! That is why I hunt with all these," he gestures at the weapon wall, "hunt a tiger with a bull-whip, and you will give him a chance!"

Rafe points to a tiger rug on the floor beneath him, "That the tiger?"

Karloff, "Yes. Bull-whipped into a trap."

Rafe, "Slim chance in the event. Weapons, traps, beaters, and radio gear I'm guessing. You're out for sport while the tiger's just trying to find a meal. Point being that in a game both are playing. A hunt is just a surprise attack in the end. Only one of you actually hunts."

Trevor, "Fundamentally, fox or tiger, they are just dumb animals."

Karloff smiles at this turn in the conversation, "You have stumbled upon a profound truth. As I have found. For I have so perfected my art that no mere beast has even the scintilla of a chance against me. Whatever my weapon, I can always outthink a mere beast. I discovered this the day I killed my thirtieth lion. With a paw trap and a poisoned knitting needle. It came upon me like a wave. The hunt presented me with no challenges! Can you imagine the horrid gloom that fact created in me? The melancholy it brought to my soul? Pondering a life without the trial of the hunt?"

Kip, "Yeah. It's like beating all the bosses on Legend level. What's left?"

Karloff doesn't quite know what that means, but he rolls with it, "The thought nearly crushed me. I saw that excess of excellence in my life's calling had upended the meaning of my very existence. Like Alexander with no more worlds to conquer. But then I realized that what I needed was not a lesser weapon, but a greater prey."

Rafe has now flashed on where all this is leading, but the other two, swimming with the port, fail to follow. Rafe yawns, "Well, looks like bedtime for me."

Kip, "How about creating new animals? Or enlarging existing ones?"

Rafe looks at Kip as if he has gone mad, but Karloff picks up the line.

Karloff, "I looked into it. Promising, but very expensive. No, the answer lay in making the prey match the man, not in size, but in wit." Karloff pauses here for dramatic effect, "What do you think is the most dangerous game?"

Kip, "Evil Dead Eight. You can't even re-spawn."

Trevor, "Well I've had some pretty wicked badminton games. I remember one rouser with Bunny Hamilton. He would balk a push shot, then sling the shuttlecock at one's head. One minute you're at the back court, the next he's pranged you."

Rafe, "He means *prey*. The animal being hunted."

Karloff smiles.

Kip, "Oh well, your lion?"

Karloff scoffs.

Trevor, "The water buffalo, deadly beast. Saw a film on them once. Very strategic animal. Foundation of Zulu military tactics."

Kip, "Oh come on, your grizzly bear eats your water buffalo for breakfast."

Trevor, "Different continents old boy."

Kip, "And then you have your mountain lion."

Trevor offers another candidate, "The mountain gorilla."

Kip, "The shark. The shark will take your mountain gorilla. I mean if the gorilla doesn't drown first."

Trevor, "The baboon. In his whole troop of course."

Kip shakes his head, "The giant sloth. Absolutely."

Trevor, flabbergasted, "A sloth?!? Are you mad!?! It can barely move."

Kip, "But it's quiet. It'll sneak up on you."

Trevor, "And then what? It's a vegetarian."

Kip, "Well so are water buffalos and you credited them against grizzles."

Rafe can't believe the conversation. Even Karloff wonders when they get back to his point.

Trevor, "A water buffalo has great horns."

Kip, "Have you ever seen a sloth attack?"

Trevor, outraged, "No one has!"

Kip, triumphant, "Right. No survivors."

Karloff, "Gentlemen. You miss my point. All those are still mere beasts. They could never have a chance against me."

Trevor is inspired, "A leopard! Silent as the night."

Kip, "Against a sloth? You'd hear a leopard coming a mile away. Now a sloth, he's right up on you—don't hear a thing."

Trevor, "It's too slow!"

Kip, "Waits till you're asleep."

Rafe has had enough, "He means *us*! Not lions, nor tigers, nor bats, nor sloths. Us, men, people, house guests, *us*!"

They look stunned.

Kip, connecting, "Ohhhh."

Trevor takes a swig of port.

Karloff, "Then we are agreed. Man is the most dangerous game."

Karloff turns to his weapons wall. The guys look to their exit, but Boris walks up behind them, holding a pistol, confirming their doom.

Karloff, looking over his weapons, "I shall use ... the bolas." He takes down a rope with heavy balls at the end, useful for throwing and entangling ... well, house guests if need be.

Rafe's hopes rise, perhaps a chance at that.

Karloff, "And ... the Mongolian short bow."

Rafe sinks a bit.

Karloff, "And, failing all else ... the Geary bolt-action." Karloff takes a big hunting rifle down.

Rafe swigs some port, so much for chances.

Karloff has found his sporting mood, "Tonight you rest as my guests. Tomorrow we begin the hunt!"

Within the library of San Monique City – night

The reading room of the San Monique City library occupies the whole of it's large attic. Its round windows overlook the bay north of the city's port. The room is paneled in wood, stuffed with books, includes maps on the walls, a large antique globe in a corner, and a telescope at the largest window. Katrina sits on the floor reading a picture book about pirates. Marcy sits at the one large wooden table awaiting a briefing from Chris, who sits across from her in front of four open books. He looks like a man who has just fallen into his best life.

Chris, "How did you come up with the code name Danger Island?"

Marcy, "My police contact, Pierre Baptiste, called it that, why?"

Chris, "It's been called that longer than it's been called San Guanaco."

Marcy, "Do tell."

Chris points to a book, his idea of proof no doubt, "The earliest recoded discovery of the Island of San Monique was by the Mayan adventurer Joplaj Wamaw. A name I believe in Mayan means, *Lunatic Who Floats on The Seas*, although my Mayan could use a brush-up."

Marcy, "Just don't ask me to say it three times fast."

Katrina chimes in, "Joplaj!"

Chris, "Now Joplaj Wamaw might be legendary, but according to the Spanish chronicles he arrived on this island hundreds of years before Columbus and erected a temple to the gods. The ruins of such a temple, so far undated by archeology, lie on the extreme western shore of San Monique. If Interpol would fund it, I could lead a dig there. Who knows what we might find."

Marcy, "Unless you find Inca gold, we cannot finance it."

Chris, "Mayan gold. Anyway, I'll write up a grant application just in case."

Marcy, "And I will fast track it to its inevitable destination in Halftrain's trash can. If we might go on."

Chris, "Right. Well, Joplaj Wamaw didn't stop at San Monique Island. According to the chronicle, he went on to what he called The Place of the Sleeping Death, described as an island he visited just after leaving San Monique—or what historians presume was San Monique. Joplaj Wamaw called his first island the Island of Red-Feathered Birds. And just such a bird was indigenous to San Monique, until wiped out during a nineteenth century French craze for women's feathered hats."

Marcy, "Survived the Mayans but not the French. Got it."

Chris, "The southwest of the Caribbean doesn't have many islands, so it stands to reason that San Monique corresponds to Joplaj Wamaw's Feather Island and that Joplaj's other island matches the now aptly code-named Danger Island."

Marcy, "Should I call the rest of the team in? They may have questions about the Mayan period of the mission target."

Chris ignores her snark, everyone has had a long trip over. "Danger Island enters verifiable history with the Spanish conquistador Pablo Barcia Castillo. Castillo began his career as a companion of Columbus on the third voyage. He set out to make his own mark. Principally, he sought to find the island of Japan in the heart of the Caribbean. He is best known to history as the last sailor on earth to still think Columbus had discovered China. The important point for us is that he obtained a ship—well stole it—and set out from the Mexican shores—thinking them China—and landed on, or more accurately wrecked his ship upon, the Island of San Monique. Whereupon the locals ate his crew."

Marcy, "Do you understand the concept of *actionable intelligence*?"

Chris, "Castillo escaped on a raft of his own making to a nearby island, which he described as rich in fruit and roots and birds ripe for hunting." Chris throws his hands forward as if to say, *there, I have proved my point.*

Marcy, "And he lived happily ever after."

Chris, "No, he fled the island in terror back into the arms of cannibals. But don't you see? An island rich in fruit and edible roots, with docile birds ripe for eating? The Carib peoples were all over these islands before Columbus. If they weren't busy exploiting Danger Island, they must have had a good reason."

Katrina blows a raspberry into her book. Marcy nods in agreement.

Chris, "What great minds must endure. The French took and named San Monique in 1636 at the behest of Cardinal Richelieu and set up sugarcane production of sufficient intensity to wipe out most of the local work force. Thereupon the French imported African slaves, which accounts for the African origins of ninety-eight percent of the population."

Marcy, "Names. You give me names of these French slavers and I'll set up prosecutions for human rights abuses. Provided the statute of limitations has not run out."

Chris, "No need, the locals handled it. Slave revolt, 1792. Over in 1804. Commemorated by the celebratory Junkanoo to be held on the streets of San Monique City beginning tomorrow night."

Katrina, "Party." She claps her hands.

Marcy's level of irritation rises.

Chris, "Anyway. The African slaves rounded up every slave owner and shipped them off to the nearest island. A remarkably merciful attitude under the circumstances—except that the slaves called the island Rock of the Sleeping Mist. Ten years after the revolt ended, the French sent a ship to your Danger Island to rescue the French population dumped there. They found nothing but bodies and bones. And, ironically, signs of cannibalism—apparently the birds didn't last."

Marcy, "So I should warn the team of cannibalism on Danger Island?"

Chris, "I wouldn't go that far. But definitely warn them of *danger*."

Katrina speaks into her pirate book, "Yar har har!"

Marcy, "Now she has local idioms?"

Chris, "Absorbing the culture. Sort of."

Marcy, "Do they have mothers in the local culture?"

Chris, "Would you like to hear about the establishment of the Voodoo Republic of San Monique?"

Marcy sighs, "Do you have anything more relevant to Karloff and the current assignment?"

Chris cocks his head with the smug look of a man about to land a bomb, "Karloff didn't build his castle."

Marcy, "Oh?"

Chris pulls out a book from the bottom of his pile and shows Marcy a page containing a painting of a goateed man with crazed eyes. "Henri de Beaufort, the Mad Orchid Hunter." Chris looks very satisfied.

Marcy, "He's crazy and a hunter?"

Chris, "Well, orchid enthusiast more than hunter I would think."

Marcy's spirits drop.

Chris, "Said to have committed several murders though."

Marcy rallies, "Do tell."

Vindicated, Chris carries on, "And he was a very big presence in the botany journals of his day."

Marcy, "You're doing police intelligence now, stay away from the botany, and keep laser-sights on the murders."

Chris, "Right. Connected though. The newspapers of his day accused him of killing several of his orchid rivals. Right there on his estate on Danger Island."

Marcy, "At the castle he built."

Chris, "Called a fort at the time. De Beaufort was an orchid obsessed madman. They do that to some people. The orchid being symbolically vaginal."

Katrina calls out a new word, "Vaginal!"

Marcy steams, "You have just one word to teach her. Just one. No other word learning till she gets that one. Got it?"

Chris, "I'm trying honey. She just has a bit of a blockage on that word. We will get there. I promise."

Katrina's stubborn vocabulary, so rapidly expanding, yet so irritatingly limited, has destroyed Marcy's mood, "And this," she gestures at all of Chris's book work, "does not help."

Chris, contrite, "I know I mostly have just deep background right now. I think something can be found in all this, but I am not there yet. I know it. Tomorrow I will talk to some of the locals. Talk to some of the fishermen. And to your contact heading the local constabulary. I will get there."

At the guest rooms in Castle Karloff – night

A hallway lit by artificial torches mounted on stone walls. A series of strong oak doors on either side. Gilded cages for Karloff's special guests. Karloff leads the way carrying a revolver and a set of keys, followed by the stalwart men of Interpol and backed by Boris holding a chained and snarling hound.

Karloff, "Your rooms. You will find your clothes dried on your beds. I shall leave you to rest until breakfast." He unlocks a door and motions for Rafe to enter. Karloff shuts and locks the door after Rafe. Karloff proceeds to open a door opposite Rafe's for Trevor. Trevor enters. Karloff locks Trevor in. Karloff hands the keys to Boris, "Deposit the last and bar the door to the main stairs." Karloff leaves.

Boris hooks the dog's chain on a metal torch and unlocks the door next to Rafe's room. He motions for Kip to enter. Kip nods at the giant. He feigns to look away toward the room. Then, with the deftness and speed of an Interpol trained martial artist he lets out a "Kiiiaaaa!" and lands a blow strait to the giant's solar plexus. He follows this up with a series of brutal chops to the giant's chest (these meant for the neck of course, but one can only reach so high) and follows these with elbows to the ribs. Each delivered with a "Haa!" Exhausting work all this. Kip tires a bit. But, undaunted, he takes hold of Boris's hand. Kip applies various control grips against the hand, bending the giant's fingers back (slightly) and turning it against its giant wrist (partially). A few more blows to the stomach to soften up the man. A bit more struggle to control the hand, which approximates to the size of Kip's head. Another punch to the big man's ribs. A rest to catch his breath, then, improbably, a turn on his heels gripping the giant's hand for a judo throw. Nothing budges. Kip karate chops the giant's arm a few times. Anything? Kip hesitates to look. Finally, though, he takes a glance at the face of Boris.

Nothing. Not even curiosity. Kip rears back for a mighty two-handed blow. Boris grabs him by his face and tosses him into the guest room. Kip lands with a thud and watches the door close. So much for plan one.

Kip looks about. He sees dark wood walls, hard stone floor—very hard—and great masses of feathers. Surprise that. Feathers and stuffed birds. Peacock feathers emerging from wicker baskets. The green feathers of the emerald Toucan and the deep blue feathers of the Victoria crowned-pigeon make up a carnival mask. A great cloak of feathers commemorates the death of innumerable Bali birds of paradise, Australian king parrots, and Amazonian Guildingii. Stuffed cranes imitate a mating dance beside a stuffed, and by all appearances amazed, male royal flycatcher, whose tuft of head feathers stands erect in hopes of a stuffed female royal flycatcher. A stuffed male crimson-rumped toucourent shows interest, but no such triply doomed mating lies in prospect. Two stuffed Quetzal birds frame the room's bed. A pair of living rainbow lorikeets chirp furiously in their small cage suspended from the ceiling. They must sleep fitfully at night in this Avery of the Dead. Kip sees his clothes laid out on the bed. He removes the robes and pajamas to dress.

In the room next to Kip's, Rafe also dresses in his now dry clothes. His room contains not a single bird nor feather. It has, rather, been decorated in classic centaur. Everywhere, human torsos stretch from horse legs. Centaurs kill bulls with swords. Centaurs grapple with resistant damsels. Centaurs flex their muscles before reflecting pools. A painting depicts centaurs battling the men of Thessaly for their women. A statue shows centaurs on the hunt, dogs at their heels. A base relief on the wall shows a centaur man in mortal combat with a woman centaur whose voluptuous torso emerges from the legs of a tiger. The tapestry behind the bed shows a centaur howling as dogs devour it. To Rafe's great relief the room has no stuffed centaurs.

Across the hall, Trevor dresses in a room neither avian nor centaurian. A brochure for the castle would call it *African tribal*. Zebra shields atop crossed assegai; headdresses of bones; necklaces of ivory. Pictures of Great White Hunters fending off angry black natives share space with others of blond jungle goddesses menaced by leering jungle savages. In such a room Chris Gainer would be inspired to write papers like *Constructs in Fear; Othering the Other*, or *Enacting Colonialism in Hunting Lodge Décor*. In Trevor, the room produces a strong desire for partition; himself from it.

Changed now into his classic tuxedo, Trevor slips out a small lock-pick tool kit hidden in the cuffs and collars. He has a try at the lock on the door. It tumbles to his skill. Trevor carefully opens the door, alert to any looming giants or the panting of immense hounds. All clear. Into the hall he creeps. So many doors to so many rooms. Trevor goes to the door behind which he saw Rafe placed and drops to his knees to try the lock. Twenty seconds of skillful tinkering and this lock too tumbles. Trevor opens the door to see a giant vase, colorfully depicting a centaur mating with a creature half-woman/half-dolphin, about to crash into his head. He shouts, "Stay your hand, man! I'm not the brute you think me!"

Rafe could about kill him, which he about did, "Are you out of your mind? Couldn't you knock? Speak through a keyhole?" Together they struggle to lower the vase without crushing Trevor. Now in the room, Trevor shuts the door quietly behind him.

Trevor looks round, "Do you think this Karloff fellow ever takes a night off? I would think that even a monstrous obsessive might like to relax now and again with a simple land-scape or still-life."

Rafe, "I would guess that he does in fact relax by contemplating the stilling of life." The two men hear a faint knocking. They freeze to listen. Yes, knocking. Faint knocking. It comes from a wall adorned with the portrait of a centaur trying to pull a monkey off its back (one of the many centaur problems to which classic painters gave insufficient attention). Trevor goes to the wall and listens. More knocking. He removes the portrait and hands it to Rafe who tosses it onto the bed. Rafe notices for the first time that the cover to the bed depicts a reclining centaur (no mean feat just that) looking seductively from a bed of orchids.

Trevor, "Have you a glass?"

Rafe finds one on a side table next to a glass carafe shaped like a man-horse. Rafe hands the glass to Trevor, who puts it to his ear and against the wall. Trevor listens, "Tapping. Most definitely tapping."

Rafe, "Thesis confirmed."

Trevor listens intently, "I think it may be Morse code." Trevor taps on the wall.

Rafe, "What does it say?"

Trevor, "I don't know." Trevor taps on.

Rafe, "What are you saying?"

Trevor, "I'm taping out *SOS*."

Rafe, "Why?"

Trevor, "Because it's all the Morse code I know." Trevor taps. Then he stops and shouts at the wall, "Tap louder!"

The tapping grows louder.

Trevor, "Excellent. Much clearer now." He shouts at the wall, "Use more words with *O* and *S*!"

Rafe looks about the room, does anyone else see this?

Trevor, "I hypothesize that, knowing but two letters, and utilizing a bit of alphabetical logic, I can eventually make all this out. I think I can guess at *P* and *T* already." Trevor listens. He shouts at the wall, "Is it *prostate*?"

Even Rafe, unaided by glassware, can hear a voice shout "No!" from behind the wall.

Trevor shouts, "Is it *posture*? Is it *posture* you mean to signal?"

From behind the wall a faint voice, "No. *Position. Position.*"

Trevor beams with pride and to Rafe allows, "I do believe I'm making progress. Is there any message you want me to send?"

Rafe, "Yes. Tap out: *I am an idiot.*"

Trevor, "I'm not certain that I command a sufficient alphabet for that. Quite a lot of *A* and *I.*"

Rafe takes Trevor by the collar, "Come on."

A few moments later they stand in a sea of feathers facing Kip. Kip says, "I think we have the whole third floor to ourselves."

Rafe, "And without making a reservation."

Trevor, "We should reconnoiter."

Rafe, "I hope that's English for find a way out."

Kip, "Should we look for more evidence against Karloff?"

Rafe, "Besides attempted murder?"

Kip, "We haven't found any unlicensed animals."

Rafe, "I wonder what could have happened to them all?"

Trevor, "We should try the door to the grand stairs from which we entered this level."

Rafe leads as they leave the feathered room and enter the hallway. Trevor tiptoes behind him. Rafe notices the cat-burglar creep, "Not that again."

Trevor, "Technique."

Kip, "They've closed the door to the stairs."

A large wooden door bars the way. Trevor kneels to work a lock but finds none. They push on the door, but it does not budge.

Rafe, "On three. All on." Rafe counts down and the three men slam shoulders into the door. No change. In the door. The shoulders will stay bruised for weeks.

Rafe, "Something blocks it. A beam or something."

Kip, "Yeah, I saw one of those leaning up behind the door when we went through."

Rafe, "We need these intelligence reports before we hurl at great massive doors."

Trevor, "Well I'm something of an expert in castle design. Favorite subject, don't you know. Never imagined it would have practical application. The world being what it is, and castle knowledge being a rather antique avocation. No real military application these days. Castle design I mean. Architecturally speaking rather past its day as well, I'm afraid. Yet strangely applicable to international espionage. Shows you never really can tell what might turn up for the better, I suppose"

Rafe, "Can we skip the introductory lecture and get on to the escape plan?"

Trevor, "Yes. Sorry. Let me think. Right now we find ourselves on the third and uppermost level of the rectangular portion of the edifice, separated from the grand stairway by this wooden obstacle, and therefore, also separated from the tower which one may access by the division of the great stairwell alternate to the one we took to these rooms."

Rafe, "Betwixt which methinks doth lie the stone redoubt upon yon pinnacle wherein one be-finds the room of radio-phonic communication."

Trevor, "My point, if I may continue, is that behind us and about the corner we should find a servants stairwell leading down to the trophy room below us. A room with an opening like this one, but, as we have seen, without a door, and through which passing, we may access the alternating stairs to said tower and possibly a radio room."

Kip, "I'm so glad we had this talk."

They carry on. Having found the servants stairwell, the three make their way down the stairs in pitch black darkness, feeling the walls as they go. Rafe says, "How big are these floors?"

Trevor, "I can't understand it. *Here.* Here should be a door accessing the level we drank port on earlier. We ought here to be even with the ground at the entrance."

Kip, "The trophy room."

Trevor, "No door. Not a sign of one."

Rafe, "The stairs go on. It's two more levels to the rear ground floor."

Kip, "The dogs."

Trevor, "But not to have a door at every level? What madman built this place?"

Rafe, "Go on down to the next level."

Down they go, finding a door at last. They open a back

stairway door and Trevor steps into a hallway. Behind him Kip and Rafe follow. They look about. Before them stands a door. Trevor looks through the keyhole.

Trevor, "Nothing."

Kip, "An empty room?"

Trevor, "Utter darkness."

Rafe opens the door. A dark room. They feel for a light switch. Rafe finds one. Not an ordinary in-your-house light switch but a whole-hand-think-as-you-flip-this light switch. Thinking, then flipping, Rafe illuminates the room in a warm and inviting glow. Before them, a library. Packed bookshelves along every wall, a door opposite them, and a table, the size of a large billiard table, on which rests a large scale-model of a small city on a hill by a bay. Kip and Rafe look at the city while Trevor peruses the books, taking them off shelves in turn to read their titles.

Rafe, "Now if you had asked me to guess at Karloff's hobbies, diorama construction would have come far down on the list. Maybe just below model trains and just above knitting."

Trevor, reading, "*Secret Force; The Division of Hunting in Plato's Sophist.*"

Kip, "Great model. Done with real love. Porcelain buildings."

Trevor, reading, "*Expedition Essentials; A Guide to Planning.*"

Rafe, "It's San Monique City. Why has he built a model of San Monique City?"

Trevor, "*The Great White Hunters; From William Finaughty to Baron Bror von Blixen-Finecke.*"

Kip notices that the San Monique City replica has flags pinned at varied locations, "Red flags on the hill and on the roads out of the city. Black flags at the south bay by the swamps."

Trevor, "*Deadfalls to Deep-Holes; The Trapper's Encyclopedia, Volume 17.* He appears to have written this himself."

Rafe looks closely at the flags, "Little arrows drawn from the red flags. Down the hill to the bay."

Trevor, "*Short-Haul Open Ocean Navigation for Beginners.*"

Kip, "Like a battle plan."

Trevor, "*Managing Remotely; How To Organize Effort at a Secure*

Distance."

Rafe, "This doesn't get us anywhere. Trevor, where are we in this building?"

Trevor replaces the book. He indicates the door opposite where they entered, "Through that door and we will be just beneath the trophy room."

Rafe, "Then that room will have the large balcony we saw from the balcony above."

They open the door and search for a light switch. When they flip it, the room fills with a soft light, and their eyes fill with a sight of horror. Shrunken heads hanging from the ceiling. Full sized heads pickling in a jar. Full sized men, immobile and with glass eyes, on slight pedestals. All tastefully done and arranged for the pleasure of the viewer.

Trevor, "Madness."

Kip, "I may be sick."

Rafe, "Do you recognize any of them?"

Trevor, "Have you lost your mind? Do you think we've been introduced?"

Rafe, "From the briefing pictures. The accountants. Agent what's-his-number."

With considerable reluctance the men walk through the room looking at faces. Very unpleasant work.

Kip, "This lies just below the trophy room where we drank port."

Rafe, "Some sort of grotesque parallelism."

Trevor points to a head, "I think this fellow might be one of those Interpol accountants."

Kip, "I mean there's the balcony."

Rafe pulls himself away from the stuffed body of Running Man Number Five, still wearing his thick glasses, standing on a slight pedestal. Rafe joins Kip on the balcony. Looking straight they see the retaining wall that surrounds and contains the lower level and the kennels. Looking above they see the smaller balcony of the trophy room—the other trophy room—recessed, and thus just behind as well as above them as they stand by the balcony railing. Looking below they see the dogs. A great heaving mass of dogs snarling up at them.

Kip, "Could we climb? Up to the other balcony? Trevor maybe?"

Rafe, "Let's try the backstairs down another level first. We might find a non-kennel lower exit. Now that we are free of Karloff, we should explore all our options."

Exploring these options leads them back to the back stairwell. The three men walk down the pitch-black stairway, Trevor and Rafe in the front, Kip a step behind. They move slowly. They feel the wet, cold, stone walls as they go.

Rafe, "Should we be at a door yet?"

Trevor, "I shouldn't think yet."

Trevor takes another step. They hear a click from below them. CLICK. Trevor steps again. Rafe steps down to his side. CLICK. Kip wonders, "Is that normal in a castle?" He steps down to join them. CLICK. CRASH. *Crash* as in the stairwell floor gives way on a hinge and drops the men crashing to a stone floor beneath.

Trevor catches his breath, "A trap!"

Rafe, "Well thank you Mr. Sinjun-Tunsby, guide to Danger Castle. Have I mentioned the need for timely intelligence briefings?"

Kip, "A light."

Above them, from whence they fell, they see a flashlight beam. A figure stands there shining the light down on what must look like their very stupid faces. Karloff speaks, "I had thought you would prefer the more comfortable lodgings above, but I suppose you ready yourselves for the sport. To each his own. I leave you to your rest. Let us hope for better sport tomorrow."

The trap door closes.

At the docks of San Monique – morning

Chris talks to a local man. Katrina picks up shells off the beach. She struggles at this since leaning in for a precise catch upsets her sometimes precarious balance. But after the distraction of pretty shells wears off, she gets the hang of it. Chris listens as the old fishman tells his tales.

Marcy and Natasha watch. Natasha marvels that Chris can listen to the old man, understand the local creole, and redirect his daughter from the odd wandering crab, without the least sign of effort. Truly the world can teach skills not even dreamed of by Russia's School of Clandestine Operations.

Chris bids goodbye to the old fisherman and hoists Katrina up on his shoulders. He heads toward the two women.

Marcy apologies to Natasha for the thin briefing, "I know it isn't the most helpful collection of facts, but I'm sure Chris has more now."

Chris, "More what?"

Marcy, "Information."

Chris, "Absolutely! Did you know that they have a version of the Voodoo religion unique to this island? Voodoo Priestess's, each called a Mama Tutu, symbolically own the entire island. They even claim possession of Danger Island, which they call *Ile de la Mort Parfumee*. Though I don't think any have ever been there. The Mama Tutus supervise and bless all the planting, fishing, and trades on San Monique. They even countersign all the contracts. San Monique is practically a matriarchy."

A man speaks up from behind Chris, "The Mama Tutus are the key to the success of San Monique." The man who says this has black skin, a white uniform, and a bearing that might suggest royalty. He speaks in a French accent. His picture previously flashed before the team during their briefing at Interpol HQ.

Marcy, "Chief Baptiste." Marcy shakes his hand. "Chris, Natasha, this is my local contact and the real instigator of our investigation, San Monique City Chief of Police Pierre Baptiste." They shake hands.

Chief Baptiste, "I must deny instigation for reasons of politics, but I gladly attest to the importance of the Mama Tutus. Through the slave years, the revolution and its aftermath, the dark days of the Kananga regime, the Cuban alliance and our struggle with the United States, always the Mama Tutus have kept our island safe. They are the customary owners of the land, the fish, and the crops. When President Duval privatized the economy, he gave the Mama Tutus half legal ownership of all the national resources. It was they who ended the sugar plantations in favor of the local gardens of our many fruits and roots. We sell these all over the world now. It was they who forbid the vast hotels and favored the smaller tourist sites. They demanded we send their children to be educated in the French universities, but always the young San Moniqueians come home to the Mama Tutus, for we are family. Today almost half the women on the island are Mama Tutus. They are our spiritual leaders. San Monique remains a poor country, but also a rich one."

Natasha, "But Voodoo? Curses, zombies, wild dancing with snakes?"

Chris and Chief Baptiste look at her like she has grown a third eye.

Natasha, again red-faced for what must be only the second time in her life, "I admit I am far from Russia."

Chief Baptiste laughs, "The snakes are not poisonous."

Chris, "Would it be possible for me to see a Voodoo ceremony?"

Chief Baptiste, "Yes, if you do not mind being sprayed in chicken blood."

Chris, "I would love that!"

Katrina claps her hands, "Love!"

Marcy intervenes, "No anthropology this trip, we need to stay focused on intelligence gathering. I asked Chief Baptiste here to meet Chris as a backup contact in case I," she chooses her words carefully here, "need to take independent action." That seemed ambiguous enough. "And to share what he knows about the *recent* history of Danger Island." She gives a hard look to Chris.

Chief Baptiste, "What do you want to know?"

Chris, "I've heard you have had a long history of missing ships around that little island."

Chief Baptiste, "It is not the favored approach to San Monique."

Marcy, to Chief Baptiste, "I thought you were principally concerned about importation of exotic animals?"

The Chief nods, "That is what rich countries and Interpol mostly worry over. I care about the missing ships, as the young man here surmises." Now it is Marcy's turn to be embarrassed, but Chief Baptiste is quick to comfort her, "You are right to worry about invasive species. On our small island they can take a great and quick toll. But Karloff on his island has not shipped any in the last few years. In that time, though, more ships have disappeared. I dread to think what has happened."

Chris, "What makes the island so dangerous to shipping?"

Chief Baptiste, "Survivors who wash up upon our shores speak of rocks beneath the waves. Almost a hundred years ago we built a stone lighthouse on the island opposite the rocks. Listed on all charts of the island, it warded off ships toward the safe passage. But we had trouble keeping it manned. The island breeds madness. In 1953 we automated the lighthouse. Karloff took responsibility for it when he bought the island."

Marcy, "I still don't see the connection to Karloff."

Chief Baptiste, "Nor do I. My men and I are ready to act. But we must know, have proof, of something illegal, before we do. Karloff has paid his way on the island, and I cannot defy his sponsors without knowing how I might charge him."

Marcy, "We intend to discover the secret of Danger Island."

Chief Baptiste, "I trust you will. But now I must bid you adieu." And so he does, nodding graciously to each in turn.

Natasha watches him walk away, "He did not wish to meet in office. He hides us." Russians may not know much about Voodoo, but political corruption they can smell whichever way the wind blows.

Marcy turns to Chris, "You should try to find the identities of survivors from these accidents. Maybe we could interview them."

Chris, "They would be tourists mostly, the fishermen stay away from Danger Island."

Marcy, "Use Interpol's Communication Directorate. They can

track people anywhere in the world." Now Marcy looks Chris dead in the eyes, "What did you find out from the locals, *about Danger Island*?"

Chris sighs, he knows he is about to disappoint, "I would call the tales ritualized." He paints a picture with his hands as he speaks, "The fire on the hill tells lies. Beware the Floating Graveyard. Death Lies in the Shallows. That's the gist of it. All of it really."

Marcy looks at Natasha, "Got that?"

Natasha, "Da. Distrust fire. Stay under or over water."

Marcy, "Then it is time to send you in."

Chris, "So soon? I've barely scratched the surface. We haven't a clue what goes on there."

Marcy, "The guys have been gone all night and no word at all. Not a peep."

Katrina tries a little peek-a-boo with Natasha.

Chris, "Maybe they lost the satellite phone."

Marcy, "No one could be dumb enough to lose their satellite phone."

Chris must admit she has a point there.

Within the breakfast room at Castle Karloff – morning

The guys eat a breakfast of bacon, eggs and fish. The fish retain their heads, eyes staring from the plates. Having lectured his guests on the importance of a high protein diet, Karloff unwinds another hunting story at them. "There I stood, afforded only the meagre protection of my trenches of gasoline, awaiting the approach of my most deadly foe. The ants! In their millions! On the march!"

Rafe looks to deflate him a bit, "Giant ants? Man-sized?"

Karloff, irritated, "No. A small variety. But in their millions! Tens of millions!"

Rafe, "But little guys, not unnatural giants. Because that would call a picture to mind."

Karloff, "Perhaps hundreds of millions! In twenty minutes, they can strip bare ten miles of jungle. They can clean a water buffalo carcass to the bone in five minutes."

Kip picks at his eggs and stares glumly back at the fisheyes. He looks up at Boris, unbruised it would seem, from the ass-kicking Kip laid on him last night. Boris holds a large pistol daintily in his hulking hands. Daintily being the only way that his massive fingers can hold a gun.

Rafe, "Still, easy to step on. Individually I mean."

Karloff, "You cannot step on them individually! In their hundreds of millions!"

Rafe, "I get it, the ants ganged up on you."

Karloff, "They launched a coordinated attack. I set ablaze my trenches of gasoline. The fire consumed them—"

Rafe, "In their millions."

Karloff has found his roll, "They used the burnt husks of their fellows as rafts to flank my position. My coolies set upon them with torches, but the ants overwhelmed and consumed them. Yet they could not defeat Karloff! I had laid my traps. Behind the army of ants," Karloff paints the picture of the field of battle with his hands.

Rafe, "Smallish ants."

Karloff, winces, "Behind the great ant army, I had soaked the ground with gasoline. And now, as they advanced upon me ... I unleashed my weapon: the ballista! I flung great fiery balls into the rear of their ranks and flung my remaining coolies, set aflame, into the advancing maw! I made of them a crimson bonfire to the glory of Karloff!"

Trevor thinks he may be sick.

Rafe, angry a bit, "Did you stuff any? The ants I mean, not the coolies. Did you stuff any of them?"

Karloff, "Alas, too small."

Trevor has an idea, a great idea, "I know, perhaps we could take drinks to the veranda, and our host, Count Karloff, could regale us into the afternoon with his daring escapades. Regale us into the evening even."

Karloff, "Tonight I have other plans requiring my attention. As for today, we have the hunt. You. You all. Shall become a tale of Karloff. I shall call you my hors d'oeuvre hunt."

Trevor has another idea, not as good as the first, but still a great idea, "Photo safari! All the pleasures and challenges of the tracking and stalking and walking about in the bush, the laying on of sights and eyeing up the target, the fussing with complicated and expensive equipment, then, snap! A picture. A thing of beauty. And no one has to get hurt."

Karloff, "No kill? You can have no hunt without a kill."

Trevor, "Well why not? As long as you aren't going to—" Trevor gulps, "eat—the kill. Why not skip that part altogether?"

Kip likes this idea quite a bit, "And the picture is its own trophy, so you save on stuffing expenses."

Rafe would like to share their excitement, but he doubts this idea will catch on where it matters.

Karloff, "The hunt cannot be complete without the kill. Without the kill you can have no frisson."

Kip, "We could order some frisson, store-bought, and eat it after."

Karloff, "You do not understand. The frisson is the sense of transgression, the exquisite knowledge of evil at the heart of the game. The frisson salts the meat."

Rafe, to his comrades, "The meat would be us."

Karloff, "There must be frisson. We must have the kill!"

And so they must.

Outside, in front of the castle door, Karloff stands before his prey. Bolas dangle from his waist, a short bow stretches across his chest, a hunting rifle rests in his hands. Rafe can make out a phrase engraved on the stock: *Ivan the Terrible*.

Karloff, "You have until the sun rests there," he points to the sky, "to make your way at peace before I begin my hunt. Free and wild, you may go anywhere, of course. But to make this a challenging hunt I must urge you not to go to the southwest peninsula, for there you shall be entrapped, and also not to venture to the northeast swamp, for death lies in the shallow lagoon. Now let the hunt begin!"

Awaiting the HMS Shark-Thrasher – day

Natasha, Marcy, Chris, Katrina, and a local oarsman sit in a rowboat out to sea but in sight of land. Chris says, "I didn't know Interpol had submarines."

Marcy, "On loan from the British."

Chris, "I didn't know you could borrow submarines."

Katrina, "submaines."

Before Daddy can offer a correction, a *submaine* appears as if on command, its conning tower breaking the calm surface. It is Her Majesty's Ship *Shark-Thrasher*. Chris nods. Manifestly, one *can* borrow submarines. Marcy checks her watch to note the time, because Interpol demands a strict accounting of borrowed submersibles. The local oarsman looks on as if submarines surface next to his boat every day.

Men emerge from an opening on the body of the sub to pull the boat closer. Above, in the conning tower, the ship's captain shouts down, "Mrs. Gainer of Interpol, I presume."

Marcy, "Yes sir. Permission to come aboard?"

Captain, "Permission granted."

Marcy and the rest, minus the local oarsman now rowing ashore with more spy stories to tell, greet the captain in the submarine control room. Captain Pierson looks exactly like you expect a sub-captain to look like. Do not cast the movie before you see him.

Captain Pierson officially welcomes his guests, "Welcome aboard the *HMS Shark-Thrasher*."

Marcy introduces her team. Katrina looks wide-eyed at the control room, the neatest playground she has ever seen. Filled with buttons, levers, wheels and sailors. This is better than a pediatrician's waiting room. She would really like to get down and run around.

Introductions done, Captain Pierson says, "If you'll give me a moment." The captain turns back to his control room duties, "Take us to periscope depth."

Executive Officer, "Periscope depth, aye. Fifteen degrees

down."

Dive Officer, "Fifteen degrees, aye. Make it fifteen."

Watch Chief, "Fifteen degrees."

Outboard Man, "Fifteen degrees."

Watch Chief, "Role negative to the mark."

Outboard Man, "Role negative to the mark, aye."

Executive Officer, "All ahead two-thirds."

Helm Officer, "Ahead two-thirds, aye. Make ahead two thirds."

Helmsman, "Ahead two-thirds. Answering ahead two-thirds."

Helm Officer, "Answering ahead two-thirds."

Executive Officer, "Answered ahead two-thirds, aye. Periscope depth Captain."

Captain Pierson, "Very good."

Captain Pierson turns to Marcy, "I understand we are to round the island at depth and deposit your agent," he nods to Natasha, "at the beach end."

Marcy, "Yes sir,"

Captain, "It may be slow going in these waters. We have an irregular bottom and no charting."

Chris, "Death Lies in the Shallows."

Captain Pierson looks puzzled. When he turns to give orders, Marcy elbows Chris in the ribs.

In the jungle – day

A dark jungle. We hear branches rustle in the wind, monkeys chatter, and panting, lots of panting. Rafe, Kip and Trevor crash, rather unstealthily, through the jungle undergrowth. Branches and bristles have torn their clothes into the locally fashionable *jungle-tattered look*. Sweat streams down their faces. They stop to catch their breath, leaning against trees, panting.

Kip, "You think we lost him?"

Rafe, breathing heavy, "Of course we did. Giant muddy footprints leading straight from the castle. He hasn't got a chance. I say we camp here for the night."

Trevor catches his breath, "Just to clarify a bit, what are the rules? I mean, how long do we have to evade him?"

Kip, "Until the sun is…" Kip looks above, but they cannot see the sun through the jungle canopy. "Well, maybe late afternoon."

Rafe has trouble believing the naivete of his young colleague. "He also said we were to be his appetizer. God only knows what he means to have as a main course."

Kip, "Let's drop the food metaphors, I'm queasy enough."

Trevor, "But there are rules, yes? He wouldn't cheat, would he? He is a gentleman."

Rafe, "He looked very gentle with his Mongolian longbow."

Kip, "Short bow."

Rafe, angry, "It'll be a rocket launcher by tomorrow morning. The guy is not exactly ill equipped. We need a weapon." Rafe inspects the raw material. Not very promising. "Leaves and branches. We don't even have a knife to cut them."

Kip, "We could make bows and arrows."

Trevor, "Or an atlatl. Throw a spear at him. That would mock his fixation on classic weaponry."

Kip, "If we had some gun powder we could make a grenade out of thorns in a coconut."

Rafe losses patience, "How about a catapult? We could launch monkeys at him."

Trevor, "Well that would be distracting I suppose."

Kip, "Take it from me, monkeys can be hard to work with."

Rafe, "Jesus, Joseph and Mary! We haven't got time to build a monkey-chucker, or invent gunpowder, or even sharpen a stick with our fingernails."

Kip, "Well we had better build some sort of weapon because we won't outrun him."

Trevor, "We could hide."

Rafe, "Brilliant. I'll hide behind you. Where will you hide?"

Kip, "We could hide in the trees. Or dig a pit and cover it with branches."

Rafe, "Forget hiding, he's the master hunter and we're just city slickers, so no hiding for us. We need weapons, and the armory is back in the castle." Rafe has a plan, "You two keep going, lead him and Quasimodo on a merry chase. I'll double back, arm myself, and come up behind the Great White Hunter."

Kip, "Can you track him?"

Rafe, "I can track you two."

Trevor, "I do think he might be alert to such a simple stratagem."

Rafe, "Right. We need to pull him further away from his fort. He wants us to stay away from the island's peninsula in the southwest and some swampy lagoon in the northeast. Can you two find the peninsula through this jungle, or find a path to it?

Trevor, "Should we disregard the warnings?"

Kip reflects, "Me, I don't trust the guy. I hate to go on early impressions, but he doesn't seem the honest sort."

Trevor, "But you do credit that he wants a good hunt, don't you?"

Rafe, "To him a good hunt ends with us stuffed by a taxidermist who really should consider a more select clientele." Rafe takes a breath. "Assume what you say, Trevor. Then you two get entrapped and I die in a lagoon. Once we split in those directions he goes for me, to frisson kill me before I die, and leaves you two entrapped to hunt later. So you two go to the peninsula, and I cut through the lagoon, avoiding death, and make the trip back to the castle. Anybody finds a boat, take the boat to get help. That's our plan. Unless anyone has a better one."

No one does.

On the HMS Shark-Thrasher – day

Tense moments on the bridge. The waters around Danger Island are as unsafe for subs as for ships. The captain gives careful instructions. Natasha, Marcy and family stand quietly to the side.

Captain, "Sonar report,"

Sonar, "Sonar aye, low depth, seventy feet, anomalous bottom."

Captain, "Bare one-third."

Executive Officer, "Bare one-third, aye. Make your mark one-third."

Helm Officer, "One-third, aye. Mark."

Helmsman, "One-third, Mark."

Helm Officer, "Answering one-third, aye."

Captain, "Sonar, report anomalies."

Sonar, "Sonar, aye. Rounded with rounded prominences. Running identification program now. Request ping for topography."

Captain, "Ping, aye."

Sonar, "Answering ping, aye. Pinging." PING.

Below the sub, in the depths, attached to a chain, a round bomb six foot in diameter with menacing looking spokes—a bomb of the classic nautical style—floats on its leash, tethered to the floor of the ocean. When the sonar pings, it sets off the trigger of the bomb. The chain detaches, letting the bomb loose to float up towards the sub. A masterful Karloff trap.

On the sub, the sonar-man watches his monitor. Sonar, "Movement from sea floor. Identification as magnetic bomb."

Captain, "Right full rudder."

Executive Officer, "Right full rudder, aye, make right full rudder."

Katrina wants to play too, "Left!"

Helm Officer, "Left full rudder, aye."

Helmsman, "Answering left full rudder, aye."

Helm Officer, "Answering left full rudder."

Captain, "Belay that order! Right full rudder! Make depth five degrees!"

Executive Officer, "Belay order, right full rudder, aye, make depth five degrees."

Katrina, "Ten!"

Helm Officer, "Right full rudder."

Dive Officer, "Make ten degrees, aye."

Dive Chief, "Answering ten degrees, aye."

Captain, "What?!? No! Ahead full! Right half rudder correction!"

Executive Officer, growing confused, "Ahead full, correction to half rudder, aye."

Katrina, "Full!

Helm Officer, "Full?"

Katrina, "Rudder!"

Seeing what is happening, Chris shooshes Katrina.

Helm Officer, "Full right rudder, aye."

Helmsman, "Answering full right rudder."

Dive Officer, "Ahead half, aye."

Dive Chief, "Answering ahead half."

Captain, "Stop! Belay all orders!"

Katrina, "Fire!"

Torpedo Officer, "Begin fire protocols, aye."

Captain Pierson, "Do not fire!"

Captain Pierson looks over in horror at Katrina. Chris takes her out. A baffled and embarrassed Marcy follows.

Below the spiked bomb approaches.

Sonar, "Bomb closing distance."

Captain, "Helm, my voice only, right half rudder! Blow ballast! Crash surface, ahead full." Alarms sound. The ship tilts to the surface. It runs silently ahead. The bomb misses the sub by inches. All in all, the whole episode a tribute to the training, discipline, and reflexes of Her Majesty's Corp of Submariners.

On a jungle path – afternoon

Kip and Trevor have found a narrow jungle path. Worn away, they suppose, by earlier people fleeing Karloff. The occasional bits of torn cloth they see along the side of the path supports this supposition but does not aid their moral. Both men look exhausted. Kip leads with Trevor close behind.

Kip, "We could obscure our trail by brushing it with tree branches to eliminate our footprints."

Trevor, "Fine master hunter he'd be if he couldn't follow a trail of branch sweepings."

Kip considers another tactic he read in a comic book, "Maybe if we walk backwards he'd think we were headed towards him."

Trevor, "And do what? Wait for us to arrive?"

Kip, "Well at least I'm thinking of things!"

Trevor launches into the air just behind Kip, ass-over-tea-kettle; he has tripped a rope snare.

Kip, "All you're doing is—" Kip looks behind him, "Flying." Kip did not expect this. "What are you doing up there?"

Trevor, "My bloody imitation of a bloody astronaut! Now get me bloody down!"

Kip grabs Trevor's shoulders to bring him to earth, "I wish I could take a picture of this."

Elsewhere in the jungle – late afternoon

Rafe struggles through thick jungle. Every tree looks like every other damn tree. Every animal call mocks him.

Easy to say: "double back." But in thick jungle, with the land navigation skills of a fungus, not so easy to do. A howler monkey blasts out a call in what, once his heart starts beating again, Rafe would characterize as derision.

Rafe notes the buzzing, excited, stinging world of insects contained in this jungle. He notes this by swatting compulsively at himself. An inventory of the local insect life, rendered in Rafe's own limited hexapodalist vocabulary, includes the flying bug taxon: the jungle buzzing-just-to-annoy-you gnat posse, the trying-to-mate-with-your-eyelid wasp, the loves-that-you've-cut-yourself-hornet. The ground dweller bug taxon contains the stings-like-electrical-fire ant, the bloated-centipede-of-death, the leach-that-somehow-attached-itself-to-your-hand (not a bug, Rafe knows, but he has no time for zoology), and the very disturbing big-furry-tarantula-looking-spider-currently walking on your foot. Rafe calculates that it will take this assembly of clearly man-eating insects all of two minutes to strip him to the bone if he only stands still, so he keeps moving.

Which only raises again the question of what direction to move in. Rafe checks the sides of trees for moss, having read somewhere that it only grows on the north side of a tree. Or the south side. At least it grows on only one side, consistently indicating some direction or other. But the trees in the jungle have no moss. Or perhaps they are all moss. Something green covers them. Rafe would guess this stuff to be a member of the slime family, taxonomically speaking, rather than a moss. It occurs to Rafe that he does not really know what moss looks like. Not life-or-death knows. He slips on slime. Or moss. Until now it had never seemed important to know the scientific designation for things he slipped on.

Rafe recalls seeing a nature show that may have said something about all animals heading toward water. He checks for animal tracks. He sees only his own. How close to the sea must you be to smell it? Rafe takes a deep breath through his nose. A mistake. Everything, but everything, smells of decay, death, and spoilage. The floor of a jungle is a compost heap that eats itself.

Rafe finds a narrow groove through the jungle that some other poor fool has trapsed out. Maybe it leads to the sea.

Within the HMS Shark Thrasher

Captain Pierson looks through his periscope. He spins around, eyes on the viewfinder, pressing a button on the handle to change the magnification. Marcy, Natasha, and Chris watch. Katrina straddles Chris. The crew watch Katrina nervously. Captain Pierson says, "We have a tug hauling a barge heading by us. Once it passes, we can position to deploy your agent."

Marcy, "Where does the tug come from?"

Captain Pierson offers her the view from the periscope, "From around the other side of your Danger Island I think."

Marcy looks through the periscope. She sees a small tugboat hauling a small barge. A green tarp covers the barge's contents. Marcy tries to adjust the view to zoom in, "I can't tell what's on the barge. If the tug hauls animal cages, we would already be onto something." She offers Natasha a look. Natasha looks through the periscope at the oncoming tug and the sub crew looks at Natasha. Natasha backs from the periscope without a word. Marcy gestures to Chris to look, "Maybe you can make something out."

Chris hands Katrina to Marcy—at which the crew holds its breath—and Chris looks through the periscope. "Not really in focus."

Captain Pierson, "These buttons on the handle, a bit tricky." Pierson helps Chris learn the focus buttons. Clumsily, Chris manages to bring the passing barge into view. "Looks like pallets. Something hanging out of them. Can't tell what. Not animal tails though."

Katrina, "Look! Look!"

Chris looks to Captain Pierson. The captain girds himself, "Why not?" Various answers to this question, as posed by a Board of Navel Inquiry, pass thorough the captain's head, but he just watches as Marcy hands the squirming Katrina to Chris. Chris leans her forward to the periscope viewfinder.

Katrina takes the periscope handles in hand. She hits the zoom buttons like a born sailor, and the crew watches as she maneuvers the periscope. Captain Pierson wonders if this child might be deployed as some sort of super-weapon. For her part, Katrina offers her assessment. "Flowers."

Curious, Chris looks again through the viewfinder. The barge has now passed by.

Captain Pierson looks at the viewfinder, "Tug's clear now. We will proceed to the deployment site." He looks at Chris, "If you will secure the child in the forward hold."

Twenty minutes later, sub safely in position off the coast of Danger Island, Captain Pierson prepares Natasha for her deployment. He and several crewmen stand in the cramped confines of the torpedo room. With them, Natasha, in a black wet-suit and scuba gear, stands ready. Marcy watches. Chris holds Katrina who pokes a torpedo.

The seamen wrap objects in cellophane to protect them from the salt water they will soon encounter.

Marcy, "We've had no message from our agents, Captain, so I'm officially ordering our operative infiltrated."

Captain Pierson gives a sharp nod to Marcy and offers his best Officer and a Gentleman smile to the lovely Russian spy.

"Our tubes are at your service." That didn't come out quite right. "That is to say, we're ready to stuff you into our tubes." Was that any better? Captain Pierson grows nervous, "I mean to say ... uh ... we mean to shoot you out our ... uh."

Natasha takes (her version of) pity on him, "Da. I go swim now."

Captain Pierson nods. He lifts up a large, yellow, waterproof duffle bag stuffed with who knows what and presents it to Natasha. "Your tow bag. It carries your gear." Captain Pierson notices Katrina's poking game, "That's an arming mechanism!"

Chris pulls Katrina in, "Sorry."

Captain Pierson returns to the briefing. "Your tow bag. It contains your gear. Satellite phone, camera, aerial photos of the island, plastic explosives, night vision goggles, Geiger counter," Geiger counter? "Supplemental com-link, fresh water, first aid kit, sanitary napkins, and a compass."

From the back Katrina yells a new word, "Torpedo!"

Marcy shoots Katrina a frustrated look at her growing, and increasingly dangerous, but still in one respect deeply defective, vocabulary.

Captain Pierson bristles and vows to himself to assign two men to watch over this most dangerous toddler. A seaman hands him a cellophane triangle about the size of a football. Captain Pierson hands it to Natasha. "Your gun. Wrapped to protect it from sea salt. Keep your weapon with you at all times. You'll find the ammo in your tow bag. For safety."

Marcy looks concerned, "Shouldn't she have—"

Natasha, "Don't worry. I am my weapon."

Marcy looks worried.

Captain Pierson holds up a yellow strap running from the tow bag to loop into a belt. "Your tow bag connection belt to attach your tow bag to your," he stutters, "b-b-body," clears his throat, "it goes around your waist." For a moment he looks to be about to put it on her, but her look warns him that such an act might prove fatal, so he hands it to her. The crew watch breathless as Natasha slides the strap across her waist and buckles it. Why are the drop-dead gorgeous ones always ones that can drop you dead?

Captain Pierson, "The tube is ready."

Marcy takes Natasha by the shoulders, "Contact us as soon as you get to the island. We can't go in without hearing from you, but as soon as we hear there's trouble: backup is on the way."

Natasha, "Who do you have left to send?"

Marcy looks away, checking the ceiling with her eyes.

Natasha, "Marcy, you are not qualified."

Marcy, "Well I can't send Halftrain."

They hug briefly and Natasha climbs into the torpedo tube. Seamen push in her attached tow bag after her.

Commander Pierson, "She'll be fine. We shoot people out of these things all the time." He corrects himself, "Well, mostly bodies buried at sea."

On a jungle trail – late afternoon

Kip and Trevor walk on, stepping carefully on the muddy path. Now Trevor takes the lead with Kip behind him. Trevor feels safer in front.

Trevor, "The rope nearly broke my bloody ankle."

Kip, "How could you have missed the trap?"

Trevor, "I had a babbling idiot in my way. I'll see the bloody traps this time."

Kip looks back behind him, "I think we lost him."

Trevor disappears down a tiger trap he has just stepped into.

Kip stops and listens. He listens very alertly, "I heard something." Kip looks around. He sees nothing. Which is odd, because Trevor is something. "Something isn't right here." Kip looks up to see if Trevor has taken flight again. He scans the trees for an airborne Englishman.

Trevor, from the pit, shouts, "Get me!!! Bloody!!! Out of here!!!"

In the submarine tube

Natasha, in scuba gear, holding a cellophane wrapped pistol in front of her and attached to a water-proof duffle bag behind her, hears the torpedo door to her rear shut and seal. The forward torpedo door opens and water floods in. For a moment she rests in a tube of water. Then, WHOOOSH. Bubbles, secret agent, and tow bag fly out of the torpedo tube. In the process the clip attaching the tow bag to the tow line breaks.

In the dark sea Natasha could never find it even if she tried.

She swims onto shore. Finding the rocky beach, she kicks off her fins. She has nothing now but her cellophane wrapped pistol. She looks about at the island. The beach around her and the jungle before her descend into the darkening shades of evening. She hears a sound. She listens. She hears the barking of what must be a small moose or a large dog. The animal heads her way. She pulls up the strap to her tow bag. No tow bag. Her gear gone with it. She looks up the beach. She sees a king-sized mastiff approaching at attack speed. She must look like easy prey to the great hound.

Natasha starts to unwrap the cellophane from around her gun. The mastiff lets out one great howl and charges harder toward Natasha. She continues to unwrap the cellophane as the mastiff closes the space between them. The mastiff is almost upon her. She frees the gun from the cellophane. She tosses the gun down and holds the cellophane in her fist. The Mastiff leaps. Natasha rams the wad of cellophane down its throat.

The Mastiff chokes and coughs. It spits up great heaps of cellophane. It shakes its mighty head and throws up. It looks at Natasha. Natasha looks at the mastiff. The mastiff sulks off. Maybe it can find some easier prey on the island. A lion or something. Natasha unzips her black wet suit. She peels it off. Beneath she wears a skintight black bodysuit. Call it night camouflage or embodied nihilism, but Natasha loves to rock the black outfits.

She takes a bearing from the descending sun. She heads inland.

On a jungle mud patch – late afternoon
Karloff leans over the world's most obvious footprint. He

looks around at the many others. He takes in the twigs and tree limbs. He snaps one to test for brittleness. He sniffs it to age the sap like a master vintner. He tears a leaf and tosses it up in the air. No wind. He returns to the earth of the track. He breaths it in, alert to every subtle odor. He pinches a bit of tracked mud in his fingers and rolls it around to test its consistency. Normal consistency it appears. He tastes it. Give him this: the man spares no effort.

Karloff stands and examines the overall pattern of the many tracks. He steps in them, imitating the action he infers from his prey. He waves his arms about as he alternates in the tracks, miming a heated argument. At one point, to confirm the heat of the dispute, he measures a track with a finely graded ruler. Yes. A footprint made in anger. Deep between the ball of the foot and the toes. Karloff has made a particular study of this. Published in the *Proceedings of the Society for Emotional Detection in Animal Spoor*. One of the Society's better essays actually.

Karloff inspects the direction of the tracks. One set leads off to the lagoon, two sets lead off to the peninsula. He sighs and shakes his head. He heads off following the tracks to the peninsula.

At a jungle stream – late afternoon

Rafe arrives at a small stream that cuts through the jungle. He cannot fathom how he managed to track his own footprints here. He half expected to find a deer, dappled in morning dew, sipping stream water in solitary contentment. He finds, in the event, mud cacked on top of fallen tree limbs. Something catches his eye. Up from the mud he pulls—night vision goggles, disabled by an arrow and a bolt. Rafe considers all the many uses one could improvise with such a device and comes up with a list of zero. He drops the goggles.

Rafe talks to himself because a lack of listeners does not keep him from talking. "Every river runs to the ocean. Right? Or a lake. No lakes on the island. So, the stream will lead to the lagoon." Seems promising. "Of certain death." Or not. "And I leave a trail a blind baboon could follow." Rafe would very much like to do something clever here. A toucan calls out and starts him. Even considering his circumstances, and his very recent conversion to vegetarianism, Rafe could just about support a hunt for loud jungle animals right about now. "Shut up!"

A voice cries out, "Shut up!" Rafe makes fists and readies to strike. "Who's that?"

A voice cries out, "Who's that?"

Rafe, "Show yourself!"

A voice, "Show yourself!"

Rafe, "Stop mocking me!"

A voice, "Stop mocking! Stop mocking!"

Rafe calms, now recognizing the tone of a parrot. "I wouldn't talk so much if I were you; you'll wind up in a guest room." Rafe relaxes on a tree. Then he has a clever idea. From his pockets he fishes out the rooster feathers stuffed there the morning before by Mama Tambo de Tutu. "I bet Mr. Exotic Bestiary does not keep roosters on the island." Rafe walks upstream, opposite his intended direction, putting out feathers on the shore as he goes. Not hoping to fool Karloff about his ultimate direction, he places them as ceremoniously as he can. He makes little feather temples of them. He arranges them with mud on tree trunks just so. Rafe deploys whatever Voodoo he can summon from memories of Saturday matinees and makes a trail upstream of rooster feathers. He inspects his work as he heads down stream. "Well Mama Tambo, let's hope this island has more than one white fool."

On a jungle path – late afternoon

Karloff looks down at the tripped tiger trap. No mangled bodies. No dumb faces staring up at him, expecting a mercy the jungle never offers. Just another day's work resetting Bengal tiger traps. And what way do the tracks lead? Like lemmings they head straight to the cliff they had been warned against. Karloff remembers his great lemming hunt of years past. Not his most challenging hunt. But consider the numbers!

Karloff reverses his trail. With the two lemmings un-trapped and headed to the peninsula he can focus on making a quick run before dark sets in to eliminate the irritating man making the other set of prints. Darkness, he knows, will bring preparations for a different hunt.

At a jungle stream – late afternoon

Footprints everywhere, water disturbed, and feathers aligned in some sort of ritual communication. What fool stops in the middle of a jungle to arrange rooster feathers? From the style of the shoe print Natasha can tell that the fool is Rafe. This might seem strange, but in fact no one graduates from the Russian Special Services Survival School unless they instinctively note every footprint of every person they encounter—everywhere. Natasha knows the manufacturer of Rafe's footwear. (Rafe can barely remember his shoe size.) But how to fathom the wayward mind of an American Talks-a-Lot?

Still, team members must be saved, so Natasha heads off downstream.

In the mangrove swamp – late afternoon

Kip can barely squeeze through the thick vines and crisscrossed mangrove roots. He heaves one foot out of the mud, fishes around for his shoe in the hole, puts the shoe back on, takes a step, heaves the other foot out of the mud, feels for his shoe…

Trevor struggles behind him, "Stay off the paths? Madness! The surrounding jungle impedes us as surely as any trap."

Kip, "We can't just walk the paths, he'll find us. Plus, he has laid all his traps there."

Trevor, "But can't you see, we've immobilized ourselves by this route. Damn! I've lost my other shoe."

Kip, "Why did you wear a tuxedo on a jungle expedition?"

Trevor, "I expected a diner party and a warm discussion of animal smuggling. Aha! I found a boot!"

Kip, "That's mine. Pass it forward."

Trevor, "A machete. That's what we need."

Kip, "I'll put it on the list after helicopter."

Trevor, "If they can't even trust us with a satellite phone, they certainly won't offer a helicopter. With a machete we would likely just lop off a limb anyway, best denied that as well."

Kip, "It's just a learning curve. We are newbies so we have a lot to learn. For instance, when assaulting the fortress of a master hunter, expect to be hunted. And always tie your satellite phone to your waist with a rope. Next time we know."

Trevor, "I've found another boot!"

Kip, "Mine again. Pass it forward."

At a jungle stream – late afternoon

Nothing screams danger like unidentifiable spoor. And not the thrilling danger of the moment before the kill, but the sick feel of danger like the ill smell of defeat. These feathers scream that kind of danger to Karloff now. He raises his sounding horn and lets out a blast. Then he turns to the feathers. Dull gray-white, like none on the island and from no bird he has imported, plucked, or stuffed. And arranged as, what? A warning? A curse? And these other tracks. Smaller feet. Delicate. Strong yet balanced. At ease in the bush. He runs a finger over these. He thrills at the thought of the feet that made these. A woman's feet. He sniffs them. Not menstruating. He takes a feather and licks it. Plucked not long ago, but how here? And why like this? He rehearses the scene. Did the woman bring the feathers? No.

Boris emerges from the jungle holding a great hound.

Karloff, "We have an insecure track. We must slow the hunt."

Boris points to his own pocket.

Karloff, "I know, but we must take greater care. You will stay with me now."

Karloff begins his tracking anew, downstream. Carefully.

In the jungle – fall of day

A cobra hisses, head wings flared, ready to strike. But something strikes it first. A hand snatches it off its branch.

Natasha, now in possession of a pet cobra, considers the tracks ahead. She sees Rafe heads straight for the stream's outlet at the lagoon. She wonders if he even looked at the satellite photos. She tosses the snake away and takes the short cut to the lagoon.

Natasha soon passes another, larger creek. She stops, sensing danger. Russian Intelligence teaches danger sensing the way high schools teach test-taking: in every class. Natasha hears a slight rustle in the mud of the creek. Dead eyes open to look at her from the mud. A crocodile. It moves slowly forward, ready to strike. Natasha jumps to an overhanging branch, swings off of it to the other side, stepping lightly on the crocodile's back as she goes. From behind it, she grabs the crocodile's tail and hauls it backward to a tree whose trunk has split down the middle. She hauls the crocodile over and through the gap in the trunk and jams the tail there, trapping the reptile. And no, they do not teach this at the Russian Clandestine Special Services Training Academy. They teach improvisation. And they recruit well.

Natasha heads on.

At a lagoon – twilight

Rafe smells the lagoon before he sees it. No need for deep breaths now, the odor of decay almost overwhelms him. Rafe has been fighting to find a footing on exposed roots for what seems like hours and has thus made quite a study of them. He sees that he no longer stagers around giant tree roots but has transitioned into some sort of lattice work of roots, seemingly designed by a vengeful god to ensnare misplaced urbanites. Almost worse than these though, are the small vines that cover the roots and squish under Rafe's feet, releasing yet more foul air at his nose. Had Karloff not gone out of his way to tell Rafe not to approach this lagoon, Rafe would now be going out of his way to avoid it. Why would Karloff bother to ward someone off of a place so well defended by roots and general ick unless it hid a boat? Based on odor, inconvenience, and general foulness, Rafe judges a whole marina must lie just past the supremely well rooted trees right ahead of him. He further judges that if he does not get there soon, night will fall on him and he will be stumbling over squish covered roots by moon shadows.

Rafe slaps his arms and neck in a now ritualized war with the Insect Nation. By this time they should have taken enough blood from him to call a truce on the basis of shared DNA. He slaps again. A sensation comes over him that he has been covered in insects, and he starts to slap all over his body. He struggles to get a hold of himself. He looks at his arms. No bugs. At the ground. No bugs. Victory in war? He looks at roots and leaves and the sides of trees. No bugs. They take the night off apparently.

Rafe listens. The jungle sounds oddly silent. Far behind him, from where he came, he still hears its now faint chatter, but ahead of him he hears nothing. Perhaps that means the ocean lies past the trees. Crawling over a lattice of roots he sees a monkey on the ground. One of the howlers that scared him to death earlier. But this one has no howl left. It looks at Rafe with dead eyes. And not a single insect feasts on the body. Rafe misses the noise.

Pressing on through the last tangle of roots, Rafe clears the forest to find that the swamp opens up to a lagoon. It reeks of decomposition. He stands on the edge of the water, all brackish and covered in weed and leaves, thick enough you could walk across it in snowshoes. To Rafe's right the land rises high to a cliff. This he hardly notices. He looks, transfixed, at the lagoon. In front of him, as the light of the early evening dies into the darkness of night, as far into the lagoon as he can see: boats. Ships even. But not a marina. Rafe, balanced on a mangrove root, looks out at a floating graveyard.

In the jungle – twilight

Karloff looks puzzled. No. He looks downright baffled. Mystified. Bewildered would not be too strong a word. In fact, none of the seven languages Karloff speaks has quite the word for what he looks like right now. So it is best to stay with particulars: Karloff looks just as you would expect a master hunter, tracking human prey, on his own human prey game reserve, stocked by his own hand, and while followed by his favorite giant, who holds his hungry hound, would look, upon encountering a crocodile firmly lodged in the crook of a tree. There are simply no other words for this look.

Karloff looks at Boris, whose expression matches the Great Hunter's, and so offers no aid. Karloff resists the urge to sniff the crocodile. "We have a most extraordinary presence on the island. We must lay our plans with the utmost care."

Boris pulls a pocket watch from his pocket. He holds it out and open for Karloff to see. Karloff looks at the time and then looks up, inspecting the darkening sky and the falling light. "Yes. I had become lost in the hunt. This quarry must wait. We must further the preparations for tomorrow night."

Karloff turns and backtracks toward his castle.

At the great wall – twilight

Kip and Trevor emerge from the jungle, clothes in tatters, scratched and bruised from head to foot, Trevor shoeless. Their joy at obtaining a clear stretch of daylight free of the jungle canopy and its insnaring vines quickly abates on seeing what lies in the clearing. A great wall. A barricade of cut jungle trees, straw and mud. It stretches to their left and to their right, well out of sight in the distance both ways. It stands roughly twenty feet high. Sharpened poles extend from its top facing upwards or inwards, away from where Kip and Trevor stand.

Kip, "Didn't expect that."

Trevor, "It's … it's … incomparable."

Kip shakes his head to clear it, "What is it about this island that makes everything grow gigantic?"

Trevor, "It must be old as the ages! Some great Mayan king must have built it to mark the out limits of his Imperium. Or, no, some lost civilization unknown to man left this as testament to its passing. We came looking for a petty exporter of unlicensed pets, and we discovered the ruins of a lost civilization! Only in the Americas!"

Kip, "It's made of mud and straw. It would need to be rebuilt after every hurricane season."

Trevor, "No, no. It's here still, don't you see? It must be secure against weather and storm in order to prevail against them for such long eons. It *is* here after all."

Kip, "Yes, it is here. But it cannot *prevail* for long eons because mud doesn't work like that."

Trevor, "Are you intimating that the builders of this enormous structure are," Trevor looks around nervously, "about?"

Kip, "Yes, perhaps I was *intimating*, so I apologize for that. Let me just *say* it: the builders are *about*. And from the looks of it, they might be giants." Now they both look around nervously.

Trevor, "Why did they build it?"

Kip walks up and pulls off some mud caked straw, "It just isn't possible. The wall must span the length between the two bays that form the peninsula. The required manpower, not to mention the materials, the island just couldn't support such a project."

Trevor, "Well I see you've come round to my way of thinking, and we may together infer that it is *not* in fact here. On the other hand, supposing it to be here, my question remains: why did they, Mayan or local, men or gods, build it?"

Kip, "Lets climb to the other side."

Trevor, "Don't be daft."

Kip, "Karloff the Terrible could appear at any moment behind us. We should at least force him to breach this wall to get to us." Kip searches for secure lashings on the structure that might assist an assent. "We can't get around it, and we can't go back. Maybe we can stage an ambush on the other side."

Trevor pulls at lashing also. "Very well, but let me lead the way. Alpine climber don't you know." He pulls on a lashing and falls on his back. "Typically use an ice axe. Won't take a moment to adjust." Trevor adjusts. He leads as they ascend the wall. They climb using the lashings and the firmer purchase of the trees that shore up the wall. Trevor loses his footing and kicks hard at the hardened mud of the wall to regain it. Mud falls on Kip just below.

Kip, "They do this in the Alps? Rain debris on the coolie?"

Trevor, "Kick into it! Your foot man! Kick into the mud! Kick it away!"

Kip does as Trevor says. Mud falls away beneath Kip's feet until he strikes metal. "What?" Kip climbs up a tree lashed against the structure until he is level with Trevor who has cleared a large space of mud revealing more metal.

Trevor, "It's not made of mud at all."

Kip strikes the metal, "It sounds hollow."

Trevor, "Shipping containers. Stacked double high and covered in mud and trees and straw to look like a native wall."

Kip, "That would save on labor and material."

Trevor can hardly contain himself, "But *why*? A peninsula bounded by a wall of containers reeks of madness all by itself, but to build it in imitation of a wall of mud and straw as well?"

Kip, "I don't know, aesthetics? Make it to respect local customs."

Trevor, "Local customs? Is there some Caribbean custom of making twenty-foot mud barricades that one might emulate?" They hear the sounds of drums in the distance.

Kip, "Up and over to find out."

They climb, more easily now that they can kick mud away to more solid footing on the seams of the containers. They crest the top and see the many sharpened poles sticking out facing toward the peninsula. Below them lies a village of dilapidated straw huts surrounded by heaps and piles of cans. Canned peas, canned beans, and an unbelievable amount of empty peach cans. They see no people. Or animals bigger than a rat. Rats they see in abundance.

Kip, "Look at the way the sharpened poles face. They built this wall to keep something in here from getting out onto the rest of the island."

Trevor, incredulous, "Something large enough to require the hinderance of a twenty-foot wall but too stupid to climb around these sharpened poles?" Drums clamor from beyond the village.

Kip and Trevor cannot see the source of the drums as more jungle obscures their line of sight. They make their way down the wall using the poles to aid their descent. They find in much easier to navigate the wall with the aid of defensive poles.

Kip, "I grant that as a security measure the poles don't work. But they look incredibly intimidating."

Trevor, "How does it matter what they look like if one may so easily master them?"

They reach the ground; the wall behind them, the village before them. Kip says, "Look at this village. Someone built the wall to keep people in. Half the art of controlling people lies in the management of symbols. Walls contain. Spear wielding walls contain even better. So the mind tells us. Build it," Kip gestures at the wall, "and they will stay."

Kip and Trevor walk through the village toward the sound of the drums. They call out periodically but receive no answers. Trevor's feet hurt with every step. From twigs to tin cans, everything in the village hates bare feet.

Trevor, "Frankly, the place looks a wreck."

Kip, "Not house proud."

They peer into a hut. Inside they see the floor covered in pink bathroom rugs, stained by mud. The back wall of the hut is made of identically sized books, also covered in mud. The mysterious builders constructed another wall of identically sized picture frames lashed together. Dried mud covers everything. Kip says, "You'd think the natives would make better straw roofs."

Kip and Trevor clear the village and head toward the sound of the drums. They can feel the sea breeze and see the sand now beneath their feet. Trevor would feel better in the soft sand were it not for all the rats he steps on. They walk past a stand of trees and over a small rise. They see the ocean.

The also see a motley collection of dancers. The dancers wear straw skirts, tattered t-shirts, and masks framed in muddy, frayed feathers. Squinting a bit, Kip can make out the masks beneath the feathers. Halloween masks of Casper the Friendly Ghost. The dancers wear no shoes, except for a few in stiletto heels.

Kip, whispering, "A lost tribe!"

Trevor, "Yes, but they are," these words Trevor struggles to find, "ethnically inconsistent."

Kip looks at him with mild suspicion.

Trevor, "And no children anywhere." He sees Kip's look, "I'm not being critical. I'm just saying it is unnatural."

Kip, accusingly, "Unnatural."

Trevor bristles at Kip, "I mean ethnographically inconsistent with the," Trevor waves his hands about to encompass a Caribbean Ocean and jungle, "the environment."

Kip, "Spoken like a true Englishman. What's the matter? The Empire missing it's days of San Monique?"

Trevor, "In the first place, San Monique was a French possession, not an English one. In the second place, I merely mean that like the wall of containers displayed as an indigenous construction, while in fact being a modern contrivance, this tribe of peoples," Trevor points to indicate the tribe, all of whom have now stopped dancing to watch the two men squabble, "displays the mark of a construct. An artifact of fancy."

Kip points to the tribe to make some point but notices that they have noticed him, "Uh oh." Kip freezes. Trevor manages a meek smile and a bit of a wave.

A large black man with a helmet of feathers, and a mask of Casper the Friendly Ghost, steps forward, spear in hand. He removes the mask and announces in a loud voice, "I am Mandinko! Shaman Chief and Keeper of the Law!"

Kip and Trevor did not expect this, though by now they realize that their expectations serve as a poor guide to unfolding events. Trevor manages a polite nod at Mandinko, head shaman.

Another man, young and Caucasian, steps forward removing his mask, "I am Old Abraham of Eternal Ages!"

A red-haired white woman, made bright pink by the sun, steps forward, "I am Vixen, Seductress of the Fjords!"

A brown skinned man steps forward, "I am Shiva, Assassin of Kali!"

"McGuffin, Savage of the Highlands!"

"Zorro, the Desert Fox!"

"Frissia, Temptress of the Forest!"

"Bistro, Wild Woman of the Night!"

An Asian man steps forward, "I am The Sinister Yong Fu of the Red Dragon Tong!"

Trevor can stand it no more, "You're the *what*?!?"

Kip has the hang of it now. He steps forward and announces, "I am Kip Carson, Maker of Strange Happenings That Light the World with Ideas!"

They seem impressed. Everyone looks at Trevor.

Trevor, "Oh, yes, well. Trevor Sinjun-Tunsby here. Englishman, rather misplaced at the moment." He sees they expect more, so: "Keeper of the Flame of the Old-School Tie!" This will have to suffice.

Mandinko raises his spear, "We are the children of the God Karloff, the Great Hunter and Master of the Seas and Waves. He who makes the rain and calls forth the cargo. He who names all things and stalks the wilds for those who disobey the Law. We serve Karloff the master. We are the Tribe of the Lost.

The tribes-people walk closer. The Sinister Yong Fu, who, frankly, could not look less sinister in his ill-fitting grass skirt, steps forward. "Have you the skill to make the great fire? From scratch? The fluid runs low!" He holds out a lighter.

Kip, "Uh, from scratch? Like from sticks or such?" Kip looks to Trevor, who just shrugs. Kip says, "I could probably figure it out in time, but I don't know the trick offhand."

The crowd roars in disapproval, "Arrgghhhhh!"

The young man who is Old Abraham steps forward. "Have you the skill to weave straw so that it does not leak?" Heads nod all around at the utility of this one.

Kip, "Again, with a little application..."

Not good enough! The crowd roars, "Arrgghhhhh!"

Vixen steps forward, holding a book, the cover of which shows a young man smiling in a kitchen and about to put ice into a boiling pot. "Have you books? We have *Cooking with Ice* by

Caeman Scott. Six thousand copies of it!" The crowd moans.

Trevor, "Well I did have my *Field Guide to Caribbean Birds and Plants*, but I lost it coming ashore."

The crowd groans. Mandinko asks with more hope than reason should suggest, "Have you ice?" Upon the reply the crowd roars as one in dismay, "Arrgghhhhh!"

Shiva the Assassin has a try, "Have you shoes? Size seven?"

Another, "Size five!"

Another, "Size ten!"

Another, "Size seven or eight!"

Another, "Any size but nine!"

As the din subsides and the tribe anxiously awaits the answer, Trevor tries to let them down easily, "I've lost mine in the mud."

Kip, "Actually, I wear size nine."

As one, the crowd screams in dismay, "Arrgghhhhh!"

Mandinko holds his spear aloft, "They are not the Gods of Salvation. To the pot with them!"

Kip, "That does not sound promising."

At the lagoon – evening

Ships float, scattered about, in the green muck of the lagoon. Ships of every description, save that of *sea-worthy*. Rafe notes that the lagoon itself must have a long entrance from the sea. Ships blown in have stuck fast in the thick, swampy water. Blown in. At the point in the lagoon furthest removed from its entrance, and most continuous with the swamp, Rafe sees nothing but sailing ships. Cracked masts, split wooden hulls, draping or decayed ropes, all half sunk or held up by the thick entangling sludge. Vines creep up their hulls.

Some must be centuries old. Rafe sees a Spanish gallon and a sloop Blackbeard might have been proud to sack. One dilapidated hulk resembles a Chinese junk. Growing plants have hoisted up, and virtually incorporated into their roots, what might be even older vessels; giant dugouts and large canoes. Further out into the lagoon rest newer ships; age of steam maybe. Pleasure cruises which ended in misery. Sport fishing boats out for a three hour tour and now forever missing. They list in the muck, never to travel the brine again. Vines cover most of these ships. The same squishy tangles that Rafe has walked over getting to this point from the edge of the swamp. For the first time, Rafe takes an intertest in jungle botany. He looks at the squishy root nearest him and traces it to a stem and then to broad leaves and a flower bud. The bud looks black, though everything has started to look that way as night grips the island. Rafe pokes the black bud, and it does not moan, or poke back, or complain in any way. Rafe starts to feel silly. He slaps at bugs that are not there and wishes they were. Better the company of even a gnat than this deathly silence.

Rafe takes stock. He knows that Karloff could be behind him right now, ready to fire a poisoned dart gun at his neck, and he wouldn't hear it coming. Nevertheless, he suspects Karloff would not favor this route to the lagoon. Rafe finds little comfort in that. Rafe has no food, surely cannot drink the water, dare not sleep in the open, and cannot move around the edge of the lagoon's swampy mangroves. On the ships before him may lie food—unlikely—or weapons or tools or at least something made of metal. He might sleep on a ship. At least the brackish water of the lagoon, and the concealment of the ships, ought to make him harder to track. Can anyone track someone through salt water?

Rafe walks into the sticky salt water, parting the weeds and rotting forest debris before him. He makes for what looks like a midsized yacht resting high enough in the water to suggest it still floats. He can walk on the lagoon bottom almost to the yacht before the green sludge gathers around his mouth. He swims the remaining distance to the yacht, or more accurately he flounders in the thick green ooze, pushing it beneath him as he passes over it, until he reaches the ship. The vines of the black pod have snaked from the shore to the yacht in loose tangles and rise up it's sides, covering its deck, leaves to the sky. This plant must grow in a mad sprint. Rafe clutches great handfuls of the rising vine to help him crest the side of the ship.

On board he walks the deck of the derelict pleasure boat, *The*

Venture, according to the round life preservers still attached to the side of a cabin wall. Rafe finds the entrance to the lower cabin and takes the stairs down. The vines have descended before him and creep through the passageways. A futile attempt to find the earth perhaps. Dumb plants. In the lower cabin the stench overtakes Rafe. No sleeping here. He finds no sign of life, but in the back at the bedroom cabin he finds a sign of death. Two skeletons, laid out on the bed. They died in their sleep; or someone gently placed them here. Covered in vines, as if resting under a blanket, they look comfortable—for skeletons.

It suddenly seems very important to Rafe that he not stay here. That he not spend the night. That he not politely ask one of the skeletons to move over for him. Rafe hurries back up the stairs to the deck. He takes a deep breath to clear his head. Remember not to do that in future. He looks out upon the lagoon for a more likely ship to rest on. The ghost fleet before him offers a wealth of unappealing options. Near the center of the mass of ships, Rafe sees a large ship with two stories of decks and very little surrounding wreckage. It sits upright in the water and has an anchor down with a climbable chain. The vines of the black pod flower stretch to it but not so thickly as to other ships he can see. It is big enough to have held lifeboats, but Rafe can see none of them remaining on the ship. All in all, about as ship shape and hopefully skeleton free a floating specter as a man could hope for given conditions. How to get to it?

Rafe retrieves three life preservers from their places on the *Venture's* outer cabin walls and attempts to lash them together with their accompanying rope. This proves futile as the ropes have rotted to nothing. So Rafe decides to just go for it and drops into the water with the three life preservers stacked beneath him. He might as well have joined the circus. He makes his way, juggling life-preservers beneath him and spitting out lagoon muck from his mouth as he kicks toward the anchor chain of the big ship.

Between Rafe and the ship lies a floating island of decaying flotsam. It looked meagre in the moonlight from the deck of the

Venture, but up close, at sea level, that little patch of green looms like a swampy Everest. Rafe weighs his options, climb over or swim around? Then he notices, tangled in the debris, what could only be a body. Limbs, head; yes, must be a body. And what but a *fresh* body could last here, even suspended in weed? Dreading what he might find, Rafe swims to the floating island of weed and pulls himself up to the body. Only not a body. A canvas suit with a round metal head. Rafe imagens Karloff popping up in an underwater ambush yelling "Surprise fool!" Then spear-gunning Rafe between his amazed eyes. But looking more closely, and gathering his wits a bit, Rafe sees that the canvas body is actually an antique dive suit; its metal head a helmet with round glass portals on every side. Looking into one, even in the light of the moon, Rafe can see a skull inside the helmet.

Enough of that. Rafe dives off the floating debris and swims in the relatively open water to the anchor chain of what, on the testimony of the big ship's side, is the *Navigator*, out of Chesapeake Bay, christened in 1924. Rafe climbs the anchor chain, a feat made harder by carrying an extra twenty pounds of lagoon waste on every part of his body. Reaching the lower deck, he walks slowly around toward the rear of the craft. He creeps beside the outer wall of cabins and below a deck above him. Rafe has for so long heard nothing but the sound of his own activity that he instantly freezes at the creak from the deck above. Just one creak. CREAK. That's even too much creak for how little a creak it was. Only one thing on this planet makes just one creak: a person trying not to creak.

Rafe struggles to remember Trevor's tip-toe technique for noiseless silly-walking. He tiptoes down the deck to the stern of the ship. There he sees that the upper deck ends, leaving a large open area of lower deck uncovered to the aft of the ship. Rafe sees the stairs going up to the upper deck. But he also sees a pile of sticks and limbs on the aft which extends well past the shelter of the upper deck walkway. Hard choice: shot by a short-bow while stupidly walking up the rear deck stairs or shot with a blowgun while stupidly getting a closer look at a pile of sticks.

Rafe chooses sticks, with the plan of turning one of them into a club to bat away short-bow arrows. He tiptoes out from under the covered deck to the wood pile. There he sees that the sticks have been arranged on a metal hatch in the form of a, no other way to put it, campfire. And the sticks are dry. That alone counts as a menacing miracle. Rafe concludes that Karloff has rowed to this ship, knowing it to be the best resting place in the lagoon, and brought a load of dry wood to make a fire, in order to mock Rafe, before splitting him with a broadsword.

But Rafe will not be mocked. He takes up the biggest stick and tries it in the air a few times to get the weight of it. A formidable weapon considering its impromptu nature. Since all this stick swinging has not attracted a crossbow bolt, Karloff must not know of Rafe's presence yet. Therefore, Rafe need only: avoid being seen, locate Karloff on the ship, take him by surprise, best him with a mid-sized tree limb, disarm him, knock him unconscious, tie him up, and score himself the first man to defeat the master hunter. Nothing to it.

Rafe climbs the steps to the top deck, stick in hand, weighing each step, and listening for creaks. He hears creaks. Because he makes creaks. CREAK. Rafe can hear nothing in this world apart from the creaks he makes. He makes the loudest, most position revealing creaks in the whole of creaking history. Boris must hear these back at the castle. Rafe backtracks to the stairs, making just the same creaks in reverse. He descends the stairs and turns back to the wood arranged as a campfire. He now means to spring on Karloff when the master bush-tracker lights his fire.

The only thing Rafe sees to hide behind is a large canvas bag. That seems odd on two counts. First, it is far too small to hide behind so why even think such a thing. And second, it has appeared here since Rafe first found the pile of sticks just a few minutes ago. Master hunter Karloff must be creeping around on these decks, not making the slightest creak. Creepy.

Rafe considers looking into the bag but suspects a trap. A mongoose springing out or some such thing. Still, Rafe cannot resist. He opens the bag. Inside: canned food, an iron pot, eating utensils, a short wooden stick with a metal point, a longer wooden stick with a metal point, and the useless, broken night-vision goggles Rafe had tossed away earlier in the day.

Rafe ponders this collection of curios. Then a chill runs up his spine. He knows, with the certainty of death itself, that someone stands behind him. Rafe releases the bag. He slowly moves his hands to take a samurai grip on his stick. He thinks out his next move. A quick turn, a deft strike, and down goes Karloff. Mr. Most Dangerous Game will rue the day he toyed with Rafe Riley.

Rafe straightens his posture. He slips one foot behind the other, turning ever so slightly on his toes to make ready the spinning strike. One deep breath. Still not advised. Then Rafe moves. He springs up, spinning and lifting the stick high. He sees the figure before him, perfect range. Rafe shouts, "Haa!" Rafe brings the stick crashing down at the figure with the whole force of his body behind the motion. Rafe continues the motion with the whole force of his body. He has lost the stick but not his momentum, which carries him upside down and leaves him crashing ass first onto the deck.

Rafe takes a moment to assess his position. Seated. Pained in the ass. Facing the stairs to the second deck. And not blow-gunned to death. Rafe turns around and sees a figure carved out by the moonlight, placing Rafe's stick back on the stick pile. And quite a figure it is. Incongruously shapely in the moonlight.

Rafe demands, "Who are you? Unfold yourself!"

A thick Russian accent answers, "You are the loudest man I have ever met."

On the peninsula shore – evening

The waves lap up on the shore as the sun sets. Native drums fill the air with jungle rhythms, or something occasionally, and likely accidentally, approaching a rhythm. In a clearing, some distance from the lapping shore, stands a pile of branches. Atop the branches lie many copies of *Cooking with Ice*. And on top of these, a large pot. A cauldron really. One might call it a two-man pot, especially seeing it now, containing as it does, two men. Kip and Trevor, stripped to their skivvies and each with arms tied in rope to their respective torsos, face each other in the pot. Native tribesmen, of a sort, fill the pot with cooking oil. Specifically, Biorni Felici Brand Quality Extra Virgin Olive Oil, poured from thousands of travel sized bottles (each bearing the smiling face of Father Tony Felici, guarantor of quality and virginity). Each native, as he or she empties a small bottle into the cooking pot, howls out a ceremonial cry to the gods—though in charity one may say that these ceremonial howls have yet to acquire a pleasing consistency.

Kip and Trevor consider their fate as the oil fills the pot.

Kip, "Maybe it isn't what it looks like. Maybe it's an induction ceremony."

Trevor, "Some sort of honorific? Perhaps we're to be made chiefs of some sort."

Kip, "An anointment! Like Kings of Israel!"

Trevor, "I say, do you think we might be expected to make a speech or something?"

Kip, "We should prepare remarks at least!"

Vixen the Seductress pours in more olive oil as the tribe shoves extra kindling beneath the pot. The Sinister Yong Fu dances around the pot holding the lighter aloft. The tribespeople dance after him chanting, "Holy bringer of fire!"

Trevor goes off on Kip, "It's all your fault! Noting the defensive orientation of the wall, and the implication of danger on its opposing side, you nevertheless urged us to crest the repulsive edifice, thereby leading us to our doom!"

Kip, "How can you build sentences like that at a time like this?"

Trevor, "Had we lingered on the contrary side of the partition, we would now face but one advisory rather than this monstrous conflation of absurd ethnographical perils! I blame *you*! I blame *you*, sir!"

Kip, "What am I supposed to do, partnered with a man who steps into every trap? You can't walk two feet in the jungle without hurling yourself into the air or falling to the center of the earth! It's like walking with a drunken two-year-old! And the incessant *whining* about how you are hanging from *here* or you've fallen into *this*! I have to evade a mad hunter and guide you blind through every ditch in the jungle!"

Trevor, "Had I not been tripping the traps, *you*, contemplative idler and theoretical mechanic that you are, would have placed us both, *even sooner*, in a condition of abject helplessness! I blame *you*, sir!"

Kip, "The only consolation I have is that I get to watch you boil!"

Trevor, struggling against his ropes, "If I could release myself, I would smite you!"

The two men struggle to strike each other, but they can't, bound as they are.

The drums sound unrhythmically; the dancers dance to match it. Vixen the Seductress of the Fjords does something one might describe as drunken office-party twerking. The young Old Abraham tries an almost convincing moonwalk. Several villagers appear to imitate a Native American dance gleaned from too many viewings of *Peter Pan*. Mandinko performs some sort of disco move usually indulged in only after too much time at a corporate retreat open-bar. The Sinister Yong Fu twirls about still holding aloft the Holy Lighter.

Kip makes vows to the heavens, "If I could just escape this pot, I'd call all the girls I've ever broken up with and get back together with them. Every one of them."

Trevor considers the life he could have led but for this tragic fate, "Missionary work. I could be an English missionary rather than an English cracksman. I could convert the heathen into … whatever it is they are being converted into now. And proper heathen too, not this lot"

Kip, "What was her name? Tanya? I broke it off after the first date. I'll call Tanya. We'll marry. Have kids. Did she want kids? I don't remember! I'll call her and find out, and then we will have kids."

Trevor, "Not one of those narrow-minded colonial missionaries either. I'll become some new, modern converter of souls to whatever belief system would get me out of this pot!"

Kip, "And Trina! I'll marry her too! And Ursula too!"

Trevor, "I say, are you going down an alphabetical list?"

The dancers move closer to the pot. The Sinister Yong Fu leans down to light the pyre cupping the lighter in his hands. Mandingo shakes his spear. The crowd chants "Umba! Umba! Umba! Umba!"

Kip, "I never thought it would end like this."

Trevor, "Well, I'm a British adventurer, so I always knew it would end like this. I just didn't think it would happen so soon."

Kip, "I wonder if there is some way I could turn this into a conceptual piece? A happening? I'm sure it wouldn't hurt less. But it might mean more."

Trevor, "I could have done so much." Trevor sees The Sinister Yong Fu trying to light the pyre. Trevor blows at the lighter, "Now I end my days boiled by absurdly draped villains." He blows again.

The Sinister Yong Fu, "Do not blow on the sacred lighter! The fluid runs low!"

The fire starts below the pot. Villagers light torches with the cauldron fire and set them around the perimeter of the clearing. The tribe moves back from the pot and hurls itself into dancing. They kick their legs up and wave their arms wide like a middle school audition for *A Chorus Line*.

Kip, "I just want to say, Trevor, that if I have to be boiled alive, there is no one I'd rather be boiled alive with than you!"

Trevor, "I so concur! I'm so glad you're here with me! Comrades in arms!"

Kip, "Partners in crime!"

Trevor, "And let me add that I am so sorry for anything I've said against your artistic heroes. This Andrew Warhol, really quite a clever chap."

Kip, "And all the things I've thought about your English affectations, I take it all back! I love British culture! The bowler hats! The umbrellas every day! I even love," Kip tears up here, "Gainsborough! I said it! I mean it! I love Gainsborough!"

Trevor, "And you as an artist! I do admire so much your artistic balloonatic attack and its underling concept!" Trevor tears up a bit in admiration, or is it the smoke? "I so wish I could see one of them."

Kip, "We *will* call this an art piece! Title: *Potted Friends!*"

Trevor, "Potted Friends!"

The two men try to hug each other, but they can't, bound as they are.

The dancers writhe and twerk. Several do a strip-tease pantomime. Mandinko leads them in a chant: "Cargo! Cargo! Cargo! Cargo!" The tribe picks up the chant: "Cargo! Cargo! Cargo! Cargo!" Then a piercing scream from the direction of the beach: "Caaarrrgooooo!" The whole tribe, dancers, drummers, and all, grab torches and run toward the beach, leaving Kip and Trevor in the pot.

The two men wait in the pot of oil for the end to come.

And they wait.

Kip sighs. A long wait.

Trevor hesitates to mention this, but, "It isn't very hot, is it?"

Kip, "No. Not very."

Trevor, "Can't really feel a difference yet, can you?"

Kip, "Well, it is a lot of oil to heat."

Trevor, "Yes, quite a task I imagine."

Crickets chirp in the distance.

Kip, "Probably not a very efficient fire, either."

Trevor, "I shouldn't think so. For so large a cauldron."

Kip, "And so much oil."

More the crickets chirp.

Trevor, "Fire seems to be going out."

Kip, "Should we mention it? Their fluid does run low."

Trevor considers this, "I shouldn't think so, not our role here really."

Kip, "No. And they seem to have left."

Trevor, "Headed out to the shore it would seem."

Kip, "Something about cargo."

Trevor, "Quite."

From the beach they can hear the tribe returning. Torches approach from the shore. Shouts of "Cargo!" fill the night. The tribe brings up the feast from the sea: three great bundles wrapped in plastic; each eight-foot square. Mandinko spreads his arms before the light of the fire and the tribe sets down the plastic bundles.

Mandinko, "Release the bounty of the sea! Gifts of the God!"

Some chant "Karloff! Karloff!" as others tear into the bundles. From the plastic encasements the villagers pull: pants. Blue jeans to be precise. They descend as one upon the blue jeans. Each grabs many pairs of pants and instantly tries them on, rolling on the ground trying to pull them up to the waist. Plaintive cries fill the night: "Size 22!" "Size 22!" Somewhere in the throng of dressing bodies a woman cries out in joy: "Size 22!" Otherwise, all moans.

Kip and Trevor watch all this in disbelief. Villagers tie blue jeans round their necks like ties. Others wrap them about their bare feet. "Scissors! Pray for Scissors!" Eventually the night calms. The tribe gathers around the pot. They look to Mandinko for a ruling.

Mandinko raises his spear, "The sea has given us cargo."

A voice, "Size 22!"

Mandinko, "Yes, but cargo. All witness. The outsiders are Salvation Gods!"

A great upwelling of "Hurrah!" greets the ears. The villagers race to the pot. They pull Kip and Trevor out and hoist them up on shoulders, slippery though they are. Off they carry the two. One fate avoided; a new one in store.

Within the Carbane a Crabe – San Monique City – evening

A rustic little restaurant, straw roof covering sturdy roof planks, lots of windows to let the air in, a counter over which beer and crabs may pass. Mama Tambo sits across that counter feeding Katrina crab and entertaining her with a homemade doll. Katrina appreciates both. Especially the crab, a new delicacy. Appropriately she has learned a newly useful word, "Crab!"

Chris and Marcy sit at a small wooden table with Chief Baptiste. Marcy grinds her teeth a bit at the order of her daughter's cultural education. Chris holds a folder from which he takes papers.

Chris, "I've broken down the data Chief Baptiste gave me," he nods to the Chief, "with the aid of the Interpol Communications Directorate," nod to Marcy, "to paint a picture of the last ten years of disappearances around Danger Island." Chris pulls a document from his folder and places it on the table, "Records from the property office show that Karloff bought the island from the government eleven years ago in a transaction of dubious legality owing to the lack of any approval from the local ceremonial authorities," Chris nods at Mama Tambo playing with Katrina.

Chief Baptiste, "The government does not recognize the need for such approval for its own transactions."

Chris, "Pity that, because the data suggests foul play around Danger Island since the sinister master hunter took over the island." Chris marvels at the thought that he has now briefly entered a profession that calls for such sentences. Moment over, he places another document on the table, "Roughly ten years ago records show an uptick in live animal deliveries to San Monique, often listed as domestic animals or livestock but coming from all over the world. Brazil, Mali, Kenya, Indonesia, India, you name it. Clearly Karloff falsified the invoices. Since the records show no export of the animals and none have been seen on the main island of San Monique, Karloff must have loaded them up on a boat of his own to take to his island. And I mean a lot of animals. Large deliveries, sometimes monthly, for about the first seven years that Karloff owned the Island of San Guanaco."

Chief Baptiste, "Yes, his man Boris made regular trips in those years, hiring locals to help with off-loading on Karloff's Island."

Chris, "Well he must have filled the place to the bursting point because three years ago the shipments mostly stopped."

Marcy, "We've gone back now to animals. I thought we had moved on to missing ships."

Chris smiles the grin of a man right on his brief, "San Guanaco has always been a hazard for ships, even after the lighthouse went up. Local fishermen stay away, and cargo ships take a different route, so the wrecks have been mostly sport-fishing vessels, yachts, corporate excursions, that sort of thing. One or two lost ships a year, maybe, since the lighthouse marked out the rocks on charts." Chris puts a paper on the table, "I did some graphs and tables. No real change when Karloff took ownership. Boats would break up— drunk captains not looking for lights or something—and people would hit the rough waters."

Marcy, "Never to be seen again?"

Chris, "Oh no. Mostly survived. Karloff would ship them back to San Monique City." Chris pulls out copies of the *San Monique News* and reads selections, "Ever so grateful to the owner of San Guanaco. Much appreciated being pulled from the torrid waters. Much thanks to the island's owner for saving us from the lions."

Concerned looks all around. Even Mama Tambo hears this. Katrina roars like a lion.

Chris shrugs, "That all stops about four years ago. No more survivors coming in on the Karloff boat." Chris points to his graphs, "Yet the rate of disappeared ships goes up. No reports as to what becomes of them but plenty more never return to a home port. Just disappear. No word, no trace. A Bermuda Triangle in the southwest Caribbean." Chris lets this sink in.

From the counter Katrina offers her latest bit of local knowledge, "Juju!"

Marcy ignores this, with effort, "Have you identified any survivors at all?"

Chris, "None. But," Chris puts pictures gleaned from news reports on the table, dozens of them, "I have photos of some of the missing." Among the many photos on the table: Vixen of the Fjords, smiling with her hair in a bun. Old Abraham posing with friends on a ship. The Sinister Yong Fu smiling at a drafting table. Shiva the Assassin wearing a lab coat next to colleagues in a promotional flyer. Mandinko in a Hawaiian shirt raising a pina coleta to the camera. "All just gone."

Marcy, "And this goes on to this very day?"

Chris, "Well, not quite. The Chief tells me no ships have gone missing for over six months."

Chief Baptiste, "Pleasure boats have arrived on San Monique without trouble this year. The Government has been much relived. Many had worried for the tourist trade. Especially before the Junkanoo. But now that the wrecks have ended, everyone has returned to normal."

Marcy, "Everyone but you. You only contacted me three months ago."

Chief Baptiste, "After so many ships lost, I had gained some leverage to investigate the Island of San Guanaco. But when the danger seemed to pass, so did my support in the government."

Marcy, "The problem solved itself."

No one present believes that. But no one present has a solution either. The Police Chief stands, bows, and takes his leave.

Mama Tambo gives Katrina to Marcy, "Some bad juju comin from that there island. When white folks don't come back to harbor and nobody care, you know the bad juju comin." Marcy notices Katrina holds a doll she can only assume to be a relic of the local Voodoo religion. Mama Tambo says, "I give the little lion good juju, so you don't worry none. And lots of crabs, cause you don't feed her enough."

Chris laughs. Mama Tambo returns to the restaurant's counter to take an order. Marcy hands the squirming Katrina to Chris and stares again at the papers on the table. Chris takes up Katrina and says, "I plan to meet with a local book-seller. I'm hoping that will clear things up."

Marcy looks at him with practiced skepticism, "Trust an academic to think that buying books will solve every mystery." She stares back at the pictures on the table, "What could have happened to them all?"

The deck of the Navigator – lagoon – night

Rafe sits by the fire. He's gone through a lot tonight. He has had to watch Natasha shake her head in derision at his kung fu. He has had to watch her start a fire with the night vision goggles he had tossed away. She did this using its battery pack and some wires running through the device to make a spark. He had made the mistake of asking where she had gotten dry wood, and had to listen to her tell him, "Tops of trees are dry." He had asked her how she managed to stay so dry and clean herself, and had to listen to her tell him, "I built boat." Which indeed she had. In her spare time. Since arriving here. A day after him. Finally, he has had to watch her make food—delicious, wonderous food—from cans she scavenged from nearby ships and a pot she retrieved from the *Navigator* kitchen. A long night already and the moon barely up.

Rafe had argued that a fire would reveal their position to the mad hunter—having explained the "game" to her. Natasha said, "Good." Rafe had mentioned Karloff's weapons, his prowess, and his stuffed victims. Natasha had said, "Yet here you are." Rafe had mentioned the plan he and the others had formed to outflank Karloff. Natasha had said, "This you call *plan*?" Rafe had sulked for a while before asking her to tell him again how she had lost her satellite phone. She always answered this with "torn strap," but he could tell the subject irritated her, so he returned to it often.

They had agreed not to sleep by the fire. Rafe based this on his need to sleep without being awakened by sudden death, but he could see that Natasha entertained a different purpose. She had set about devising a trap by the fire with a trip wire and her metal tipped sticks pulled from the night vision goggles. Rafe had mentioned that Karloff was a master trapsman. Natasha had replied, "Me too."

So now Rafe sits sulking, poking at the black bud of a plant hanging from a bit of wiring debris. Natasha sits as well, having finished her trap setting. Rafe pokes at the fire. He says, "So tell me about yourself." From her expression he can tell he might as well have asked her to lecture on particle physics. "Right. Not your thing." Rafe reaches for a stick to throw onto the fire.

Natasha, "Take care. Trap."

Rafe pulls away from the stick, "Jesus. As if we didn't have enough danger lurking around us." He looks about. "I can't even see how you set the trap, and I watched you do it."

Natasha, "It cannot trap if it can be seen."

Rafe, "It immobilizes me with its invisibility."

Natasha, "When we leave for other boat, walk close behind me."

Rafe, "You know, I am competent. I may not be an expert at blunt weapon jujitsu, but fully rested, not drained of blood by illegally imported mosquitoes, I generally manage to take of myself."

Natasha, "Yes. You are very strong man." Her voice suggests a lifetime of soothing bruised male egos.

Rafe may be unsophisticated about traps, but he mastered subtext a long time ago, "Okay. Few words but well chosen. I get it. I'm not saying I wish you didn't rescue me, though I could stand a little less judo. I don't begrudge you all the trap-making, karate, and shots out of torpedo tubes. Frankly, I love the fire building and food scavenging. I'm saying that being on this team requires holding one's own end up, and I feel my end dragging."

Natasha says nothing.

Rafe, "You'll see. Somewhere on this island we will find an animal vulnerable to Rafe Riley. When we do, Natasha the Covert Commando will appreciate the help."

Natasha stares into the fire.

Rafe, "*Do you not know I am a woman? When I think, I must speak.*"

Natasha, "What is this?"

Rafe, "Shakespeare. Or irony. I'm not sure what your *this* points to."

Natasha, "All men who commit fraud with words are trained in Shakespeare?"

Rafe, "See. That's part of the problem. Few words and all action; what do people know about you? Words can be very useful. Let me show you. I'm not a confidence man. Not for a long time. Interpol recruited me as a security consultant. No hustling little old ladies out of their retirement for me. And as for Shakespeare, I'm a failed actor, not a failed swindler." Rafe leans back on the pile of cushions he brought up from below deck. "It's not like I haven't tried to get to know you."

Natasha stokes the fire. She tosses her stick into it. "We will move to boat next to this one." She dislikes how that came out. "I think we should move to boat next to this one." Better. "Karloff will come here and find trap, not us." Natasha looks around the dark deck. She looks at the bulb of a flower hanging from the broken guy lines. An orchid waiting to bloom. Symbolic of something she thinks. She hesitates. This comes hard. "I am trained in Russia since very young age. I am, you say it, *prodigy*? Not in violin. Not in ballet. I am recruited very young age because I make boys cry who hurt me. And I am clever with many things. So they take me away to school. School to make Russian enemies suffer. I am very good at this school."

Natasha speaks slowly, "But I am not so good at knowing who is real enemy; those they say are enemy, or those who put me in school." She sighs, "And always to be hard. Against so many boys that hurt you. To be clever; against so many. And these things I am good at, maybe they are not such good things. But I am made to be this. I am prodigy. Then, one day, I say no. *I* will say who is enemy. I will think on such things and not just do as ordered."

She stabs the fire, "But now in the West I am alone. And I am trained to be hard. And hard way I find easy way for me. But I do not wish to be hard always." She puts down the stick. "So I do not mean to be so hard on you Rafe Riley. I am afraid of being so alone, and that I must think on so many things and not just do. I am glad that you try to be my friend. I will try too."

Natasha, having shared more in this moment than at any time in her life, waits for Rafe to answer.

From Rafe: the sound of snoring. He has had a long day.

Natasha lies back. She could use a rest herself. Just for a few minutes until they reposition on the adjacent boat. It felt good to let things out. A lifetime of restless eyes looking for danger. It felt good to be vulnerable. Just this once. Natasha looks above her at the flower bud in the moonlight. It opens, slowly to her eyes, but very quickly for an orchid. The bud spreads its pedals. Streaked in white and black. Delicate and fragile. Its stamens out. Other buds around her open up. Natasha grows sleepy. She sees a bee fly about above the open orchid in nature's gentle dance. The bee hovers for a moment, then falls dead from the air onto the deck. Natasha closes her eyes.

Within a jungle temple – night

Temple might stretch the matter a bit. Closer to bungalow in the form of Disney Land's Tiki Room. It has a secure faux straw roof and proper wooden poles made of faux trunks. It has cool tile floors and plenty of proper windows to let in the air. The bungalow lies off the shore facing the sea and thus receives an ocean breeze. Whoever built this did not build the village huts.

Whatever its initial purpose, it serves now as a temple. At one end torches burn around the idol of the god which rests on a pedestal: a stature of Karloff. It stands three feet tall, and it shows the Great Hunter leaning on an elephant tusk while standing on a dead lion, itself resting on a dead rhino. He holds an Arquebus.

Before this idol, facing a selection of important villagers, Kip and Trevor lie on the floor, leaning on pillows, still in their skivvies. Frissia and Vixen scrape oil off their bodies. If Kip and Trevor find this erotic, they hide it well.

Trevor, "I do urge caution Ms. Temptress, as the blade appears rather sharp."

Kip, "Takes the dirt right off—ahh! A bit scrappy that time. Uh oh. I can do there if you like."

Trevor, "I just mean to say, I believe you are removing hair as well as oil. Not that I mind, but my skin lies just beneath." Trevor squirms.

Kip, "The Romans did it like this. Ow! That was deep."

It probably bares mentioning that neither Frissia nor Vixen have been trained or properly equipped for the ceremony.

Villagers lay out the clothes of Kip and Trevor, now with the dried mud beaten off, before the squirming adventurers. Kip and Trevor look out at the assembled village dignitaries sitting around them. Mandinko raises his spear, "All hail Karloff!"

"Hail Karloff!"

Kip and Trevor look behind them at the statue of the preening hunter.

Kip, "Not a chance."

Mandinko, "The Salvation Gods must hail the Supreme God."

Kip, "If he's a god, then the gods must be crazy."

Trevor offers a helpful suggestion, "Could we perhaps forego divine orders and just join your little band as honored members?"

Mandinko nods in approval, "Bring the masks!" The Sinister Yong Fu and Old Abraham each bring a plastic mask of Casper the Friendly Ghost forward and place them at the feet of the inductees. Vixen the Seductress and Shiva the Assassin of Kali bring forth bottles of Weld-Rite PVC glue. Mandinko ceremoniously waves his spear over the masks. "To join us you must make the dance mask. You must hunt down the feathered birds, and pluck their feathers out, and bring the feathers here for the mask."

Trevor, "Yes, well, while that would be something, I fear that a feather plucking expedition at this time might be a little difficult."

Kip, "We have issues on the other side of the wall."

Mandinko, "You must have feathers for a mask, or you must boil in the pot!"

Kip has an idea, "If it's feathers we need, I think we might have that." Kip searches the pockets of his clothes laid before him. Trevor seizes on the idea and searches his own clothes. Each produces a bundle of feathers stuffed into their pockets by Mama Tambo.

Kip, "Holy sacred feathers. Properly blessed and everything."

Trevor, "Sufficient unto the day."

Mandinko looks at the feathers, "These will do."

In short order Kip and Trevor have made themselves proper tribal Casper Feather Masks. The villagers in the temple dance around them chanting. Kip and Trevor enter into the spirit of the thing, dancing in place. Mandinko does his disco moves. Vixen does a standing lap dance on The Sinister Yong Fu. Kip and Trevor feel very much a part of their new tribe. Then Mandinko proclaims, "Now the drawing of blood!" Whoops and shouts follow as members of the tribe bring pocket knives and a bright red plastic bowl. All shout, "Draw the blood! Draw the blood!"

Trevor has had enough, "I should say not!"

Everyone freezes.

Trevor, "You will not draw any blood from me!"

Kip, "Same here! Just use what you got scraping the oil off."

Mandinko, "There will be blood!"

Trevor shows his fists, "I shall pummel the first man, or Vixen, that attempts to knife me. Not withstanding your numbers."

Kip sticks his chest out, "Standing tall with my man Trevor."

The crowd hesitates. Mandinko attempts to reason with his guests, "The God Karloff demands blood initiation."

Kip, "I can't say that surprises me one little bit."

Trevor tries reason as well, "You can't really believe the things you say. You can't actually believe in the divinity of that preening predator."

Shiva the Assassin, "Karloff brings the Cargo!"

Trevor, "Preposterous. Cargo ships leeching containers into the sea does not require Karloffian wizardry."

Old Abraham, "Karloff is the Master Hunter!"

Trevor, "Granting that, it does not explain all this." Trevor gestures at the tribe. "How have you come to be here? What makes you act this way?"

Vixen the Temptress of the Fjords, "We are the Lost Tribe."

Trevor, "Again, granted. But from where were you lost?"

Kip takes a soft approach, "Think back Vixy. Who were you before?"

Shiva protests these doubters, "I am Shiva the Assassin of Kali!"

Kip, "But before. Before Karloff. Who were you then?"

Mandinko, "The strangers speak heresy. To the pot!"

For one tense moment the tribe seems about to seize hold of Kip and Trevor. But then, from the back, a voice breaks through the bonds of Karloffian mind games. "I am *not* Old Abraham of Eternal Ages!"

Everyone freezes.

"I am Joel Leibowitz!" Joel speaks with the pride of a man free at last, "I am Joel Leibowitz, Occupational Health and Safety Compliance Officer for Lubrica Chemical Corporation!"

A tense silence falls over the tribe. Shock, awe, and soul searching. A hesitant voice speaks up, "I am not Zorro the Desert Fox. I am Pedro Garcia, Vice President of Brand Management for Uglixi Corporation of America."

The dam brakes, "I am not Shiva the Assassin of Kali. I am Prashanta Bhatt, Intellectual Property Director for Etherege and Wycherley Publishers."

"I am not Frissia, Temptress of the Forest. I am Rebecka Finn, Account Maintenance Consultant at Bovine Processed Foods of Ohio."

Vixen slides up next to The Sinister Yong Fu. She takes his hand. She says, "I am not Vixen, Seductress of the Fjords. I am Linda Cravitz, Assistant Director of Human Resources, Maleween Services and Placement Corp."

The Sinister Yong Fu shuffles his feet and grips her hand, "I am not The Sinister Yong Fu of the Red Dragon Tong. I am Peter Hu, Graphic Design Coordinator for Listless Images Corp." He smiles shyly at Linda Cravitz.

Linda—formerly Vixen—tells Kip and Trevor, "We met on the island." She blushes.

All eyes turn to Mandinko. A hush falls over the assembly. The world seems to turn on what happens next. Mandinko struggles a moment. He takes a deep breath. He offers his hand to Trevor, "I am not Mandinko. I am Arthur Washington Carver, Chief Financial Officer for Tatacom Industries." Trevor takes his hand, everyone cheers.

Kip, "How do you come to be here?"

Mandinko—sorry, Arthur Washington Carver, "We fell off boats. Or crashed on the shore. Or drifted into the Lagoon of Death." A chill spreads over the assembled at the mention of this. "Karloff hunted us. But spared us. Again and again. Until we had become his obedient playthings. He put us here in the village, baptized us anew, and gave us the Law."

"The Law!"

Carver, "No! It was all mind tricks. He tortured us with the hunt and bent our minds with the relief of survival. He placed us here to stay behind the wall."

"Not to leave the stockade! That is the Law!"

Carver, "No! We have sprung free of the Law."

Trevor puts his hand on Carver's shoulder, "Brave fellow."

Kip, "This is all great. And so timely. But the rest of them, in the village, will they go along with this ... reawakening?"

Peter Hu, "They still follow the God Karloff."

Carver, "Karloff is no god!"

Trevor, "Good fellow."

Kip, "But can we bring them all along? With the new understanding? Will they follow your lead, leaders as you are?"

Carver, "I don't know. It is quite an ask."

Linda Cravitz offers hope, "The Elite Believers have gone. Without their interference the rest may follow the Great Mandinko."

Kip, "The Elite Believers?"

Carver, "Yes, The Elite Believers. Karloff divided the tribe by loyalty. The Elite Believers were his fanatical devotees."

This generates renewed excitement:

"They could leave the stockade!"

"They held the gun on the hunt!"

"They never stepped on the orchids!"

Trevor feels he is losing them a bit. It has been a long day for everyone and a big shift in religious belief for the assembled. "Yes, and you're saying they have left the village, these Elite?"

Carver, "Days ago. Karloff took them to work the boats. To set his great hunt in motion."

"They beat for the hunt!"

"They set the fires on high!"

"They tend the orchids!"

"Not to swim from shore! That is the Law! Are we not prey?"

"Praise the God Karloff! Praise the God Karloff! The Great Hunter!"

Carver, "Stop! Stop! This madness must end!"

The group calms.

Trevor, "Good man!"

Carver walks to the stature of Karloff, "This is not the god!" Carver topples the statue. It falls onto the ground leaving the great hunter now nose to the floor. A dead silence falls over the temple. Carver lays down the law to the assembly, "Karloff is not the Great Hunter. He has failed in his hunt. Only once, but still he failed. We all know it. One has escaped even his deadly aim. Karloff has been matched. He is no god. Karloff is not God!"

Trevor, "Well spoken!" Trevor feels inspired himself.

Carver, "Sredni Vashtar is God!"

Trevor, "What?"

All, "Sredni Vashtar." They say this with such fearful solemnity that Kip almost says it with them.

"Sredni Vashtar. Sredni Vashtar. Sredni Vashtar. Sredni Vashtar."

Trevor, "Wait. I've become rather lost I'm afraid."

Carver beckons, "Come." Carver turns and heads to the door. He leaves the temple. Kip and Trevor follow him out. Behind them the assembly follows, quietly chanting, "Sredni Vashtar. Sredni Vashtar. Sredni Vashtar." They walk into the moonlit night. A sea breeze blows warm on their faces. Carver takes a torch in hand and leads them all a short way from the temple towards a small building built in stone blocks. It looks like a tomb fit for a Russian expatriate hunter when his final hunt has passed. Carver stops before the entrance. "We are the Vashtari of the Lost Tribe. The followers of the One True God. The god that defies Karloff. The hunted one that escaped his hunt. The great foe of Karloff, and the greater god than he. The ultimate master of the bush. We are his keepers and his secret acolytes."

Someone says, "Shhh."

Carver, "I, Mandink—" He corrects himself, "Author Washington Carver, CFO of Tatacom Industries and High Priest of the Secret Order of the Vashtari and Servant Special of the God Sredni Vashtar, bring these men to see the great foe of Karloff. The one true god of the island." With that he enters the crypt. Kip and Trevor follow.

Inside, lit only by a torch, Kip and Trevor take a moment to adjust to the dark. The crypt forms but a single small stone room with a stone table at the back, placed there to someday hold the coffin of the great man himself. On that stone table now lies a small cage, covered in a cloth. Carver sets the torch in front of the covered cage, its flame illuminating the cloth covering. Kip and Trevor draw close as Carver walks behind the table and stands over the cage before him. He grips the cloth to unveil the cage. "Behold, the god Sredni Vashtar." He pulls away the cloth. Revealing:

A ferret.

Kip and Trevor look at the ferret. It looks back at them, perhaps vaguely godlike in its own ferretish way. Trevor's spirits sink.

Kip, "And we were making such progress too."

At the junkanoo – streets of San Monique – evening

When the Africans of San Monique were slaves to the French, they would creep into the forest at night and make sacrifices to their gods, renamed as Catholic saints so that the French would not know. They did this because human beings cannot live in a world that doesn't mean anything to them. They will make a meaning if none exits. They will take your meanings if you steal all of theirs. The African slaves, out of sight of their masters, would drink and dance and make a world of knowing like the one they once knew. If a master stumbled upon the scene he would see blooded animals, charms, and writhing bodies. The sight would terrify the masters. What slave's free moment does not terrify the slave's master?

One day a French master found the Voodoo dolls, the headless chickens and the blood sacrifice in a forest clearing. As always he called the slaves together to listen to the Catholic priest. The priest told the slaves that animal sacrifice was evil. A Mama Tutu, Mama Tutu de Tongo to be precise, rose up and asked, "Do you not pray to a human sacrifice?" The master beat her, there and then, on the spot, blessed by the priest in the act. Mama Tutu de Tongo took her beating. She knew the price for what she said; she paid it to have her say. The master went to his bed. The priest went to his bed.

That night, in the forest, the Mama Tutus put on their hidden feather headdresses. The Voodoo priests donned their feathered cloaks. The drums sounded in the night. Rise up. Rise up the drums said. A thousand times they had sounded before, but never had the slaves risen. This time they did, because one day, people will.

The slaves of San Monique fought their masters. Much blood, of chickens and men, was spilt. The Christian saints fought the African gods over who would own the names; who's meanings would rest on the Island of San Monique. You could call it a draw. The people of San Monique would speak the tongue of the French, but by blood they had made it their own tongue too. They had earned their right to it. They spoke it their own way, beautiful to their ears. The African gods would go by the names of Christian saints, but they would be praised by writhing bodies that would feel no shame in their dancing.

And as for the masters? Well, the former slaves gave them an island of their own.

In celebration of the liberation of San Monique, the people held a junkanoo every year. They would put on their feather headdresses and cloaks and play their drums and dance in the streets all night. The French were welcome to come too. Anyone could come. There were no masters now.

On the streets the people of San Monique City dance in their feathered costumes, lovingly crafted. They play drums, blow whistles, clang cow bells and carry on like free people. Delighted smiles fill every face. Among them Marcy dances with Chris, who carries Karina on his shoulders. Locals come up to them, removing feathers from their beautiful cloaks to give to these visitors so that no guest need go without the sacred feathers; a tribute to the generous spirit of the people of San Monique, who bear no masters and bear no grudges.

Katrina stuffs yellow and red feathers behind her ears. Her parents dance. They dance to the drums until they arrive at their destination. Katrina does not understand why the party must end here.

Within the library of San Monique City – night

Chris and Mary sit at the table, filled with books and papers, while Marcy plays with the giant globe. The sound of the junkanoo drifts in through the windows. All the world celebrates but these three.

Chris, "No word at all?"

Marcy, "I've lost every team I've sent in."

Chris, "Natasha might have matters well in hand by now. Maybe she just lost her satellite phone."

Marcy, "No one, but no one, is stupid enough to lose their satellite phone."

Chris, "Well, I leave commando stuff to you special agent types. But in my capacity as Adjunct Researcher/Interpol Nanny I have good news. I've cracked the case."

Marcy, "So now you lay it all before me."

Chris, "From books I might add. Papers and books. And the locals. Things you read and hear."

Marcy, "Okay. Go."

Chris pulls out a paper, "The last message of Agent 117: love, peace, and flower power."

Marcy, "A bit more hippie than I'd expect."

Chris, "Trained professional. Keep it in mind." Chris pulls out a menu, "Here, a diner menu from a ship that went missing two years ago, the pleasure craft *Life of a Salesman.* Mostly chartered for corporate bonding excursions. A local found the menu stuffed in this bottle," he holds up a champagne bottle, "on the shore of San Monique."

Marcy, "So?"

Katrina, "So."

Chris, "A message written on it."

Marcy, "Invisible ink? By a spy?"

Chris, "Blue ink. It says: send shoes."

Marcy looks unimpressed.

Chris, "Admittedly, ambiguous at best. But significant that it exists at all. A survivor of a charter cruise which went down with all aboard put that message in a bottle and set it out to sea. And not just that one." Chris pulls out a collection of odd bits and pieces of paper. "A fishing charter receipt in a bourbon bottle. Stationary from a yacht that went missing. Notes on the pages of a cookbook stuffed in bottles. All messages washed on shore and held onto by locals. Each one traceable to a missing ship."

Marcy, "And what do the messages say?"

Chris shifts uncomfortably in his chair, "I would describe their content as—cryptic." Chris reads from his list, *"Send shoes,"* he looks up, "Again. Uhm, *the fluid runs low. All praise the god Sredni Vashtar*—I haven't identified that god yet. Still another on shoes. And a heart with an arrow through it containing the initials L.C. and P.H."

Marcy looks skeptical.

Chris, "I admit the messages don't help, but the bottles had to drift in from nearby just based on the tides and currents. No one threw them into the water off the coast of Mexico."

Katrina points to the globe, "Mexico."

Marcy cannot believe this, "She can identify places on a globe, but she can't say *mommy*?"

Chris, "No. She just repeats things."

Katrina spins the globe, stops it, and points, "Thailand."

Chris quickly goes to pick her up, "I just showed her a few things on the globe earlier." He carries Katrina to the table. "She pointed nowhere near Thailand by the way. Closer to Vietnam, really." Chris puts Katrina on a chair at the table and instructs her, "Just listen." He turns back to Marcy, "I can see you are not impressed. But I have more. I have this," Chris holds up a paper with a list on it. "I went to the *San Monique City Libraire*, which is French for *bookstore*, as distinct from the *San Monique City Bibliotheque*, where we now sit. Not the most transparent language if you ask me." He notes her impatience, "I hold here a list of books. You see I figured if Karloff were a reader he would need to special order his books from a local source, one that could fill the orders world-wide. A customer like that, they would keep track of his orders. Chief Baptiste helped out. Put me in well with the owner. So here I have it, every book Karloff has ordered since he moved onto Danger Island. Journals, articles and newspapers too. Not only that, but I acquired some of them here at the *Bibliotheque* and had a look over." He points to the books.

Katrina points also, imitating her father's expression.

Chris, nods at Katrina, "She helped. Mostly by not breaking things for half an hour."

Katrina nods, "Candy."

Chris motions to her to clam up.

Marcy, "What did you two find?"

Chris, "Lots of hunting stuff, as you would expect. Nothing else but that for several years really. But then, about four years ago things get interesting. Or maybe just weird. *Lighthouse Construction and Maintenance*—though I allow he does have a lighthouse. *Social Organization and Primitive Man*—I own that one myself."

Marcy, "You own half the books in creation."

Chris, "*Jungle Foragers and Their Mores. Social Hierarchy in Early Man. Creation and Development in Early Legal Codes, Pilates*

For Men—I admit it can be hard to separate the signal from the noise here."

Marcy, "I didn't hear a signal."

Chris, "Well he must be sending them, because he ordered full tech specifications for a radio transmitter." So there.

Marcy, "So what?"

Chris, "Ordered his last hunting book three years ago. His next orders were: *The U.S. Army Manual for Psychological Warfare, Psychological Manipulation of Prisoners of War, Brainwashing in Communist China*, and maybe a dozen other titles along the same lines. Many in languages I don't read, but the bookseller helped me out. And don't get me started about orchids."

Katrina, "Start."

Chris, "Okay. Karloff ordered orchid books from day one, not a lot, but he must have been a collector." Chris looks at Katrina as if they have recently discussed this between them, "I figure he got wind of the island in the first place knowing about its orchid history."

Katrina nods in agreement.

Chris, "But around two and a half years ago, books on orchids show up by the dozen."

Marcy, "Spare me the titles."

Chris, "Specific requests for botany papers published by the mad orchid hunter de Beaufort. I couldn't make much of the titles, but a synopsis I found suggests that de Beaufort had crossed an orchid from the island with a distant member of the Venus flytrap family. Orchid branch. I don't know exactly. But what he had was," Chris points to Katrina:

Katrina, "Death."

They high five each other.

Marcy shakes her head. "An orchid that eats flies?"

Chris, "Releases a toxic pollen. Kills the insect. Insect falls to the ground, then the orchid sends tendrils out to absorb its nutrients. Very creepy if you ask me. De Beaufort bred these for toxicity. To believe his papers, and many didn't, he had these things taking out small lizards at a distance of two or three

161

feet. And the orchids would bloom at night, maybe five nights in a row, around the time of the full moon, which is when the bugs were thickest in the air, I suppose. That part the botanist credited least, apparently. Orchids don't like to bloom. Also, some skepticism that the toxin could knock a bat out of the air, as de Beaufort claimed." Chris pulls out a book and opens it, "Here, look at this illustration."

Katrina, "Illstraton."

Chris starts to correct her but Marcy cuts him short, "If you teach her the word *illustration* before the word *mommy* I will scream." She looks at the pictures of de Beaufort's orchid. She reads its name: "The Death Orchid."

Chris nods. Katrina mimics his grave nod.

Marcy, "So Karloff reads up on all this?"

Chris, "For six months. After that, all his books cover toxicity. Like the growing library of a morbid chemist. Then he stops ordering those too, about a year ago."

Marcy does not like where this is headed.

Chris pulls out a book and shows her, "Six months ago he orders this, *The Infernal History of San Monique City*. I looked this one over. *The Infernal History of San Monique City* is the only book about San Monique history or culture he ever ordered. Just this one, living off the coast eleven years."

Katrina points to the book and nods knowingly.

Marcy flips through the book. She notes pictures of charred devastation.

Chris, "San Monique City has burned down to the ground at least four times; 1750, again in 1870, again in 1921 and finally in 1943. They even have a tradition on the island of how to escape when the fires get out of hand."

Katrina holds out her hand to show what a hand is in case the adults need that.

Chris, "Run to the south bay. Which is to say to the undeveloped part of the bay in the swamp lands. Which makes sense."

Marcy, "Where do you mean all this to go?"

162

Chris presses on with the zeal of a prosecutor closing his case, "If you know a man's reading list, you know his mind. His book list gets very focused in the last six months. After—mind you—after—he has the book on the history of San Monique City fires, he orders books on arson, incendiary devices, more books on brainwashing, as if he didn't have enough already." Chris pulls out some samples of these books, "*Tides and Currents Around San Monique, Topography of San Monique City, Diorama Modeling in Porcelain*—mind you I haven't made that fit the theory yet —*Emergency Procedures of the San Monique City Police for Fire, Hurricane, and Riots,* and every map of the city in existence."

Marcy, "But what do you think it all means?" She asks this as if already suspecting the answer.

Chris, "A hunting obsessive cycling hundreds of animals a year through his private game reserve. He stops just as the ship sinkings increase and survivors no longer survive. Brainwashing, Death Orchids—"

Katrina, "Pilates."

Chris waves that off, "Toxins, fires, the tides of the bays, the escape routes to the swamp. It can only mean one thing."

Katrina, "Buffalo hunt."

Chris and Katrina fist-bump.

In the shock of the revelation Marcy barely registers Katrina's linguistic milestone. "You're sure of this? You could put this before the San Monique Interior Minister, and she would have to accept it?"

This deflates Chris, "Well, no. I mean it requires a few leaps of logic. It is just a book list. At least shallow minds might see it that way. No offence to the Minister."

Marcy, "Then what can we do with it?"

They sit in silence. The sounds of the junkanoo seep into the room. The sounds of liberty. Katrina looks at her mother's worried eyes. She slips down from the chair and toddles over to her, holding out her arms. Marcy picks her up and sets Katrina in her lap. Katrina embraces her mother. Katrina's eyes grow heavy. She has had a long day.

On the deck of the Navigator – night

Natasha feels refreshed. Content. She sits naked in a grotto, on a verdant bed of leaves, as orchids bloom around her. They offer their pedals as gifts to the gods. They whisper promises of new life, fresh soil, decomposed bodies. The orchid pedals darken. They turn to thorns. They turn to teeth. Natasha would let them bite her. They promise so much peace. The peace of dead flesh.

But a violent motion disturbs this lovely world. An earthquake. A volcano erupts and tosses the garden of Eden into chaos. Natasha can feel herself pulled from its drowsy embrace. She hears a voice. It calls her name. Natasha. Natasha. Wake up. Is it the god of flowers?

"Natasha! Natasha! Wake up damn it!"

No. It is the voice of that most irritating man, Rafe Riley.

Rafe, "Natasha! Wake up!"

Natasha opens her eyes.

Rafe, "Something's happening."

Natasha looks around. She sees the deck. The moon. The orchids in the moonlight. She sees Rafe Riley holding a dead bat in her face.

Rafe, "It fell on me."

Natasha jumps up. She really looks around now. "Karloff?"

Rafe, "Just what I thought at first, but I don't think so. I don't know."

Natasha sneezes.

Rafe, "Me too."

Natasha, "The orchids!" She pulls a few flowers off stalks, but she sees the hopelessness of disarming the lagoon of black orchids. She looks up at the radio pole rising from the *Navigator*. "We must get higher!"

She and Rafe race up the stairs to the second deck and climb a ladder to the roof. Natasha motions Rafe to the radio pole. It has small rungs for the convenience of repairmen long lost to the lagoon. Natasha climbs, Rafe follows. Not halfway up they feel the pole sway, its guy-lines long snapped.

Natasha, "We must get to the top."

Rafe, "Why?" Natasha doesn't answer but Rafe follows her, as one does in the company of sound instincts. At the top, Natasha above Rafe, each holding on against the sway of the pole, they can see the moonlit lagoon laid out before them. Ghost ships abound. Off in the distance they can see faint lights and hear the purr of an engine. More ominous than that, they see below them, covering the lagoon and rising higher, a mist. Particles puffing about.

Rafe, "The mist? You think that's it?"

Natasha, "Do you feel it?"

Rafe, "Nauseous, faint headed and like death hugs you breathing pollen into your nose? Or maybe I dreamed some of that."

Natasha, "We must stay above the mist."

Rafe, "It's rising."

Natasha points to a sailing ship adjacent to the *Navigator*, "We must get there."

Rafe, "The mist will cover its deck in a few minutes."

Natasha, "We climb its mast."

Rafe, "I'm already hanging from a pole thank you."

Natasha, "Masted ships lie in a row to the hill at the shore. We climb each one."

Rafe, "And fly between them?"

Natasha, "Yes." She leans out toward the adjacent sailboat. The pole sways with her and she leans back. "We must lean together, at the boat, and sharply so that the radio pole snaps at the base and not the middle."

Rafe sees her plan, "On three. One. Two. Three."

They hurl themselves together towards the sailboat, holding on to the radio pole. It bends and lowers them until it snaps sending them to the sailboat deck. Rafe pulls up the stunned Natasha and they both race up the sailboat mast. They see the mist rising below them. Next to the sailboat another masted ship rests in tangled weeds. They lean the mast over and tumble to the next boat. A sail and tangled rigging breaks their fall and provides a quick means up the boat's highest mast.

Rafe, "This luck can't last."

Natasha, "Just three more and we make the hill."

The next two boats they make. But tipping over the last mast Rafe falls toward the sea. He will not make the deck. He hits the water of the lagoon and plunges to its bottom. Rafe holds his place beneath the water. He has no way to crest the side of the boat next to him. What to do? Die under the water or die breathing in the mist of toxic pollen? An anchor hits the water above him and drops to his feet. He climbs up it to the surface and keeps climbing without releasing his breath. On the deck Natasha helps him up.

Rafe looks at her face. She does not look good; grim, weak and sick. Rafe bends down and lifts her onto his shoulders. He carries her up a ladder to the base of the next mast. Rafe lets out his breath and takes another. He resists the urge to sneeze, healthy as such a response may be, to avoid taking another breath. Ropes hang down from the mast. Rafe pulls on the ropes to test them. They seem sturdy and fresh. This boat must have become trapped more recently than those around it. A testament to the sailor who guided the ship through the maze of derelicts. Pity he's dead now. Natasha grabs the rope and pulls herself up with great effort, Rafe behind.

Rafe calls up to her, "We won't be able to break this mast. Climb above the mist and try to get your head clear." He marvels that she can climb these ropes at all the way she looked. He wonders how he must look. Above the thickening mist they cling to the mast. No ships lie now between them and the rising shore covered in Mangroves. They do not have far to go, but Rafe knows that between them and the shore a thick carpet of sludge must float. Natasha looks down at him from just above. Rafe can't tell if she looks better. He asks, "Did you come this way to the *Navigator*?"

Natasha, "Thick with floating vegetation."

Rafe, "We can't make it over the flotsam. Hit the water and

swim under."

Natasha jumps. Rafe notes that she does not exactly need a long time to psych herself up. He thinks out his swim for a moment, then he follows her into the water. He swims against the bottom of the lagoon toward, he hopes, the shore. The sludge floats over him as he swims. Lungs bursting, he makes the surface. A hand grabs him and pulls him to the roots of a tree. Natasha puts her arm under his and lifts him up a root. He grabs tight to her and pulls her up the next. In a few minutes that feel like a lifetime, they pull each other above the mist of pollen. They rest a moment and then scramble up a bit of rock to the land above. It rises before them toward a crest. They ascend until they are on a plateau looking down at the lagoon. They sit and rest.

Rafe laughs. Natasha looks at him in wonder. Rafe says, "All that time you were setting up a trap for Karloff, we were sitting in his trap for us."

Natasha, "Yes. I underestimated him."

They look down at the ghost fleet of Danger Island, enwrapped in its bed of orchids and blanket of mist. They relax, breathing easier. No sound of crickets. No sound at all. No mystery there now. But as Rafe relaxes he does hear a sound. In the far distance.

Rafe, "Do you hear an engine?"

Natasha, "A tugboat." She points to the far end of the lagoon, closest to the sea, "Lights."

Rafe sees the lights but cannot make out the craft. "I see the lights." Rafe can see that the ocean breeze at the far end of the lagoon disperses the mist of pollen. Watching the lights Rafe makes out what must be a tugboat. "What does it do? Can you see what's going on?"

Natasha, "Men attach the tug to a small barge. I hear one shouting once. In Russian. A curse."

Rafe, "Karloff." Rafe turns over and lies on his back. "He's cutting off our escape."

Natasha drops down beside him. "I do not think he bothers

with us right now. He does not need to forestall the escape of the dead."

Rafe laughs, "*Forestall*? You have better English than you let on."

Natasha, "Old instinct. Never show all you know."

Rafe tries to raise himself, "We should double back and beat him to his castle." He collapses back down again. "I mean later. Post nap."

Natasha rests her head on Rafe's shoulder, "We rest a moment."

Rafe puts his arm around her and closes his eyes, "Just for a minute. Gather our strength."

They fall asleep. In the lagoon the tugboat heads to sea, hauling a small barge with pallets filled with plants.

Orchids.

On a rocky cliff – morning

Morning finds Rafe and Natasha walking along a cliff. Behind them, now blessedly out of sight, lies the nightmarish lagoon. Before them, in the crisp light of day, stands the ruins of a building. It has been reduced to its foundations. Before its demolition it had commanded a lovely view of the sea. The open ocean lies before it, and another cliff sits just to its north, thus further still from the lagoon. The waves below the ruined building crash unimpeded into the cliff face from the open ocean. From the cliff to the north, rocks from the island stretch into the churning waters, forming a jagged spear of stone jutting well out to sea, washed by the changing tides.

Rafe walks behind Natasha toward the ruin, "Not a can? Nothing? A scavenged biscuit even?"

Natasha, "No."

Rafe, "I know I didn't suggest grabbing any canned food at the time, but I didn't prohibit it either. I suppose people filled with their dinner are apt to neglect preparing for breakfast."

Natasha, "Also poison death-mist."

Rafe, "What about roots? Eating roots for breakfast?"

Natasha spreads her arms wide, "Eat any root you wish."

Rafe, "I just thought that with all the Russian commando training in humiliating colleagues and vaulting ships they might have taught you something about edible roots."

Natasha, "Carrots you can eat."

Rafe, "You have carrots?"

Natasha, "No. But if you see carrots. Eat them."

They hear the sound of an orangutang. Rafe says, "How about monkeys? Can you kill a monkey? You can throw me at it if you want."

Natasha, "Tempting. No time. We must make circle to Karloff fort to support comrades in what you call plan."

Rafe, "Made in haste I agree. Before we knew all that we know now. By the way, what do we know now?"

Natasha, "Karloff moves death orchids off island."

Rafe, "Yes. But why?"

Natasha, "To make death."

Rafe, "They like to keep it simple in Russia. See target; destroy target. But we in the free world like to see the reason of the thing. We also like breakfast." Rafe gives up on food. Clearly Natasha has not sequestered a pair of bagels with cream cheese in her body-fitting commando suit as a surprise meal at the top of the cliff. "How does he work tugboats? I just know of him and Boris on the island. It would take more than that to run a tug. And forget about recruiting disaffected Interpol agents. I can tell you right now Karloff is not a man you want to work for. Ten minutes of Karloff—hell just a visit to his living room—and you know he won't be giving out a Christmas bonus."

Natasha, "You talk so much."

Rafe, "I talk when I'm hungry. But riddle me this: who runs the tugs?"

Natasha, "Cadres."

Rafe, "Once again, brief, Russian, and unhelpful."

Natasha, "I do not know. So we circle round. We survey. We find the place of weakness. We gain our edge."

They stand now at the ruins, overlooking the sea, on the edge of a cliff. Rafe picks up broken pieces of brick and examines them. Just as he suspected: he knows nothing about bricks, or ruins, or structural forensics. But he refuses to look incompetent again in front of Natasha. So: "Something stood here once. Made of brick, or a brick like substance. A structure or building of some sort."

Natasha, "A lighthouse."

Damn. "How did you jump to that wild notion?"

Natasha, "Circular foundation. Overlooks ocean. And I see one on that cliff."

Rafe looks where Natasha points. Across a small chasm, a lighthouse. "So you think someone moved it? For a better view?"

Natasha, "Come, we look."

Rafe, "Should that be our priority? Mad hunters and missed meals be damned?"

Natasha, "Perhaps we find weapon for you. Heavy stick or short metal pole for you to make *Haa* at enemies."

They skirt around the edge of the cliff, past the small gorge that separates the ruins from the lighthouse. The opposing cliff upon which the lighthouse stands also boasts a view of the sea. Here, though, the rocks of the cliff span outward into the ocean. A sublime vista and a hazard to shipping. Rafe examines the lighthouse. He rubs his hands on its brick surface. He says, "Bricks. Or a brick like substance." He taps the bricks. "Is this new construction? Can you tell?"

Natasha, "I don't know."

Rafe looks out to sea, "More rocks here. Do you know anything about lighthouses?"

Natasha, "No."

Rafe, "I wish Interpol had shot someone out of that torpedo tube with a more relevant skill set. Do you know anything about shipwrecks?"

Natasha, "Do you?"

Rafe, "Well I survived one recently. On the basis of that I know two things. First, do not make Kip Carson responsible for the equipment case. Second, always have hold of your satellite phone before you make the jump."

Natasha, "Yes. A good lesson."

Rafe draws conclusions, "I think Karloff moved the lighthouse. Tore it down over there and rebuilt it here. Still flashing its safe channel message, but leading ships onto the rocks."

Natasha, "Why?"

Rafe, "I hope you get to meet the man, because once introduced, questions like that won't even occur to you." Rafe looks to the lighthouse entrance. "We solve the mystery in there." He pushes on the wooden door. It squeaks open. Within they see an empty lighthouse; wooden floor covered thick in dust. The brick walls, painted white, have no adornment but for a mirror across the room at the foot of a spiral staircase.

Rafe and Natasha enter. Rafe says, "Okay. Not thick with clues yet. Except that mirror seems out of place." Rafe steps into the room toward the mirror.

Natasha, "Wait."

Rafe takes another step. CLICK. Rafe knows that nothing good follows *click*. Beneath the two of them the floor gives way cracking into pieces and pitching them into a stone pit below. Natasha roles out of the rough landing, ending on her feet. Rafe falls on his ass in the traditional manner.

Natasha, "What is English word for *zhadat*? It is *wait*, no?"

Rafe, "I almost waited. Then I decided to trip the trap and jar my spine into my brain."

Natasha takes him by the shoulders, "You are injured?"

Rafe, "No, I'm pretty callused there by now." He smiles at her, "Glad to see you care."

Natasha, "Unbroken man must stand so I may climb out of pit."

Rafe finds his feet. "Okay. I suppose once out you can make ropes out of vines to pull me out."

Natasha pats his shoulder, "And I will find root for you to eat."

Rafe laughs, "I should have trapped us sooner." He stands back against the wall nearest the door and cups his hands for

Natasha. She steps onto his hands and then with a heave she launches up to the edge of the trap. Rafe watches as she propels herself up in one motion, pulling with her arms and kicking off the stone sides of the trap. She lands, back to the trap, feet just under her like a cat attaining a kitchen table. A marvel of grace and balance.

A rope flies across the gap from the other side of the trap. A lasso. It perfectly catches Natasha and tightens in an instant, sending her back down toward Rafe. Instead of dropping to the trap floor, she swings to the other side of the trap, landing hard against the wall. The blow of the impact knocks all the air from Natasha, leaving her stunned.

Rafe lunges at her legs. They disappear before him. Something has plucked her up over the top of the trap as if by superhuman force. Rafe pounds the wall, "Bastard!" He tries to climb the stone in a futile attempt to reach the top. From above he hears the laugh of the master trapsman. He sees the giant figure of Boris look down at him. Rafe shouts, "Natasha!"

Karloff, "Natasha. And a Russian. Better and better."

Boris tosses a bag down at Rafe. Rafe dodges it assuming it a trap or a net, but it just lies on the ground.

Karloff looks down at Rafe, "Fear not. You will yet have the honor to be a kill of Karloff the Great. You must stay here for a time. I shall entertain this masterful lady. I shall make my great hunt. When I am satisfied I will return and treat you as an after-dinner mint."

Rafe, "Natasha!"

Karloff, "She cannot answer. But do not fear. I am Karloff. I do not take this prize to hunt. She will serve another appetite." Karloff laughs and disappears from Rafe's view. Rafe struggles against the unyielding wall. He cannot climb it. He looks about at the wooden detritus littering the stone floor of the trap. He tries to stack it into a platform, but Karloff meant his trap to keep his prey stuck in place and so the wood lends Rafe no aid.

Rafe looks at the bag Boris dropped into the pit. Snakes probably. Rafe nudges it with his foot. He can hear Natasha in his head telling him not to nudge a bag of snakes. What would Natasha do? Pull them out of the bag and tie them into a rope. But what can Rafe do? He gently takes hold of the side of the bag. He puts a hand on the opening, drawn shut by a string. Rafe envisions snakes hurling themselves as one upon him the minute he pulls open the bag. He hopes that this rehearsal of nightmares will prepare him mentally for the deed. He does not feel prepared. But without aid of something he cannot save Natasha, so he opens the bag. He does it in a single motion leaping back from it as soon as a gap appears so that the snakes have no target to strike. No snake emerges from the bag. Rafe gently takes the bottom of the bag and prepares to lift it up to overturn it and dump the snakes onto the floor. A plan probably not much better than "circle round back to Karloff's castle." Still, he can't just stand here. He dumps the contents of the bag.

Sausages. Bread. Apples. A canteen of water. Karloff brought him breakfast. He studies the material at hand. Rafe cannot climb the wall with a sausage. He tries to think like Natasha, who by now would have probably built a rocket out of all this. But all Rafe can see is animal food. What if he built a fire out of the wood on the floor and inflated the bag with hot air to ride out as a balloon? How does one ignite a sausage? It occurs to Rafe, not for the first time in the last few days, that his own particular skill set has yet to find a use on this mission.

Within an igloo – morning

Kip sits in the igloo. His snowshoes rest against the ice walls. He feels warm in his caribou parka. He carves the walrus tusk. Nanook and his wives marvel at his skill. Kip adds the final touches to his little statuette. Nanook asks him what he carves. Kip answers, "I carve the idol of my god." Nanook asks to what animal he offers prayers? Kip shows Nanook the figure. Kip says, "The mighty ferret god."

Kip's eyes snap open. He sees the muddy thatched roof. He sits up and looks around. Not an igloo. He looks at his clothes. Tatters. He looks to his side. Trevor snores. Outside the hut Kip hears raised voices. Some sort of argument in progress. Probably to decide their fate. A common occurrence lately. He shoves the snoring Trevor. "Wake up."

Trevor wakes from a dream, "Don't tickle. Don't tickle."

Kip, "I'm not tickling, I'm shoving."

Trevor, awake now, "Kip." He grabs Kip's arm in thanks. "You wouldn't believe the dream I had. We were boiled alive in a pot. Then we became gods."

Kip, "That happened. More or less. I dreamed I lived in an igloo."

Trevor looks around, "You might have included me."

Kip, "And I worshiped a ferret."

Trevor, "More or less the case."

They hear the voice of Carver—once Mandinko—outside the hut. They haul each other up.

Trevor, "Once more into the breach."

They walk outside to see the whole village roused in the late morning sun. Carver and the Acolytes of Sredni Vashtar face off against the rest of the village. The point at issue appears to be theological.

Carver, "Karloff is not God."

Representing majority opinion against Carver and the Vashtari is a small stout man with a comb-over. Kip vaguely recalls he introduced himself the night before as *Torgon, Barbarian of the Steppes*.

On the matter of Carver's new order of spiritual enlightenment, Torgon begs to differ, "I Torgon, declare you apostate! You, Keeper of the Law, have defiled the Law! I, Torgon, declare you outcast! You, leader of your people, have betrayed your people! I, Torgon—"

Carver, "Cut all that crap, Eugene. I'm Arthur Carver and you know it. We worked together at Tatacom."

Torgon, Barbarian of the Steppes, "Bring back the great Mandinko, imposter!"

Carver, "I was never Mandinko. It's an insult. And you have never been Torgon, Barbarian of the Tundra, it's an absurdity."

Torgon, "Of the Steppes! Trikina is Battle-Mistress of the Tundra!"

Carver, "I used to let you beat me at tennis."

Torgon, "No one defeats Torgon! Torgon lays waste to the plains and laughs as his enemies perish beneath the hooves of his horses!"

Kip interjects, "Not to speak out of place, but if you are all that, how can you also be a slave to Karloff?"

Torgon, "No one defeats the god Karloff."

Kip, "Are you not his prey?"

Many, "Are we not prey?"

Carver, "Stop that."

Trevor has a go, "My colleague has a point. Such extraordinary titles just to supine yourselves so utterly to the man Karloff."

McGuffin, Savage of the Highlands, "Who are these interlopers to speak here?"

Linda Cravitz, "They are Salvation Gods!"

Trevor, "No, I think that might be step backwards."

Carver, "They speak sense, let them speak."

The village concurs and silently awaits inspired speech. Kip looks at Trevor and Trevor at Kip. Kip says, "Go ahead, you have the English accent."

Trevor steps forward. He clears his throat. Where to begin. "I would first like to thank Mr. Carver and the members of last night's very productive meeting for this opportunity to address you all. It is, of course, an immense privilege to be asked to speak at such an august assembly. On such an important topic too. An urgent topic as well, all the more so as time—as they say—may be running out. Not, in any event, on our side—as they say. So thank you all for ceding the podium so generously." Trevor takes a deep breath, "I have not prepared anything, taken aback as I was by the invitation itself, so I will need to speak extempory. Also please excuse me, I don't think I know everyone's names —" (A clear misstep.)

"I am Sumo, The Mad Wrestler!"

"I am Velcron, Binder of Wounds!"

"I am Fatima, Sultress of the Veil!"

"I am Darktanion, Master of the Black Stiletto!"

Carver raises his hands, "Stop! Let him speak!"

Trevor carries on, "Yes, thank you very much Mr. Carver. Where was I? Oh yes, as I said, I have not had the opportunity yet to learn everyone's—"

Kip very strongly waves Trevor off from this.

Trevor, "Uh, that is to say, that, uh, putting aside further introductions for the time being. Getting to the meat of the matter. I believe it of the first importance that we enter this discussion with an open mind. Matters of faith often provokes great passion, and we all fancy ourselves possessed of some right opinion of grand theological themes, often in fact beyond our keen. I recall my own grandmother used to say ... what was it now? Grandmama used to say it all the time, tip of my tongue..."

Kip, "I think it was *I have an idiot for a grandson.*"

Trevor, "No, but very much in that spirit. I think it went more like—"

Kip steps forward the relieve Trevor, "If I may."

Trevor steps aside.

Kip, "I'm new to this island and its strange pantheon. But from what I've gleaned, this Karloff's godhood rests solely on his being the Master Hunter. He is a god only if everything is his prey. He has no claim to divinity beyond being undefeatable. I don't think you could describe him as a nice sort of fellow, so benevolent deity is out."

The mass of the village must concur with this.

Kip, "Therefore, if any have escaped his hunt, then he is not the Lord of the Hunt. I'm sure I heard that. If he is not Lord of the Hunt, he is not a god. Thus, only evil oppressor remains to him."

Torgon, "No one defeats Karloff at the hunt."

Kip, "Someone has, as I understand it."

Kip and Trevor look at Carver. A sense of unease descends upon the village. Carver steps forward and speaks, "The stranger speaks truly. We all saw. We all remember the day. Karloff stalked the village for his prey. He tracked it everywhere. We saw his prey swing round to watch him. We saw his prey escape his bow; escape his pistol. Karloff hunted and could not track it. Karloff can be beaten. Karloff *has* been beaten."

Murmurs. Torgon speaks up, "But what proof have you of this? How do you know his prey escaped? He may have found it later, out of our sight?"

Carver speaks to his Vashtari, "Bring forth Sredni Vashtar." Two of the Vashtari bring up the covered cage of the ferret god Sredni Vashtar. The village gathers tight round. Carver grasps the cloth cover, "Behold!" Carver lifts the cover, revealing the god Sredni Vashtar, nibbling a carrot.

A stunned silence follows. All the village, Vashtari and Karloffians alike, bow down before the ferret. The chant starts low, but rises: "Sredni Vashtar. Sredni Vashtar. Sredni Vashtar. Sredni Vashtar." Then they dance, writhe and whirl, converts all. "Sredni Vashtar! Sredni Vashtar! Sredni Vashtar!"

Trevor, "Good fellows!"

Kip, "Now what?"

Within a stone pit – morning

Rafe digs away at the dirt floor of his stone prison with a small block of wood on which he walked in the glorious before-times, those he now refers to as *Pre-Click*. He has dug a hole almost a foot wide and two feet deep. This testifies to the power of desperation over good sense. It did occur to Rafe that a major principle of escape tunneling is to dig *to* someplace and not just toward the center of the earth. A sound principle that. But from it Rafe could not deduce an alternative to *just dig*. And since Rafe refused to go with *sit and digest his meal so that Karloff will have good sport*, he needed to do something. Half an hour pondering wood-based levitation devices yielded nothing, so Rafe digs. Thus, while up remains the only direction Rafe needs to go, down is the only direction he heads.

But now Rafe can feel eyes on him. Someone above, looking down. He considers his move: grip the wood block firmly but lightly, set feet ready for a spinning turn, slowly curl the body into a spring, then up and around in a single motion and hurl the woodblock right between the stalker's eyes. But Rafe has had enough of the amateur karate theatrics. Whoever stands there watching can just hit *himself* right between the eyes. Rafe has digging to do.

"Freeze."

A man's voice, but Rafe does not recognize it. Rafe digs on.

"I said freeze."

Rafe, "It must be a hundred and two degrees down here buddy. I may evaporate but no way will I freeze."

"You're digging your own grave there."

Rafe, "If you mean that as a threat you will need to come back in about six hours because I am a long way from grave size right now."

"The hunter is the hunted now."

At last Rafe sees an opening. As Natasha would say, a point of leverage. Rafe drops the wood block and stand up. He turns around to address the man looking at him from the top of the trap. "Take a good look buddy. I am all hunted and no hunt. I'm guessing that puts us both on Team Victim. If you ask me, alone up there, waiting to fall helpless into the next trap, that seems like a bad plan for you. I'm dead certain squatting over this dent in the ground won't help me. So I strongly advise against joining me down here. On the principle of stronger together—which I know I read off a coffee mug once—I urge you get me out of here."

"How do I know I can trust you?"

Rafe, "In my back pocket I have my resume, four letters of recommendation, a citation for good citizenship from the Alameda California Chamber of Commerce, and a small polygraph machine with operating instructions. Happy to show it all to you. Failing that, I can only refer you to human decency, the Categorical Imperative, and fear of a common enemy."

"I have no enemies."

Rafe, "Karloff. I refer to Ivan Something-o-vich Karloff, Master Hunter and enemy to mankind. Animal kind. All kind—he probably hates plants as well."

"Karloff is a god."

Rafe, "Got to quibble with you there friend. A god, Hindu, Christian, Greek or Roman, does not sport hunt his guests. Even gods of questionable character respect the law of hospitality."

"Karloff is a god."

It occurs to Rafe that he has seen this man's face before. Rafe takes a new tack, "You might as well take *me* for a god. I at least can peer into the misty veil of time and see who you are."

"I am the lowly dirt, less than a ferret, the prey of Karloff."

Rafe, "Granted. But you are something else as well. You have a number. Not every man has a number. Not like you do. I know your number."

"What is my number?"

Rafe, "First you get me out of here, then I say your number."

"Tell me first."

Rafe, "Okay. But you have to swear that if I give you the right number, the one that you are, you get me out of here. Swear on the Great God Karloff if you like."

"I swear. May he make me his prey."

Rafe looks the man in the eye. Yes, he means it.

"What is my number?"

Rafe, "117."

Within a castle washroom – day

Washroom might be too polite. Really a small bathroom with cold stone walls and fixtures from the nineteenth century. It now resounds with declamations.

"You are the fly, caught in the spider's web." Karloff speaks into a mirror, "I am Karloff, the spider!" Karloff tugs on his Czarist officer's uniform, and stands even more erect before the mirror, inadvertently raising the hem of the coat once again. "Karloff the spider!" Again, he tugs the tunic down. Something about this seems off to him. Is she really a fly? He tries again, "You are the prawn, caught by the frogfish's lure. I am Karloff, the frogfish!" Luring, all to the good. But maybe not frogfish.

He throws his head back, "You are the bee, tricked by the orchid mantis' colors. I am Karloff, the orchid mantis!" Good association that, Karloff and the orchid mantis. Very fitting. But perhaps his guest will have had enough of orchids for now. Karloff points his open hand at his image in a rhetorical gesture fit for Cicero, "You are the shrimp, mesmerized by the display of the cuttlefish. I am Karloff, the cuttlefish!" A neat suggestion of cuddling. Cicero would be proud. And mesmerizing works too. But maybe Karloff should not self-style as a cuttlefish. "You are the sea slug, drawn by the glow-worm's bioluminescence, I am Karloff, the glowworm!" That went wrong on both sides.

Karloff gathers himself before the mirror, tunic as tucked down as its old fabric will allow, "You are the hermit crab, stunned by the electric eel. I am Karloff, the eel!" He likes hermit crab for her, she seems solitary and given to the sideways attack, but maybe not eel for him. To close. "You are the marmoset, deceived by the cry of the margay. I am Karloff, the margay!" Nice alliteration, but it leaves him explaining what a margay is, and detailing the latest research into its deceptive cry. And he feels none too sure about marmoset either. So, no. "You are the Amazon milk frog, caught in the teeth of the snapping turtle. I am Karloff, the turtle!" Amazon fits her to a tee, but Karloff dislikes the crude hunt-craft of the snapping turtle. "You are the dung beetle, stuck in the chameleon's saliva. I am Karloff, the chameleon!" Certainly, he is Karloff the Chameleon—indeed he ought to write that down somewhere—but dung beetle fails to strike the right romantic note. Now inspiration strikes, "You are the spider monkey, squeezed by the boa constrictor, I am Karloff, the constrictor!" Karloff thrills at the idea of squeezing his new prey, and Karloff the Constrictor sounds grand.

Odd that he made his way back to spider though. Still, good enough for a first date.

Outside a lighthouse – day
Rafe stands above a seated Agent 117 on the cliff outside the lighthouse. Rafe tries to find his bearings. So does Agent 117.

Agent 117, "I had it all man. The babes, the cars, the guns, the action. I would scuba knife-fight all morning and break roulette wheels all night. In between; the women. Scorching hot. Stab-you-in-the-back-ruthless-but-you-don't-care level hot. And what an excuse I'd carry. Hey baby, I'd love to settle down, but the world's got to get saved and I'll be dead tomorrow. Turn them on and turn them out. Back to sniper shooting from a parachute."

Rafe, "I appreciate that you've begun a period of reflection, but—"

Agent 117, "I had the skills baby. The only sound I made was the click of my gun."

Rafe grimaces at *click*.

Agent 117, "And the gear. Best gear. Gadgets to die for. To make the other guy die. Take his babe. Man, when you can rock the gear you feel like you own the world. You get the right tactical on you, makes you hard. You snap on that camo vest, it's like clicking on manhood."

Rafe, "Can we stop with the click stuff?"

Agent 117, "But that night against Karloff. Game over man. He broke my gear. He broke my skills. He broke me all the way down."

Rafe, "You've been here what? A week?"

Agent 117 grabs Rafe's leg, he clings to it, frantic to be understood, "He broke me, man! I begged. I wept. He promised me a new place in the animal kingdom. Said he'd give me the law. Turned me loose. I thought I'd made it. Fool him to let me go. But wherever I went, there he was. Finds me hanging from a rope or caught in a net, or just puts an arrow next to my head. What do you call that? He says god. In my world that makes sense."

Rafe pulls Agent 117 off his leg, "Shake out of it. We need to focus. Work as a team."

Agent 117, "Karloff laid down the law. Like a man he laid it down. Like a god. He's got this law, don't step on the flowers. It like blew my mind. I just thought, yeah. Like don't step on the flowers. Smell them. Don't step on them. Get the beauty. Stop and just smell the flowers."

Rafe, "I think he may have had something else in mind."

Agent 117, "He said there'd be more laws. Like a god sets down laws. And names. God gave everything names, right?"

Rafe, "That was Adam." Rafe can feel the pull of his madness. "Not that that's the point here."

Agent 117, "Like a god he gives the names. He gave me a new name. Called me Kraken, Breaker of Stallions. I can't even ride a horse—doesn't really come up in my line—but he gives the names. Until you said 117, I thought I *was* Kraken, Breaker of Stallions."

Rafe, "He brought you round to all this on what? Day three? And already you'd forgotten you name?"

Agent 117, "Secret agents do not weep, man! Testosterone-fueled men of action do not beg! Women beg! Babies cry! Men just give it out hard and take it with a war face on."

Rafe tries to calm Agent 117, "Listen, they wound you tight making you into the secret agent superman. I see that. Now adversity has unwound you. Your macho fell away and left you a bundle of raw nerves and self-doubt. No one's immune to that. But your duty didn't change just because failure unspooled you. I can see you are not fit for a confrontation. You can stay here and, I don't know, guard our rear. Protect our backs. But I need you to point me in the right direction. I have no time to waste on jungle navigation. And no skill at it. And no gear. And I now jump at even the *word* click. So how you feel, I say: same."

Agent 117 looks up at Rafe, ready for yet another new god.

Rafe continues, "Even so, we need to carry on. People count on us. Karloff has some horrid plan we need to stop. I have to save a damsel in distress. Or unleash her to reap a terrible vengeance, I'm not sure which. But I need to get to her, and I need your help to do that. Collect yourself, and show me how to get to the castle."

Agent 117 stands up. He wipes his eyes.

Rafe offers him a bit of his shirt, "Here, blow."

Agent 117 blows his nose. He feels better. "You don't have far to go. But you must move slow. Traps everywhere."

Well of course, Rafe thinks, it wouldn't be Danger Island without traps.

At the jungle village – day

The Lost Tribe dances to their new god, who seems to enjoy the show. Kip tries to get the attention of the village, but ecstatic celebration rules the day.

Kip, "Listen! Listen!" No good. The crowd dances and whoops. All but Vixen, now Linda. She hears. She grabs Peter Hu and they run to a hut. Together they haul a large gong to Kip. They set it next to him. Peter offers Trevor the mallet. Trevor hits it. GONG! Everyone stops dead and turns to the two adventurers.

Kip, "Listen. Wonderful to witness your liberation—"

Trevor, "Very spirited. Good show!"

Kip, "But I think, and I'm sure Sredni Vashtar would agree," the ferret makes no objection, "that we now need to take decisive action."

Torgon, "Build a new alter!"

Sumo, "Elect priests!"

Bistro, "Make sacrifices! Carrots! Find carrots!"

They almost take off on this quest, but Kip brings them up short, "No! We must defeat Karloff. And now. Before he finds out about your new ... deity."

Torgon, "First a sacrifice! For cargo!"

Carver speaks up, "We don't need cargo. We need to defeat Karloff."

Kip, "And not later. Now. He has some plan in mind."

Carver, "He has taken the Elect!"

Trevor, "Yes. To make fires. Or tend flowers, I'm not entirely clear on it to be honest."

Kip, "But it will be bad. Evil even. I mean Ivan Karloff and his fire-cult do not plan to bring toys to disadvantaged children."

Torgon, "But what can we do?"

Carver speaks with the voice of the Law, "Rise up!"

Trevor, "Well said Mr. Carver, well said!"

McGuffin, "Dare we?"

Carver, "Rise up! Sound the drums!"

Tribesmen grab drums and begin drumming.

Carver commands again, "Rise up! Hear the drums!" excitement grows. Carver commands again, "Rise up! Follow Sredni Vashtar!" Hands pass forward the ferret god.

Carver, "Rise up!"

The rest pick up the chant, "Rise up!"

Kip, "That's it! That's the spirit. Rise up!"

Trevor, "Yes! To arms! Arise!"

Carver, "Rise up!"

"Rise up!"

Kip, "Go team, go!"

Carver, "Rise up, and take the castle of the false god!"

Trevor, "Arise village arise! Grab your pitchforks as it were!"

Kip likes the sound of that, "Rise up! Grab your pitchforks!"

Carver, "Grab your pitchforks!"

All, "Grab your pitchforks! Grab your pitchforks!"

Villagers run, in mass, away from the village, away from the wall, away from Kip and Trevor, into the trees of the forest about the village. In an instant Kip and Trevor stand alone, but for Sredni Vashtar. Kip has not noticed. He continues the inspired chant, "Rise up! Take that castle! Rise up! Bring down Karloff! Rise up! Love that ferret!"

Trevor, however, has noticed that the gang's all gone. He tugs on Kip's shirt as Kip continues to sing, "Rise up! Early in the morning! Rise up! All the little children! Rise up!—What the hell?"

Trevor, "They rose and left. Every one of them. Simply melted away." Trevor indicates the abandoned village. A soft sea breeze stirs the dust of the ground and ruffles the hair of rats licking cans. Nothing else in the village moves in the silence.

Kip, "And we were making such progress."

Castle bedroom – day

A bedroom, to judge from its four-poster bed draped in

animal skins, which serve as curtains and as a warning to unwary unskinned animals. Thick furs cover the bed. Bears, polar and black; deer, white and spotted; beaver pelts, heads still on; chinchilla pillowcases. At the foot of the bed, red panda slippers rest on a heart shaped pillow, made from a panda's heart. Next to the bed in size, Boris, holding a gun; but presumably he is movable rather than furniture.

On the room's stone walls: Assegai crossed to frame a Zulu shield. A tapestry of a centaur flexing its arms. An ostrich plum. An empty plaque, suitable for framing an animal head the size of a weasel. A mounted skinning knife. A bolt action rifle. And a picture of Karloff's mother, looking on in disapproval.

Apart from the great bed—and the armed giant—the room is sparsely furnished. An open wardrobe reveals Karloff's evening wear, his hunting suits, his crocodile belts with ivory belt-buckles, and an albino alligator jacket fringed in squirrel tails. A curio cabinet displays stuffed bats, each sporting a dart sticking out between its eyes. A candle strewn table serves as a shrine to a bearded old man holding a rifle.

And oddly most disturbing of all, a mahogany chair shaped as a seated man, headless. Tied to this, no less disturbing, Natasha. Cleaned, combed and wearing a traditional Russian wedding dress; white, with beads of yellow and baby blue, and only a few old blood stains. A crescent headdress tops the outfit, with beads hanging down at the sides. A thick rope coils around her arms and waist, securing her to the chair.

Natasha looks calm. She does not struggle against the ropes. She relaxes in the chair and studies her captor. To her way of thinking, if your enemy offers you a shower, clean clothes, fresh fruit, and a comb, you take it. Freshen up a bit. Tied to a chair, you relax. You save your strength. You do not try to dig your way to China. You sit quietly and study your foes for weakness.

Karloff enters, uniformed and haughty, sidearm in holster. He sees Natasha in all her cold beauty. He stumbles a bit on his rehearsed introduction: "You are the web, trapping the wary dung beetle. I am Karloff, the constricted!" Two hours preparation dropped and broken. Still, on home ground, allied with a giant, in uniform, untied, and male, Karloff sees himself holding the psychological advantage. "I apologize that only now have I been able to properly introduce myself."

Natasha, "I forgive you, wary dung beetle."

A slight loss of edge there. Karloff will retrieve it, "I see you wear the dress as ordered. You are the first Russian to wear it since my mother."

Natasha, "It is with pride I take your mother's place."

That had not quite been Karloff's sense of things. He tries again, "I mean to honor you as I have honored few other women."

Natasha, "Myself. Your mother. Who else?"

Karloff, "You need not bring my mother up!"

Natasha, "You brought your mother up."

Karloff sees that he has lost a bit of ground in the psychological chess game. Mother's dress; a misstep. "Leaving aside my mother," Karloff struggles to suppress thinking of his mother now, "it is my intention to honor you with the person of Karloff," he puffs like the adder about to strike, "to give you the pleasure of the hunter in his glory; you: the prize of his hunt. He: the hunter sated with his prize."

Natasha nods her head at Boris, "He?"

Karloff, knocked off his stride, "He?"

Natasha nods at Boris again, "*He* is the hunter that I prize?"

Karloff, "What? No. *I* am the hunter." Karloff thought that obvious.

Natasha, "And who is he in this?"

Karloff, "He is Boris, he is not in this."

Natasha, "Then he is not the pleasure?"

Karloff, dumbfounded, "*Him*? No. *I* am the pleasure. No. I *give* the pleasure."

Natasha, "And I am the prize? The hunter's, not his?"

Karloff, "No. He is not a part of this at all! Forget he is here." It does occur to Karloff how hard this might be considering the dimensions at issue.

Natasha, "So we have it all straight now."

Karloff has honestly lost track. How did he get his chess pieces so bunched up? He isn't even sure whose move it is. Time for a new tactic. Some short, sharp moves to weaken her resolve.

Karloff, "My dear Natasha, I have you at my mercy."

Natasha, "You have no mercy to have me at."

Good point that, "You see that I have won every round against you."

Natasha, "For those lessons I thank you."

Karloff, "You take defeat well."

Natasha, "Why not? Your defeat does not bother me."

Karloff, "You are mistaken, I possess the high ground."

Natasha, "Lit by the sun behind you."

Karloff, "I bear arms." He slaps his holstered weapon.

Natasha, "I am my weapon."

Karloff, "You are my helpless captive."

Natasha, "I am your captive. But you give me all the help I need."

Karloff, "No one can save you now."

Natasha, "What of you? Who will save you?"

Karloff, "I need no saving. I am strong, you are weak."

Natasha, "You have me tied to a chair, locked in a room, guarded by an armed giant, while you slap your pistol at me. Who is the strong one here and who the weak? Perhaps you should suspend me above a pit of crocodiles, just to be safe."

He should have gaged her. He debated that point with himself all the way back to the castle. But he had longed for the sound of his mother tongue—Damn! Mother has come up again.

Karloff, "Bah! I tire of this game."

Natasha, "I can see that you would. Perhaps checkers?"

Karloff tries to reorient his thoughts. Had he been wrong to stalk this quarry? Karloff had envisioned this encounter since he found her tracks. A worthy opponent; a capable woman. But by this point in his plan he meant for her to lay helpless in his arms, intellectually dominated, emotionally crippled, and pleading for the love of Karloff. Perhaps she would be better gardening orchids. Or hunted in the proper way. He notices that she looks at him. Like one might a pinned insect. With eyes that weaken a man's breath. Her stunning body roped tight to a chair. Karloff says, "I had thought we might have become l-l-lovers." He blushes at the stutter, "But I see now that is impossible."

Natasha's look softens. Her body relaxes. Her visage takes on the hint of a smile, "Oh, I had not thought of that."

Karloff wonders how he could have baited his trap so poorly. Apparently, though, she sees his trail now. "It is that with which I thought to honor you. Thus, the dress."

Natasha, "Your mother's dress."

Karloff, "Let us leave my mother out of this!" How does this all keep coming back to mother?

Natasha, "I am sorry." She sounds it. Very sorry. In a seductive way. Intriguing combination. Apologetic and lustful. "I did not mean to raise constrictions to your passion."

Karloff cringes, but Natasha comforts, "I did not take your meaning before. You can understand my confusion. I am brought here, to this place so sensual, and you come, so full of your manhood. But here with us stands this brute." She nods to Boris. "What am I to think, if you do not come alone, full of your manhood?" Her voice carries an undertone of soft and naked bodies. How on earth does she undertone that?

Only mostly distracted by her voice, Karloff sees her point. And he feels the fullness of his manhood. He turns to Boris, "Leave us. Go to the observatory and keep watch. Remember that we have several new guests not yet fully processed. Watch for them."

Boris departs.

Karloff, "Now my dear Natasha, nothing will disturb us."

At the jungle village – day

Kip and Trevor stand alone. Not even crickets for company. Kip says, "Where'd they go?"

Trevor, "They just took off."

Kip, "Was it something we said?"

Trevor reviews events, "I made some opening remarks. We heard a few introductions. You presented a most eloquent case against the mad Karloff. I thought we witnessed something of a spiritual revolution. You made some remarkably good points about the direction events might take. Carver gave a most inspired speech. A general rising of spirits. They brought the god here to our feet." Trevor indicates the ferret. "Then some talk of grabbing pitchforks—I don't know how that got started— followed by a collective vanishing."

Kip, "Wait. Listen."

They listen. Noises from the jungle beyond the village. A great rustling of leaves. Then bursting forth from the trees, the villagers return. Each one carries a brand-new pitchfork, individually encased in a clear plastic shell.

Carver, "We have the pitchforks!"

Torgon, "Hardware 'R Us brand!"

They all seem so eager now, awaiting further orders. Kip and Trevor now command the Vashtari Army, inspired by the ferret god, armed with hay-sorters. This, apparently, is what progress looks like when you really make it. Kip can't think of what else to say, "Release the pitchforks!"

The Vashtari struggle to open the shell casings. They role on the ground trying to defeat the loss-prevention packaging. They poke plastic sheathed pitchforks with other plastic packed pitchforks to no avail. Someone deploys a pocketknife and at last the armory begins to open.

Trevor, to Carver, "Can you find our way to Karloff's castle?"

Kip, "Without tripping traps?"

Carver, "We shall prod the ground with our prongs and make our way to the castle. Vashtari, follow! Release the god Sredni Vashtar!"

They open the ferret cage and follow Kip, Trevor and Carver. Sredni Vashtar runs from his cage and up upon the shoulder of Arthur Washington Carver, High Priest of the Secret Order of the Vashtari and Servant Special of the God Himself.

They begin their climb over the jungle wall.

Marcy Gainer stands on the tarmac of the San Monique City Airport with Police Chief Baptiste. No longer in business attire, she wears a jumpsuit and full parachute gear. She holds a camo patterned haversack at her side. Chief Baptiste wears his khaki uniform and looks skeptically at Marcy.

Chief Baptiste, "Mrs. Gainer, rather than all this, let me take a launch to the island and look around."

Marcy, "I only need to make contact with a team member, and I can confirm at least some of the account I've given you."

Chief Baptiste, "But so many of you have gone missing. I can't let you take the risk. I should go in spite of my superiors."

Marcy, "*I* can't lead your people here in San Monique. If our suspicions turn out to be correct, you will need to act at once. I'm convinced the threat is imminent."

Chief Baptiste, "We have staked out likely locations. But I will need to put forth the results of your inquiry, along with your declaration against Karloff—should you confirm illegalities—before the Minister will permit extensive action."

She puts her hand on his shoulder, "That is another thing you must do that I cannot. And another reason we need to go by air. But I thank you for the offer Chief."

He nods to her, "You are very brave Mrs. Gainer."

Marcy, "The paperwork will be murder if I don't get my team back."

Marcy turns and walks toward a modest sized plane on the tarmac. From its door Chris waves at her. Katrina waves too, from her Baby Bjorn.

The *E* team readies for deployment.

On a jungle path

The Vashtari make their way down the jungle path, pitchforks held high, drums sounding—along with the odd tambourine. They prod the ground before them, springing traps.

Trevor, "I say, what do you think has become of Rafe? You

don't think he's fallen to the mad hunter do you?"

Kip, "He has the luck of the devil. I'm more worried about Natasha. Marcy would have sent her in long ago, and we've seen no sign of her. She doesn't even know what's going on. It chills me to the bone to think of what Karloff might do to a woman."

Trevor shudders at the thought, "Poor woman. She'd be helpless before him."

Castle bedroom

Karloff stands close to Natasha, who remains tied to her chair. He inspects her. He rolls his eyes across her like a surveyor over an uncharted landscape. Softly, cooingly, he declaims at her, "I am Karloff, your master. I tempt myself with you now, to whet my appetite for when my great hunt has brought me full to overflowing. I tempt you with my presence, to prepare you for the moment of ecstasy to come."

Natasha, "Do not tempt me. Come closer."

Karloff steps close. Natasha slips off her shoes under the seat of the chair. Or rather, she slips off Karloff's mother's shoes.

Natasha, "Kiss me, darling."

Karloff leans forward. Then stops himself. He shivers. He says, "So much greater shall it be when I come to you, covered in the blood of my prey to mingle with your own."

Natasha, "Untie me."

Karloff, "That would never do. You are the helpless animal, I the lusty hunter."

Natasha hooks her left foot around Karloff's right lower leg and puts the ball of her right foot on his toes. She has him trapped. "But darling, I must feel you." Her tone has gone from sexy to threatening. Her eyes remain locked on his.

Karloff tries, without losing his dignity, to pull away, "I must prepare for my hunt." He cannot escape her grip. "If you will excuse me, my good Natasha."

She does not excuse him. She holds him fast by his foot. Tears of pain well up in his eyes.

Karloff shouts, dignity be damned, "I shall strike you!"

Natasha keeps her left foot hooked to Karloff's lower leg. She raises the other off his toes to just below his knee. In a single motion she pulls her left foot forward and pushes her right toward Karloff. She upends him, sending him sprawling to the floor. Natasha rocks back on the chair to gain momentum, then violently forward, flipping herself and the chair toward her fallen prey. She rolls with the momentum until she sits upright over Karloff's sprawled body. She remains tied to the chair, but now the chair pins Karloff to the floor beneath her, his hands constrained by the chair legs. Natasha crosses her feet against his throat.

Karloff writhes and gurgles.

Natasha, "Where do the orchids go?" She, at least, understands the concept of actionable intelligence.

Karloff gurgles as he chokes. He turns red.

Natasha, "Burble your answer louder. I cannot hear you."

He turns blue.

Natasha lets air into the weakening Karloff, "Where do the orchids go?"

Karloff gasps out, "I am Karloff the great—"

Natasha has heard this one. She cuts him short with her feet, chocking him again.

The door to the bedroom swings open. Boris enters. He lifts the chair, and Natasha, and throws them against the bed. Natasha lands on her side, stunned and still tied fast to the chair.

Karloff struggles to his feet. He breaths heavily. "You dare to defy my—" He takes a few more breaths, it never felt so good before. "My hunt." Karloff looks at the giant. "Why did you return?"

Boris makes signs to Karloff. He points to his eyes, and then away. He presses four great fingers against his chest, four times, and then walks two fingers down his arm.

Karloff nods, "I see. More defiance." He motions to the mounted gun, "Take down *Ivan the Terrible* and come with me. We shall put this down in short order."

The giant retrieves the gun.

Karloff addresses Natasha, "You shall know soon enough of the orchids. And when they have done their work, I shall return to you and claim my prize!"

Natasha, "My pleasure."

Karloff shutters at this. He leaves, followed by Boris. The door locks behind them.

Silence. Natasha takes her bearings. The giant has damaged the chair. Natasha twists and turns, uncoiling the rope over her shoulders. With persistence she frees herself. She picks herself up off the floor and leans for a moment on a post of the bed. She takes a deep breath. She walks to the door and tries it. Locked of course. She inspects the lock, but it looks secure, the door itself strong, it's hinges on the other side and no tools within to use. She goes to the window, it has been secured and not meant to be opened. Karloff must not like fresh air.

Natasha goes to the wall and removes an assegai from behind the Zulu shield. She uses the blade to pry open the window. Looking below, she finds that she is in the tower, second story on the side. The stone of the tower offers little to stand on, but no worse than climbing a sheer rock face. So doable, if rightly equipped. She uses the assegai and the skinning knife to cut the skins and firs into a rope, roughing up the ends for better friction and tying them together end to end. She ties one end of her animal skin rope to a post of the bed and the other around her torso, making a harness of the crocodile belts. She uses candle wax to add some stick to her hands.

She steps out the window.

A jungle path

The advance reconnaissance line of the Vashtari stab the ground with their pitchforks. Behind them Arthur Washington Carver walks, bearing their god Sredni Vashtar on his shoulder and carrying the tribe's flag, a palm leaf festooned with tinsel. Beside him Trevor walks, nervously, tossing a rock ahead of him to trip what he knows must be a catapult trap ready to launch him off the island altogether. Behind them Kip leads the tribe in the only marching song he knows.

Kip sings to the marching Vashtari, "Heigh-ho! Heigh-ho! It's off to burn we go!"

The Vashtari know the tune, "Heigh-ho! Heigh-ho! It's off to burn we go! Heigh-ho heigh-ho heigh-ho heigh-ho heigh-ho, heigh-ho. It's off to burn we go!" At last, a bit of culture they pull off convincingly.

Ahead of marchers, up the trail, Karloff watches them with growing concern. He picks up a bit of dirt and throws it in the air, but the wind offers no clue. Karloff looks at Boris. Boris only grunts.

Karloff, "There are too many. And somehow they have armed themselves with tridents! A most formidable weapon in the right hands. And hear their deadly cadence! We will return to the castle and utilize its fortifications. We shall set up the maxim gun and mow them down. Then let the hounds loose to chew away the bones. Come." Karloff heads back home at double time, Boris behind him.

Within an airplane

Marcy and family cruise on the pride of Interpol's Air Infiltration and Exfiltration Reconnaissance Flight Fleet Task Force—Air Service Division. It is in fact the only plane Interpol owns. The Luxembourgian Air Corp and Dirigible Division donated it to Interpol when drone technology rendered the entire Corp/Division obsolete. Up till then the plane had served as Luxembourg's total air defense system. The plane has full airborne unit compatibility—drop doors, chute lines, and jump signals in place—and seats six comfortably. Interpol takes pride in the plane for two distinct reasons. First, it can infiltrate special agents and administrative assistants anywhere in the world within an eighty-mile radius of any commercial airport —and provide comfortable seating for their families (up to five members). Second, Interpol's Air Infiltration and Exfiltration Reconnaissance Flight Fleet Task Force—Air Service Division provides employment to one hundred and sixty-two Interpol support and supervisory personal; plus two pilots. Marcy directs it on its second mission ever.

Chris wears Katrina in his Baby Bjorn front-pouch. Katrina wears kids-version pilot goggles. Marcy checks her straps and connections. Marcy says, "It will take only ten minutes to return to San Monique City after they drop off the Assistant Director of Operations for Interpol's Washington, DC headquarters on a bit of unauthorized daring do."

Chris, "How did this commando stuff fall to you? I thought you were strictly administration."

Marcy, "It's either me or the janitorial staff, and they make too much money to chance on an airborne assault."

Chris, "You really need to ask for that raise."

Marcy, "Police Chief Baptiste must wait for my call. He needs to hear it personally before he can move."

Chris, "No heroics. Find a team member and make a call."

Marcy makes a silly face at Katrina. Katrina makes it back at Mommy. Marcy then picks up a bag—pink, covered in blue and yellow cartoon elephants. Marcy says to Chris, "Don't worry I'm fully equipped." She kisses Katrina on the cheek, "Bye-bye little one. Mommy will be back soon." Marcy commands Chris back from the door. He steps back. Marcy opens the door letting in the rushing air.

Katrina smiles and points at her, "Mommy!"

Marcy's jaw drops. She lights up like a Christmas tree catching on fire. Tears form in her eyes. "Did you hear that? *Mommy!* She said *Mommy!*"

Chris, "Clear as day."

Marcy kisses Chris. She kisses Katrina. She says, "I'll be back."

Marcy jumps.

Outside the giant castle door

Rafe approaches the great door to the great hall. He has made his way through the jungle with tips from Agent 117. Now he stands alone before Karloff's castle. He wonders how he will open these doors by himself. He hears something. Someone behind him. Rafe readies himself. Set to spring. With a shout he spins around hands outstretched wrestler style.

Rafe, "Ah Ha!"

Six feet away he sees the unsmiling face of Natasha. She sees him. She has seen more fearsome sights in her life, "Why do you *ah ha* me?"

Rafe slumps in relief, "You scared the hell out of me."

She looks honestly perplexed, "How?"

Rafe, "Any Russian on this island will do it." Rafe notices something amiss with Natasha. For instance, she wears a wedding dress. "I must have missed a lot while in that pit. Are we still on the same side? Should I have brought a gift?"

Natasha, "Karloff wishes to be good friend with me."

Rafe, "You must be the first."

Natasha, "No. I think his mother also."

Rafe looks her over again, "Can we back up a moment, because I think I may be orchid-dreaming again. Where did you come from? Heaven? A wedding cake?"

Natasha, "I escaped Karloff's castle."

Rafe, "Did you pick up any weapons? Because he has a few."

Natasha, "I am the weapon."

Rafe, "Well are you the radio transmitter too? Because I think we have cause to call for help."

Natasha, "I have no radio."

Rafe, exasperated, "Well how are we going to get help? Will it just drop from the sky?"

Marcy lands between them, her parachute enveloping them all. Rafe and Natasha struggle out from under the chute as Marcy unhooks from the rig.

Rafe inspects the sky wondering what else will soon arrive.

Natasha, to Marcy, "Wonderful aim."

Marcy, "Thanks. Rydell High School Women's Sky Diving Team, State Champions." Marcy beams a moment with Rydell High pride. "So what is mission status?"

Rafe, "Highly successful, Karloff's trying to kill us."

Marcy, "Great!"

Natasha, "Also he has death orchids."

Marcy, "Chris will be so proud!"

Rafe, "He's moving them off the island."

Marcy, "To wipe out San Monique City. We haven't a moment to lose." This though, raises a question, "Why haven't you called in?"

Rafe, "Phone sank."

Natasha, "Phone sank."

Marcy looks incredulous.

Rafe, "Satellite phones become very slippery in the surf." He looks to Natasha for support here. She nods her concurrence, very slippery.

Marcy looks about, "Where are Kip and Trevor?"

Rafe, "They set out yesterday to draw Karloff away while I doubled back here."

Marcy looks skeptical. Natasha folds her arms to look at him.

Rafe, "The best of bad options as we saw it. We faced Russian thugs. Very bad people these Russians," he looks at Natasha, "saving your presence. Where Kip and Trevor got to I cannot say, but as decoys they leave a lot to be desired. By now their fate ranges somewhere between murdered and island kings. I'd go with *entrapped,* to judge from the Karloff warnings we ignored."

Marcy, "Where is Karloff?"

Rafe turns to Natasha, "Yes, where did he go after the wedding?"

Marcy notices Natasha's new look, "Did you marry Karloff?"

Natasha dislikes this turn, "No."

Rafe, "So he jilted you? Left you at the alter?"

Natasha, peeved, "No."

Marcy, "Have you and Karloff met before?"

Natasha would really like this to stop, "No! I wear his mother's dress."

Marcy, "Okay … Is that a Russian thing?"

Natasha goes for a tactical change of subject, "I saw the giant Boris sign to Karloff that many men approached the castle. Karloff left to find them."

Marcy, "The lost castaways."

Rafe, "Castaways?"

Marcy, "My husband has all this locked down. At a theoretical level. Which brings us back to the main point. We need to get the cavalry here."

Rafe, "Aren't you the cavalry?"

Marcy, "No, I'm Team," She counts it on her fingers. "*E* ... I think. I brought the satellite phone." She scolds a bit, "The third satellite phone."

Natasha and Rafe avert their eyes and shuffle their feet.

Marcy, "With which we call Chief Baptiste. You don't think Karloff can get away before help arrives?"

From behind, they hear the loud and commanding voice of Karloff, "So! We have interlopers." He stands some fifty yards away, where the trail breaks onto the clearing, holding a very big gun. Boris, also very big, stands behind him.

Rafe sees him, fully armed and accompanied by a colossus, "No. He won't escape. We have him trapped."

Marcy, "No worries. I came fully equipped." Marcy reaches into the haversack covered in cartoon elephants. She hands Rafe a diaper bag, "Satellite phone." She hands Natasha a milk bottle "Grenade." Marcy looks confused. She checks the bag. Elephants, not camo. "I grabbed the wrong satchel."

Rafe, "Door!" They charge the castle door.

Karloff watches from the distance, "Come." He orders Boris, "Capture the new woman to find why she comes. Capture the old prey to discover the plan of his comrades. Capture the woman Natasha for my pleasure in celebration of the great hunt on San Monique." Karloff takes off at the jog toward his three intended victims who now heave at his castle door. Boris just takes slightly longer strides behind him, more his natural pace, really.

Rafe, Natasha, and Marcy push with all their might against the great doors, swinging them open enough to slip through. Inside they push the door closed. Marcy looks about in the castle entrance hall at Karloffian interior design, "After all this I expected more trophies."

Rafe, "By the time you complete the grand tour you will rue those words."

Natasha concentrates on practical matters. She finds a thick plank beside the door frame and lays it across hooks on each door. The plank and hooks together serving as a bar on the door.

Natasha, "That will keep them out."

Rafe, "You may be a little over-optimistic." The doors creak inwards towards them. The large plank starts to splinter.

Marcy, "Chris thinks Karloff has a radio transmitter in the tower."

Rafe, "Right. Up the stairs, bear to the left, beware of traps."

Marcy, "Traps?"

Rafe, "The man loves traps. If you hear a click, jump backwards."

Marcy looks at the winding stone staircase. An unlikely venue for impromptu acrobatics. "I should have kept my chute on." The door creeks again. Again the plank begins to splinter. "Should we all go up?"

Rafe, "You go call for help, we'll lay ambushes down here."

Marcy heads for the stairs that lead up the tower.

Natasha looks at the splintering door, "It won't hold."

Rafe, "That way to the trophy room. Karloff probably doesn't want to splatter it with blood." Rafe and Natasha run to the trophy room.

The great doors heave again. The plank shatters, and the doors swing open. The giant Boris steps in. He steps aside and bows slightly as a very pissed-off Karloff steps through the great doors and into his baronial stone foyer. Boris turns to stand behind him, a human frame to Karloff's greatness. Karloff motions at the broken beam on the ground. "Secure the doors."

Boris closes the doors and jams a beam against them.

Karloff sees a stranger, female, in a jump suit, making her way with cautious speed up his grand stairs. Then he hears a familiar and irritating voice.

Rafe calls from the trophy room, leaning on its door jam, "Hey, Kerfuffle. I'm going to have some more port while you keep master-hunting me. A drink with your new wife. Though I understand she's looking for an annulment based on conjugal non-performance. Something about your rifle jamming? I think maybe you just over-polish it." Rafe returns to the trophy room.

Karloff steams at the insult. His rifle never jams. It gives the greatest satisfaction a man can know. It fells its prey with a single shot. And over-polishing? Absurd! A day spent polishing *Ivan the Terrible* is a day well spent. Karloff grips his well-polished rifle firmly. He would very much like to teach this fellow a lesson right now, but he sees the crude trap laid out for him. Karloff motions Boris towards the trophy room and heads himself to the tower stairs after Marcy.

Boris grins.

Outside the castle door

Kip and Trevor stand side by side looking at the formidable doors and stone walls of Karloff's castle. Behind them the Vashtari argue, as usual. The adventurers take no notice as they consider strategy.

Trevor, "But is he even in there? For all we know he could be out and about on the island."

Kip, "In there, I'd say."

Trevor, "What would he be doing in there?"

Kip, "Sleeping up for a night hunt. Stuffing Rafe with sawdust. Aiming at your forehead. Could be anything. We find out by going in."

Trevor, "Into the monster's lair? With all its snares and implements of wounding? And this parachute canopy lying here, I'm certain it hides a pit. Who knows what else he may have added to foil us within his fortress?"

Kip, "We get help prodding for traps just as we got this far." Kip turns back to seek the aid of the Vashtari, only to find them deeply divided.

The recent converts busy themselves gathering wood for a bonfire while the older and wiser Vashtari, more fully reverted to civilized behavior, discuss committee assignments.

Linda, "The Planning, the Action, and the General Strategy Committees should each have representation on a Steering Committee."

Joel, "As should the Resources Committee."

Prashanta, "And the R&D working group."

Linda, "No, that just replicates the Control Committee."

Peter, "Will we need separate reports?"

Carver, "Brief memorandum, please."

Pedro, "Form the Action Committee and the R&D Group into a provisional reporting committee responsible for memorandum edits. We did this at my last company, and it cut paperwork in half."

Joel, "Analytics? Have we placed that yet?"

Behind them the primitives build their sacred fire pile.

Torgon, with the zeal of the converted, "Fire for Sredni Vashtar! Honor to the great ferret god! Bring more wood! Make the effigy of Karloff to burn in the fire of the truth! More wood! Dryer wood! Who has the lighter?"

Someone starts beating the tribal drum. Dancing breaks out. The Vashtari loft their pitchforks high as the fire begins to smolder.

Kip, "We seem to have lost focus here."

Within the trophy room

Natasha marvels at the single-mindedness of the castle's master. The man has no off switch. "Death lust."

Rafe enters, "I would have gone with *kill craze*. You should see the bedrooms." Rafe considers, "But then I suppose you have."

Natasha throws him an ugly look.

Rafe gets a lot of those, "I have him pretty steamed, we should position ourselves for action."

Natasha, "The balcony."

Rafe, "Dog kennels at the bottom. Though maybe we could make the lower balcony." Before he can elaborate, Boris enters the trophy room. Rafe takes his best martial-arts-master pose. Natasha shakes her head. Pathetic.

Rafe, "All right Boris. You, great pile of Russian puss. You great clump of Cossack clutter. You stack of stupidity. You knoll of nuisance. You dung-heap of doom. You hillock of hinderance. You mound of malignant menace. You..." Rafe begins to falter, how can he be expected to fight without a thesaurus? "You tumulus tumult." Good. "You embankment of embarrassment." Getting harder. "You breakwater of bile." Now something to really sum things up, "You. You. You planetoid of pusillanimous puffed-up, piss-pouring, putrid pistachios." Okay, maybe a bit of a drop off at the end. Still, surly enough to distract the giant with rage.

Boris remains impassive.

Rafe proceeds to taunt, "That's right, I said it! What are you going to do now? No Karloff to hide behind. You're nothing without your master's voice."

Natasha, "Rafe."

Rafe, "Don't worry Natasha, I got this."

Boris approaches, apparently unwounded by Rafe's taunts and unworried by Rafe's karate stance.

Rafe, "I'm legally required to warn you, I have a blue belt in strip-mall karate."

Natasha is about to take over, "Rafe."

Rafe, "Not now honey, I'm dealing with this."

Honey? Fine. Natasha will let Rafe handle this.

Rafe, to Natasha, "Just stay behind me, you'll be safe."

Boris is almost upon Rafe, his great mass casting a shadow over his foe.

Rafe holds his hands up to Boris, "Deadly weapons, don't get to close."

Boris grabs Rafe's hands and hurls them, and the rest of Rafe, thankfully, over a stuffed chair covered in hyena hide.

Rafe lands with a thud atop the skinned remains of a mountain lion. He winces with the pain. But he jumps back to his feet in a flash. "I let you do that! Giving you every chance here."

Boris flings the chair between them across the room. It

bounces off a stuffed aardvark and comes to rest against a ceramic pot depicturing an angry speared hippo.

Rafe, "You know the boss isn't going to like you breaking the furniture. Particularly after he killed it all special for this room."

Boris grabs Rafe by the neck and lifts him into the air.

Rafe has trouble making himself heard through the giant's grip. Rafe says, choking and kicking for emphasis, "I prithee take thy fingers from my throat, for though I am not splenative and rash, yet have I in me something dangerous, which let thy wiseness fear."

Unfamiliar with Shakespeare's collected works, or with Horace Binkley's Anthology *Great Quotes by the Chocked*, Boris offers only a puzzled look.

On the tower stairway

Marcy makes her way up the stone stairs trying to find the right balance between searching for traps and avoiding death at the hands of the crazed hunter. Since Marcy's total education in traps (perhaps mercifully) comes to nothing, she can do no better than pound the stone with her hand prior to taking a step; neither effective trap detection nor swift progress. She blames improper briefing. She vows that on the next Silencers mission, proper intelligence, constant communication, and thorough, careful briefing will be the rule.

Marcy hears something. She pauses. Footfalls behind her. She looks over the spiraling staircase, down the central tube of the tower. She sees Karloff in hot pursuit. He sees her and sneers. Marcy takes off up the stairs in bounds. Never mind traps, now she looks for a hiding place. She sees a door off a small platform beyond which the stairs continue upwards. She opens the door and runs through it into the room, closing the door behind her.

Karloff pursues this latest, and frankly unaccountable, quarry. He reaches the door to the observation room. He pauses, unsure what weapons and tactics await on the other side. But he is the great Karloff, and no woman can defeat him. He will proceed with steady deliberation. As against the dwarf panda.

A disarmingly gentle and harmless seeming creature, but one Karloff credited with subtle cunning. Until he shot it while it snuggled his leg. Here again, as with the dwarf panda, he will take care before achieving his triumph. He takes the door handle gently in his hands. Be still, little dwarf panda.

Inside the room, Marcy has the door closed but little good it will do her, it has no lock. What does she have to match Karloff's gun? The room itself contains only a telescope pointed out a window into the distance. No help there. She rummages quickly through her baby bag. She pulls out a bottle of baby powder. She snaps off the lid. She sees the handle of the door slowly turning.

On the opposite side of the door, Karloff has his gun at the ready, his hand slowly turning the handle. The bolt clears its nesting place. Karloff swings the door open and leaps into the room.

Seeing Karloff at the door, Marcy lets fly with the baby powder: a direct hit to Karloff's face. Who's the master marksman now!

Perhaps you have never had baby powder flung in your face, but be assured, babies use this impromptu weapon for a reason. Disorienting at the least. Karloff staggers backwards. He struggles to understand why it now snows under his eyelids.

While he struggles, Marcy squeezes past him to the door. For good measure, as long as he is not himself, she steals the gun out of his hand. Clearing the door to the stone stairwell she throws the gun down the stairwell and takes off to the top again.

Aghast, Karloff watches as *Ivan the Terrible* splinters on the stone. She will pay for this! No woman can treat the great Karloff this way! No other woman. Neither of them can. And an unarmed woman at that! Unarmed women. What a day of firsts. Karloff rubs his eyes to make them water. What is this fiendish powder? Tears of rage clear his eyes. He heads up the stairs after her.

Within the trophy room
On the wall a mounted raccoon head looks on impassively

through glass eyes. Rafe lands hard against the wall, replacing the raccoon head with his own. As Rafe-fights go this one seems about average to him. He losses, but slower than the handicappers would have predicted. It would be a good deal less painful if it were not for the fact that everything in the room seems to have horns attached. Rafe considers a change in strategy. Blows and kicks leave the giant unfazed. Perhaps a quick shoot to his legs and a wrestling take down.

Boris reaches for Rafe. Rafe shoots to the giant's legs. He nearly knocks himself unconscious against the tree-trunk sized thigh. Rafe presses forward. He tugs back. He grips one giant leg with both arms and tries a dead lift. Maybe some more taunting would help. "You great heap of helpless—"

Boris pulls him free of his leg and hurls him again across the room.

Rafe lands at Natasha's feet. To her he says, "Could you at least sell popcorn?"

Natasha, mockingly, "Oh please Rafe, save me. Save me from the big bad man."

Rafe, "I suppose you think you could do better."

Boris grabs Rafe and hurls him into a chair. At least a softer landing this time. Until the chair falls backward, dumbing Rafe's head on the floor.

Natasha shakes her head in pity for them both.

Boris starts towards Rafe for a new round of man-throwing when Natasha's words bring him to a quick stop.

Natasha, in Russian, "You have arms like jelly and the breath of a Cossack's ass. I shall now make you scream in pain and pee yourself."

Rafe can't make this out, but Boris certainly does. Leave it to a Russian woman to find exactly the insult most apt to infuriate a Cossack. And imagine thinking ill of a Cossack fart; perfume of the plains. Boris turns to face Natasha.

Natasha stands before the wall of weapons, framed by the armaments. She turns to the wall. She inspects her options.

Boris smiles. He fears no weapon known to man. Especially

wielded by a woman.

Natasha considers. What to choose: battle axes and broad swords, dirks and daggers, maces, morning-stars, and great mauls. Such an endless array of classic lethality. She picks out a swagger stick. It is a short, thin cane suitable for urging your horse on or pointing to the enemy during an inspiring speech to the troops. Even Karloff would not select it for a fight.

Natasha tries it out by slapping it against her thigh. SMACK. Good sharp sound.

Boris does not understand; of every weapon she might pick —but oh well. He decides to dispatch her in short order and get back to redecorating the room with Rafe's body.

Boris moves in on Natasha quickly, huge and menacing. Invincible.

Natasha calmly raises the swagger stick above her head taking the stance of a Wushu sword fighter.

Boris lunges at her.

At the last possible moment before he grasps her throat, Natasha steps in and lands the tip of the swagger stick straight into the giants left eye.

He clutches his face and falls back. He howls in pain, holding his eye. "Arrrrrgggggggghhhhhhhh!!!"

Rafe, "Well, sure, if you're going to use a *stick* on him. I didn't know weapons were allowed."

On the tower stairs

Marcy rushes up the stairs, a well-powdered Karloff close behind. At the top she sees another strong wooden door. She turns its handle and swings it open. Inside she sees the glory of her efforts. A great, if rather old fashion (Karloff calls it classic) radio panel. You could bounce radio waves off the stratosphere and call Portugal with this rig.

Marcy slams the door. Again, no lock. Clearly this man does not have children. How to secure the door? Marcy searches the baby bag. She pulls out a large metal fingernail clipper. She jams it like a wedge between the frame and the door. She drives it firm using a board book of *Good Night Moon* as a hammer. There is nothing mommy cannot do with a baby bag. Marcy turns to the radio and begins her message. In Morse Code: Dot-Dot-Dash-Dot-Dot-Dash.

On the stairway a white-faced Karloff reaches the radio room door. He pushes on it hard, but it will not budge. What could possibly be blocking it? He tries again, but it holds fast. Then he hears a terrible howling from below. A deep baritone wail. Boris? How could that be?

Karloff rushes down the stairs.

Outside the castle door

Kip tries to reason with Vashtari Inc. "We need immediate action! Against the castle!"

Carver, "Absolutely. But in my experience, and I think we all agree with this," Carver's new management team nods in uniform concurrence, "action initiated without a proper organizational structure tends to undercut itself in the fullness of time."

Kip, "Attack the castle! Now!"

Trevor, "At the very least if you could just aid us in opening the doors. Our efforts have been to no avail."

Linda, "I think Joel's group has done some work on that."

Joel, "Well that's just not fair Linda. We are barely up and running, and door opening represents a big lift for our small group."

Linda, "I just hoped for an initial feasibility study."

Kip, "If we all push at once, it's feasible."

Carver, "My point exactly, our key to success lies in coordinating action."

Kip, "Attack!"

Trevor has an inspiration, "I say, perhaps we might consult the god himself? Perhaps he might cut through the tangle of bureaus."

Kip latches onto this and addresses the ferret, "What do you say Sredni Vashtar? Feasibility study or attack Karloff?"

Sredni Vashtar, still on Carver's shoulder, grows agitated. The ferret twitches. It barks and hisses. Then it rushes off Carver's shoulders and onto Kip's. The Vashtari look on in amazement.

Trevor, "A decisive passing of the torch, I'd say!"

Kip seizes the moment. He takes the ferret from his shoulders and places it on the ground before the great doors of the castle. "Okay little buddy. Show us the way. What do you want us to do? Beat down the castle doors?"

The ferret takes off toward the castle. It avoids the doors altogether and finds a small hole in the stone wall of the castle. The ferret slips through this gap and out of sight.

Mysterious are the signs of the gods. Best to secure a decisive interpretation at once. Trevor says, "There, you see? The god storms the castle! We must follow."

A moment of thought, then Carver declares, "Sredni Vashtar has spoken! Swing open the doors!"

The adventurers and their Vashtari charge the doors at last.

Within the trophy room

Boris is mad now. Hurt, but mad. Now that he knows the dangers of a riding-crop he won't fall for that again. He makes his way back toward Natasha, his face a mask of fury. He raises his hands to show their great size. He throws out his chest to show that the rest of him matches.

Natasha calmly kneels down.

Boris smiles at her meek surrender; it won't help her. The Cossack language does not even have a word for mercy. The closest it gets is one for hurt-more-slowly. Boris makes a quick check to see what Rafe does. Rafe looks at him with pity. Odd that he will just stand and let Boris destroy this woman. Boris turns his attention again to the kneeling Natasha. Boris looms over her. He reaches down to grasp her.

Smoothly, the way water runs over glass, Natasha springs to a stand between the giant's huge hands, pushing the swagger-stick straight up the giant's nose. He howls and pulls back. Boris, nasally, "Ohhhhhhhhuuuuuuhhhhhh!!!"

Natasha leads him around by her stick for a few moments. Boris goes wherever she pushes; it hurts that much.

Having had her fun, Natasha pulls the stick from his nose and lands it straight in his crotch.

The big man crosses his massive legs and his eyes roll. He doubles over in pain.

Natasha slams the base of the stick into the base of his exposed neck and Boris goes down.

Rafe, "I love the way you Russians, wherever in the world you meet up with each other, you right away get along."

She drops the riding crop and walks over to the side table on which still lie some of last night's delicacies.

Boris sees the swagger stick fall. He has her now, she has disarmed herself. Fool! Boris stands. He faces Natasha.

Natasha sucks a piece of lemon off a tiny lemon fork.

Boris lunges at her, hands outstretched to throttle her.

In one deft move she jams the lemon fork between his finger and fingernail.

Boris howls like a dying Minotaur:

"Aaaagggggaaaaahhhaaaaaggghhhgghhhhhhhgggghhhh!!!!!!" (That's just how a dying Minotaur sounds.) Boris crawls off. His worst day as a henchman ever.

Rafe, "Well, that about wraps things up."

From the doorway, the voice of Karloff sounds, "I think not."

Rafe, "Oh, right."

Karloff stands holding two fencing swords, one by the hilt, the other by its shaft, "I do not know how you have beaten my giant, but you shall never defeat ... Karloff!" He enters the room.

Rafe, to Natasha, "Maybe he'll tell you his theory of danger-hunting. Leopards, lions, frightened unarmed men."

Karloff, "Ah, but I shall arm my opponent now. You, madam, may defeat the brute, but not my skill." Karloff, irritated, must slightly amend this, "Now that I know your prowess with chairs." The secrets women hide. Karloff tosses the blade to Natasha, but Rafe intercepts it in mid-air.

Rafe, "Try me Kerfuffle."

Natasha looks concerned, "Rafe?"

Rafe, to her, "Do you know how to use one of these?"

Natasha, "Rafe."

Rafe, "It has a pointy bit at the end."

Karloff grows impatient.

Rafe, "You need to stay away from the pointy part. I read that somewhere."

Natasha, "You are a man of words, not weapons."

Rafe, "That hurts. I have my pride. I don't mind you beating up the gorilla for me, but don't just assume I'm incompetent."

Natasha, "You are a man, no one expects you to do everything."

Rafe, "Give me a little credit."

Karloff tries to reassert himself, "I am Karloff!"

Rafe and Natasha pay him no heed, they are just talking to each other.

Natasha, "I do not wish you to be injured."

Rafe, "So far as I can tell, you are 0-2 against Crazy Ivan."

Natasha looks at Rafe with concern.

Rafe, "Just say the word, have you ever fenced before?"

Natasha, "No."

Karloff has had enough. He will just finish Rafe with a thrust. Karloff thrusts. Without even looking away from Natasha Rafe parries the thrust.

Rafe, "I have."

Rafe taps Karloff's sword twice and takes a very legit looking fencing stance. Karloff tries another thrust, Rafe parries. Then another, Rafe shrugs it off.

Natasha looks perplexed.

Rafe now takes an aggressive fencing stance. Karloff gets serious too. Rafe stands up looking oddly at Karloff's head and shoulders. Rafe says, "What is that? Dandruff?"

Karloff wipes at the powder on his face.

Rafe, "Do you have a skin condition?"

Angry, Karloff lunges at Rafe.

Rafe parries.

Natasha, "How do you do these things?"

Rafe talks as he fences. That's easy, Rafe talks while he does everything, "Acting classes. Ten years of them. Make-up, voice, diction." He thrusts Karloff back, "Loved the fencing best."

Back and forth they go, parry and thrust, thrust and parry. Blade clinks off blade. Exotic fencing moves flow full force. Karloff executes a D'Artagnan Double. Rafe answers with a Porthos Parry. Karloff attempts an Aramis Advance. Rafe retorts with a Rathbone Riposte. Karloff tries a Scaramouche Simple. Rafe replies with a de Bergerac Balestra. Karloff completes an Ivanhoe Insistence. Rafe responds with an Earl Flynn Feint.

Rafe, "You should have seen me in *The Count of Monte Cristo*."

They go at it full-on. Three Musketeers style. All across the trophy room. Karloff backs Rafe up, then Rafe springs back and backs Karloff up. Karloff makes a deadly lunge, but his blade empales a stuffed beaver, right between the eyes. (Again.) The beaver clings to Karloff's blade as the master hunter struggles to free it. Finally tossing the beaver away, Karloff tries again at Rafe, who now faces him by the grand fireplace. A lunge and a parry and then Rafe topples a giant elephant tusk onto Karloff. Karloff struggles away, backing into the horn of a rhino.

Karloff, "By gods!" Which is just what you say when you feel a rhino horn up your butt.

Rafe uses the tip of his foil to skewer stuffed birds from the mantle. He flings each in turn at Karloff. A whole attack wing of glass-eyed fowl descends upon the mad hunter. A stuffed square-tailed kite hits Karloff on the nose. A taxidermized tawney eagle slams into his shoulder. A sawdust packed peregrine flies into his forehead. A filled Fiji goshawk hits him square in the chest. A crammed crusted Cape-gyrfalcon strikes his arm. An upholstered honey-buzzard bashes his skull. The stuffed flying squirl flies again, into Karloff's eye. Karloff retreats under the assault, recovering only when Rafe has cleared the mantle.

Then the men circle each other again. Karloff lunges, but his sword strikes a moose head on the wall. Retracting his blade, the head crashes down onto him. More fight than the moose had put up in life—admittedly then facing a remote-controlled assault rifle. Karloff turns to face Rafe. Karloff advances on him.

Rafe lays his own trap now, backing over the animal rugs, swinging his sword in the air wildly, "Could it be Karloff's comeuppance? Because it looks to me like a general uprising of the annihilated animal kingdom."

Karloff, enraged, lunges. His foot catches on the teeth of his tiger skin rug, sending him to the floor. Looking up he sees the startling sight of polar bear teeth. Another rug, but startling to see in a sword-fight nonetheless. He reaches to lift himself up and puts his hand on the porcupine foot stool. That has really got to hurt.

Karloff, "Ooowwww!"

I thought so.

Rafe cringes, "Payback's a bitch."

Karloff pulls a few quills out. He prepares another lunge. A fly buzzes up his nose. Karloff dances around the room trying to clear his left nostril from the vengeance of nature. Even Rafe feels a little pity. Karloff smashes the bug in his nose and has another go at Rafe, but it is no use. He is undone. Rafe takes command and backs Karloff to the balcony doorway. Karloff looks desperate now. Rafe plucks a button from his shirt. Karloff lunges. Rafe disarms him. The fight ends.

Karloff, "No one defeats Karloff!"

Rafe, "You haven't been paying attention."

Karloff stands for a moment, proudly puffing himself, "You shall never find me on my island! I am the Master Hunter!" Then he turns and rushes off the balcony.

Rafe stands a moment, stunned. Natasha rushes to the balcony. Rafe follows. Both look down over the balcony railing. Below them, Karloff stands on the balcony beneath theirs as the dogs howl excitedly on the ground below that. Karloff gives them a scoff. He walks from the balcony into the room below the trophy room, which is to say, into his room of human prizes.

Karloff feels victory snatched from defeat. He has his plans in hand. His escape route. His hidden boat. A first aid kit to remove this damned fly. He remains—somewhat—undaunted. A bad day to be sure, but not his last. He counts this a draw. He remains undefeated in the hunt. All is well.

But then, before him, appearing as if by magic, his greatest foe. His one failure. His nemesis: Sredni Vashtar, the ferret.

Karloff, "You!!!"

The ferret charges. What can a mere man do in the face of a charging ferret? Karloff backs away in fear, "No! No!"

The ferret leaps up and bites Karloff on the neck. Karloff backs onto the balcony and to its railing.

Above, Natasha has climbed onto the balcony railing, preparing to leap to the balcony below in pursuit, when she and Rafe hear the mad hunter's plaintive cry. They watch as he back-peddles to the balcony edge, trying to snatch away an attacking … ferret.

Karloff screams and pitches off the balcony. He lands amidst the howling mastiffs. They descend on him at once, teeth flashing. Rafe and Natasha see only dogs piling on dogs. A ferret scurries from beneath the pile to rush up the wall and out of the kennel.

Rafe, "Looks like someone forgot to release the hounds."

Beside them Marcy appears, "What did I miss?"

Natasha tries to explain, but her English fails her.

Marcy looks down at the mass of dogs.

Rafe, "It's Karloff under all those teeth. His mastiffs feed on poetic justice."

From the trophy room entry, they hear two familiar voices.

Kip, "Ah ha! We have you now!"

Trevor, "Not a move from anyone!"

Natasha, Rafe, and Marcy turn to the voices. Kip and Trevor look a mess: covered in mud, clothes in rags, sharpened sticks in hand. They could be cave men. Seeing their colleagues, Kip and Trevor look first confused, then relieved.

Kip, "Rafe!"

Trevor, "Natasha."

Kip, "Marcy?"

Marcy, "What happened to you?"

Kip and Trevor look each other over, realizing what a sight they must present. Trevor says, "We have been elevated to the status of Cannibal Gods."

Kip, "Where's Karloff?"

Rafe nods at the balcony, "Dog food. He was toppled by some sort of ... mink."

Trevor and Kip high-five each other. Kip says to Rafe, "And look at you. Doubled back and took the castle. The plan worked."

Rafe thinks, "Uh. Yeah." He looks at Natasha, "Yeah! See. The plan worked."

Natasha shakes her head, "But what of Karloff's plan?

San Monique City

And the word went out, and it was good: Dot-Dot-Dash-Dot-Dot-Dash. Chief Baptiste set loose his men, and with them the city's Mama Tutus. They descended as one on the hilltop houses and storage sites where Karloff's mindless minions waited for darkness, lighters in hand. The police kicked in doors; the Mama Tutus whipped the Karloffian Elite Believers from their fuses. Afro-Caribbean Voodoo worshipers drove out white cultist before they could bring down a fiery hell to San Monique City.

They took them to the soccer stadium to process. The police held up pictures of missing persons lost at sea to the confused faces of the Karloffian Elite, identifying the captives and returning to them their old names. The Mama Tutus gave out tin cups of water along with a firm scolding. Sometimes a Karloffian would shout out "Karloff is god!" but the San Moniqueians just ignored this. They were a people possessed of many gods, none of whom sought to burn their city down.

Soon the fanatics settled. They let the Mama Tutus draw crosses in blood on their foreheads. They listened intently to stories of the Voodoo gods. They rejected Count Karloff for Baron Samedi. After the shock of the change wore off, they began to ask about stock options, benefit packages, equity spreads, tax structures and accounts receivable. They had been cured.

In the south bay, men in gasmasks hooked barges filled with death orchids to boats and hauled them out to sea. They sank the barges, sending their deadly flowers to the ocean floor. A Mama Tutu offered a Voodoo spell and spread feathers on the ocean surface, holding the evil fast in the sea.

On the beach

The Silencers, Marcy, Rafe, Natasha, Kip and Trevor, stand on the beach as the marines come ashore. Literally. The San Monique Marine Corp Reserve hike off a landing craft. Following them, the Mama Tutus. Old Mama Tutus spreading blooded feathers and saying spells, young Mama Tutus waiving Writs of Possession and Warrants of Arrest.

The Vashtari greet them with dances and songs. A policeman struggles to handcuff a compliant Boris. These cuffs will clearly never fit round his wrists. Boris offers his thumbs. The officer cuffs his thumbs together.

Kip uses a washcloth to clean mud off Trevor. Trevor flicks leaves from Kip's hair. Natasha pets a well-fed mastiff.

Chris, wearing Katrina in the Baby Bjorn, approaches Marcy.

Marcy lights up with joy, "Baby!"

Chris, "I'm going to pretend you mean me."

Marcy, "Both my babies." She kisses them both.

Katrina, "Mommy! Mommy! Mommy!" Katrina squirms to get into Mommy's arms; and she does.

Marcy holds Katrina close as Rafe and Natasha look on. Rafe puts his arm around Natasha. At first Natasha bristles, but then, oh well.

Halftrain enters from the landing craft. He has arrived just in time to administer. Halftrain generally finds that the best way to avoid confusion in the press about the distribution of merit is to show up before the photographers. Halftrain finds some things difficult, like opening doors and brushing his teeth, but he has a natural instinct for taking credit.

Halftrain, "Excellent. Excellent."

Moans all around.

Halftrain, "I'm happy to announce: I've saved you."

Natasha, "My hero."

Marcy shoots her a restraining look.

Halftrain, "I think we'll get the press out here. Some pictures. Of me. Maybe some of you too." He looks at Trevor and Kip, "The cleaner ones."

Chris prods Marcy, "Go on, ask him."

Marcy, "Not now."

Chris, "Why not now? Hour of great success. Go on."

The Silencers take note and gather closer.

Marcy gathers her courage, "Mr. Halftrain. I would like to ask you—"

He cuts her off, "Of course you would, of course you would."

Marcy, uses her mommy voice, "No."

Halftrain stops, stunned.

Marcy, "I would like to ask you for a raise."

Halftrain smiles, finally a task he fully understands, "I would love to, naturally. But we have budgets to get around. Job evaluations to consider. Meetings to attend. I wish I could. I truly do." He sounds very sincere. This takes hours of practice, but he finds it well worth the effort.

Natasha slides up behind Marcy, she looks dead at Halftrain. This look alone has shattered lesser men than Halftrain, few though such men are.

Halftrain gulps, "If I only could, nothing I'd like better."

A dirty Kip and a filthy Trevor post themselves on each side of Halftrain. Kip even throws a muddy arm around him.

Halftrain, "Gentlemen, I want to, I really do..."

A smiling Rafe puts a hand on Halftrain's shoulder and beams reassuringly at him. Halftrain warms at finding a supporter in the crowd.

Rafe, "But Mr. Halftrain, you already have. You've filled out the papers. You've turned them over to Marcy."

Halftrain, "I did?"

Rafe, "Yes, you were very generous."

Halftrain, nervous, "I was?"

216

Rafe, reassuring him, "Of course, it was only fair, only what she deserved."

Halftrain, "Well, of course it was only fair. I stand up for my people." For the record: "How fair was I?"

Rafe, "Very. How much of a raise did Mr. Halftrain give you Marcy?"

Marcy, "Oh. Uh. He was very fair. He doubled—"

Chris clears his throat.

Marcy, "Tripled. He tripled my salary."

Halftrain is shocked at his generosity, but he can always fire a few interns. "Oh well, what's done is done. Let's find the press." Halftrain wonders off into a tree.

Katrina calls after him, pointing, "Fathead!"

Marcy, "Honey, in the adult world we call that a chief administrator."

Katrina points at him again, "Moron?"

Marcy laughs.

Katrina, "Idiot?"

Kip, "She's coming along fast."

Trevor, "Most impressive, in spite of the Americanisms."

Katrina, "Nitwit?"

Natasha, "She has many words."

Rafe, "Something of a prodigy." He winks at Natasha who responds with a cockeyed look.

Katrina, "Nincompoop?"

Marcy, "Where does she get this from?"

Chris, "I've tried to make clear the source of her problem."

Katrina, "Halfbrain."

Marcy, to Katrina, "Between you and me, that's an overestimate."

Katrina points to Marcy, "MOMMY!"

Marcy, tears in her eyes, hugs Katrina close. "I feel like it's Christmas!"

I feel like that too.

ABOUT THE AUTHOR

Whip Lipsey

Whip Lipsey grew up in Georgia, came of age in Missouri, and dropped out of high school in California. He holds a bachelor's degree in history from the University of California at Irvine and a PhD in philosophy from the University of Rochester. He left academia to work as a screenwriter (and was shocked to learn that writing for Hollywood does not require a doctorate). After twenty years raising his three children as a full-time father, he has returned to writing.

www.ingramcontent.com/pod-product-compliance
Lightning Source LLC
Chambersburg PA
CBHW072051170626
46813CB00004B/1308